Empath

S. Usher Evans

Sun's Golden Ray
Publishing

Line-editing by Regina West
Dragon design by Cassondra Stevens
Copyright © 2015 Sun's Golden Ray Publishing
ISBN: 0986298123
ISBN-13: 978-0986298127

contents

"Fear makes the wolf bigger than he is."
German Proverb

chapter one

"So, I think it's probably best that we just cut our losses and move on."

The moping just had to stop already.

Even the dust bunnies were mocking Lauren at this point, all lined up against the wall and reminding her she hadn't vacuumed since before the break-up.

When everything was perfect.

She moaned and rolled on her belly, the mattress squeaking beneath her. Her thoughts were at war with each other as they rehashed the same old song and dance. Things *weren't* perfect, or else they'd still be together. She was just glorifying and catastrophizing the situation, as she always did. She couldn't just feel the normal range of emotions; she had to feel things deeply, painfully, fully.

But it was time to stop feeling that way and get the hell over it already. Everyone was tired of hearing about it. She was tired of hearing about it. It was over, done, finito, kaput, ended, credits rolled.

He was never coming back.

That thought sent a fresh wave of tears down her face, and she kicked herself for thinking it.

Because if he *was* going to come back, he would have come back already.

empath

Or maybe he was—

She stopped that thought before it could continue.

She sat up in her bed and brushed the tears out of her eyes. Her mother's voice came floating into her head now, telling her she was being overly emotional. It was why she excelled at drama, before she decided to hang up her character shoes after college and get a real job. Data entry wasn't suiting her very well, and yet it did. It was dull and monotonous work, repetitive so that she didn't have to think much. She could get through an entire day forgetting that she'd just had her heart smashed a few months before.

There she went again, over-dramatic.

"GOD!" she screamed into the empty room, furious at herself. She was the one who ended it in the first place; she did this to herself. They'd been together since their freshman year of college, and after a year of beating around the bush, it was pretty clear to Lauren that they weren't going to get married. He wasn't ready, and she needed to move on with her life.

Right?

So why wasn't she moving on with her life already?

She guessed it would have been easier if they'd broken up in a fight or he'd cheated or done something awful to make her hate him. But he was a good person, a decent human being. During their five years together, they fought a grand total of three times. They were best friends and ended their relationship as best friends.

Best friends that didn't want to be together for the rest of their lives, a nagging little voice in the back of her head reminded her.

She was stuck in this limbo of knowing it was right to leave him, but being swallowed by the pain of missing him. One half of her was dragging the other half along kicking and screaming, and the depressed half was winning.

She caught sight of herself in the mirror hanging on the wall and blanched. She looked worse than she thought. Her dark hair was balled on top of her head, her skin was slick and pasty. To top off the look of total homebody, she was wearing a ratty t-shirt and pajama shorts, just now realizing that she hadn't gotten dressed all day. Come to think of it, she couldn't remember what she had done all day, other than spending too much time in the humor section of Pinterest and refreshing her Facebook over and over again. But it was Saturday night, and pretty soon her feed would be filled with white dresses and smiles of girls who were actually wanted by the loves of their lives.

She closed her eyes and stuffed that thought into the back of her mind, in the space where she kept things she was too afraid to think about. She hoped that if she buried it deep enough, beneath other, happier thoughts, she'd get over it more quickly.

She turned to her phone, hoping for a distraction, and refreshed her Facebook again. Her heart pounded in panic when her eyes ran over the name of his best friend, and she wondered if she'd see his name or his face. Unwilling to look, she quickly scrolled past and saw a post from one of her friends talking about going out to a bar that night.

"Oh shit." She slapped her palm to her head, remembering that she had agreed to go with them. Lauren wasn't looking forward to it. In fact, she would have preferred to sit at home in the same clothes she slept in the night before, rather than get into the shower and attempt to look like she cared.

Then again, maybe getting out was what she needed after all. She was so tired of crying, so tired of being *sad* all the time. She just wanted to be as happy as she used to be and for everything to go back to normal. There had been this dark cloud hanging over her head, and she wanted someone to make it go away.

Wandering around her room, she found something decent to wear and walked over to her vanity to find some jewelry. Instinctively, she went to grab the diamond necklace that had been her staple piece for the past few years, but she stopped, tears welling in her eyes. *He'd* given it to her on their first anniversary. Then the bracelet the next year, then earrings. In fact, the only piece of jewelry missing from his collection was the ring that he didn't want to buy her.

He used to think of it as a funny joke—the Josh collection, he'd called it, and she'd been too quick to point out that it was missing an integral part. She remembered how he'd get more annoyed every time she brought it up.

See? She reminded herself. *It was a good thing.*

She closed her jewelry box and sniffed back more tears. She was *not* going to cry tonight; she was *not* going to be pissy and moody and passive aggressive.

She was going to enjoy herself, damn it, even if she had to fake it.

***

Lauren walked into the crowded club, plastering a smile on her face as she weaved through the people. She hated going out. There were too many people and too much noise, but for tonight, she forced herself to accept that she was here. Scanning the club, she spotted the gaggle of girls that she knew and made her way over. They were all prettier than Lauren, but perhaps she was just feeling dumpy lately. They had beers and were standing around a positively beaming girl with a beautiful diamond on her left hand.

"And next week, we're going to look at different places, I'm *sooooooooo* excited," the girl said, her voice high and nasally. "I mean, my mom is flipping out about all of this, and it's *sooooooooo* much work. I was *soooooo* shocked when he

10

proposed!"

"Lauren!" Lauren's friend Aubrey, the one who had invited her out, smiled when she spotted Lauren standing outside of the group. "You came out!"

"Yeah," Lauren said, forcing a smile on her face.

"How've you been, girl?"

Lauren wondered if she should tell Aubrey about the low times, the every day crying, the way that nearly everything in her *life* hurt now, but she decided against it.

"I'm good, you know," she shrugged noncommittally. "Considering."

"Have you seen Josh?"

The name was enough to ignite a flame of nervous butterflies in her chest. "Nah, we haven't spoken really since...well...since then."

"Yeah, he's supposed to come out tonight."

Lauren's heart fell into her stomach and she found herself unable to breathe. He was going to be here? Was he already there? She looked around anxiously, wondering if every face in the room was his, and played out in her head a million overly dramatic scenarios of what would happen if he showed up, each one more nerve-wracking than the last.

After she had checked every person, disappointment settled on top of her. She heard the nasal-sounding girl continue her babbling about her stupid engagement.

"And I mean, I've started going dress shopping, and I started looking at monogrammed things. I can't wait to be Mrs. Howser!" she sighed, adjusting the ring on her finger happily. "I just...there's so much planning to do, and I just don't know how I'm going to fit it all in!"

Lauren forced another smile onto her face and said, "Well, if you need any pointers, I have a whole wedding-themed Pinterest board I'm not using. Spent six months on it!"

The girls paused to look at Lauren as if she were a bomb about to explode.

"Kidding!" Lauren grinned, wondering why they were looking at her like that. "Just kidding. I'm totally fine about it. No big deal."

The girls laughed at her, and Aubrey put a hand on her shoulder. "You're handling this all so well. We're all really proud of you!"

The conversation turned back to weddings, boyfriends, trips, friends, and all of the things Lauren didn't want to talk about right now. She selfishly wanted someone to ask her how she was really feeling, but she'd also just told them that she was absolutely fine.

Because she was fine. The more she told herself that, the truer it would be, right?

She took stock of everyone around her and spotted diamonds on half of the girls. Everyone else seemed to be following the same script, the one that she'd been trying to get Josh to follow. Find boyfriend, get married, have babies.

And yet, she couldn't help but wonder, if they *were* so perfect, why didn't Josh want to—

Fear dripped in the back of her mind as she squashed that thought before she could finish it. Hoping for a distraction, she began looking around the club for anyone who caught her eye. After all, everyone and their mother told her that *they* had met the love of their life within a year of ending a long-term relationship. So it was just a matter of time before Lauren found the person she was *really* supposed to be with.

Perhaps that's what she needed—a knight in shining armor to save her from her misery.

She sauntered over to the bar, trying her best to look

attractive as she waited for the bartender to walk over and take her drink order. This was how it happened in the movies. Girl at a bar, guy comes up to her and starts chatting, and then they ride off into the sunset.

The bartender walked right by her without stopping.

She grumbled and leaned forward, scanning the room for Josh's face.

No, not Josh. Someone else.

She realized no one was noticing her, and the dark cloud of disappointment that had settled in her stomach spread across her chest. Everything suddenly was incredibly annoying, from the music they were playing to the people standing too close to her at the bar, to the damned girls with their damned diamond rings that Lauren didn't have.

She was overcome with the strong desire to go home, get in her sweatpants, and cry.

She walked back over to the girls, who were still laughing and talking about something Lauren wasn't interested in.

Lauren put a fake smile on her face. "Hey, I think I'm going to bail," she said to Aubrey.

"What?" Aubrey frowned. "Why?"

"Just...tired." This was her go-to lie for excusing herself from situations. "And this place isn't really my scene."

"Okay, are you sure?"

"Yeah, no worries," Lauren waved her off. "I worked out really hard today, and I just feel really tired."

It was a boldfaced lie, but it seemed to work.

"Oh, okay." Aubrey smiled. "Drive safe, honey!"

Lauren left the thumping club, her ears still ringing as she walked the dark streets to her car. Almost every person she passed was a couple, and it made her want to throw up. Just as the tears spilled over her eyes, she got to her car and climbed in, grateful to be in the solitude of her front seat, in the dark, where no one would know how much she was feeling right now.

She was disappointed that she didn't meet someone new, disappointed that he didn't show up, angry that nobody seemed to care that she was drowning, annoyed that everyone else in the world was getting married and she *wasn't*, fed up with herself and her out of control emotions, and just done.

Just.

Done.

She turned the key in the ignition and as the tears fell harder. In the silence of her car and the privacy of the night, she let herself fall apart.

***

Mondays were always shitty, but that Monday was extra terrible. The dark cloud over her head had refused to dissipate all day Sunday. When Monday morning rolled around, it was painful to even pull herself out of bed and look halfway presentable for work.

And now she was staring at a spreadsheet and couldn't find the mental focus to start typing. Her eyes drifted to the spot on her cubicle shelf where the photo of Josh had sat since she first started work there. She remembered the day after they broke up, walking in and tossing his picture in the trash (then covertly sticking it in her purse...just in case).

She looked to the clock and decided to take a lunch break. Grabbing her purse, she walked out of the dreary office into the blinding sunlight. The sun made her feel somewhat better, as it was hard to be unhappy on such a pretty day.

She walked down the lightly crowded streets, not finding any place to eat that very much interested her, and trying, but failing miserably, to not remember what Josh had said about all of them. After all, every single one of these restaurants was on "the list" of places that they'd jokingly agreed never to return to again.

She angrily turned down a side street, needing to get off the main drag and out of her thoughts. This row of shops was mostly antiques, nothing that Lauren ever found very useful. She wasn't a trinkets person like her mom, but she also never went into an antiques shop with Josh, so they probably wouldn't remind her of him.

She opened the door quietly, listening to the soft jingle of the bell. She noticed an old man standing behind a glass counter. He nodded his hello to her but didn't move to get up. Lauren liked it better that way; Josh always called pushy salesmen "hound dogs."

Damn it, she hissed at herself.

She slowly walked down the aisles, wishing she had a reason to purchase some of the unique trinkets. Nobody she knew had a birthday coming up, and nothing piqued her fancy enough to get her to fork over money.

That is, until her eyes landed on a beautiful ruby necklace.

She almost missed it, situated between china figurines in the back corner of one of the display cabinets. But a stray beam of light hit the necklace at just the right angle, drawing her toward the glass to get a better look.

"Oh, that is a fine piece, indeed."

Lauren jumped out of her skin, forgetting about the old man. He had followed her to the case, obviously hoping her interest would result in a sale.

"It's a pretty necklace," Lauren said.

"Yes, I've had that for a while," he said, cocking his head to the side. "Perhaps it was not in a good place."

Lauren smiled, her eyes drifting down to the stone again.

"Would you like to try it on?"

15

"Oh, um..." Lauren hedged, checking the time on her phone. She really couldn't take more than a half hour for lunch, and she'd already wasted twenty minutes. Not to mention, she wasn't sure how much the necklace would cost, and she hated to bother this man and only to put his merchandise back.

But it was pretty. And she *did* need a new necklace to wear every day, since she couldn't even look at her old diamond one without breaking into tears. Maybe buying a new piece of jewelry would be just the thing she needed. A line in the sand to say, "no more sadness."

"Sure," Lauren said, even though the man had already pulled it out and was gently offering it to her. She took the gold chain in her hand and wrapped it behind her neck, struggling to fix the clasp.

"Here, let me," the storekeep said. Lauren held the ends of the necklace and handed them off to the man. As his fingers danced against the nape of her neck, a chill ran down her back.

I desperately need this sale. If I don't start making some money soon, the shop will go under and we'll have to start all over. I do hope that she—

His fingers left her neck and the strange thoughts abruptly ceased, leaving Lauren staring back into her wide eyes in the mirror, wondering what the hell had just happened.

"Quite fitting on you," the man said.

Lauren knew that he was desperately hoping she would buy it, and for some reason she *wanted* to buy it from him, just to help him stave off bankruptcy. But how the hell did she know that he was about to go through bankruptcy?

"Well?" he asked, oblivious to her internal conversation.

"Oh, yes," Lauren said, dropping her hair behind her back. "Lovely."

"Would you like to wear it out of the store, or shall I wrap it up for you?" Again, Lauren felt a strong urge to just *help* the man for God's sake. She somehow knew he was worried for his wife at home, who was sick.

And *how* did she know that his wife was sick?

"I think I'll...wear it out," Lauren said, knowing (again, how did she *know*) that if she put this necklace back, the man would be heartbroken.

The entire place was giving her the creeps and she just wanted to get out of here before she started hearing more voices.

"Excellent, excellent. That will be two hundred dollars."

··*·*

Lauren hustled down the street to make it back to work on time, arguing with herself about the merits of spending so much money on something so trivial. It was a pretty necklace, sure, but *two hundred dollars* was a lot of money.

More perplexing was her strange feeling about the man, and knowing that she needed to purchase this necklace from him to make him happy. She'd always had an inner compass, a voice that told her the right thing to do, the wrong thing to do, and how things would turn out. The voice told her it was time to break up with Josh, the one that had taken over on that terrible May morning after she'd ignored it for three months.

The memory threatened to replay and she forced herself to stop as she slid into her desk just as the clock struck one in the afternoon. Instinctively, her hand flew to her phone to send a text message. She stopped herself just as she unlocked her phone. She and Josh used to text constantly during the day. Most of it was inane conversation—discussing the latest with his favorite football team, wisecracking lines from their favorite television shows—but it passed the time. He used to be the first person she told about everything, the only person interested in her boring little life.

Just as in the club on Saturday night, her loneliness pulled at her like a sinking stone and the dark cloud returned. She hated herself for letting the darkness in, but at the same time, it was nice to let herself feel it. Faking happiness all the time was exhausting; even more so to attempt to fool herself.

"Let me take your burden..."

Lauren sat upright so fast her back cracked. She had just heard a voice, one much different than she'd ever heard. It was hissing and guttural, almost snake-like. And it sounded like it came from *inside her mind.*

She paused, her ears searching the room for the sound of the voice. When it did not come again, she realized that she must have been imagining things. She turned her attention back to the numbers that beckoned her, and realized she had spent the entire morning moping and was now behind schedule. She placed her fingers on the keyboard and began to work.

Look to the left screen, highlight the numbers, copy, paste in the right screen.

Look to the left screen, highlight the numbers, copy, paste in the right screen.

Look to the left screen, highlight the numbers, copy, paste in the right screen.

The monotony put her into a trance, and her mind wandered again. She needed a vacation, she thought, continuing to move back and forth between the screens. Some time away from this place and these memories and the sadness. Maybe in a different place, she'd be able to move past everything without having to actually endure the pain of dealing with it.

Or, maybe he'd just come back home and then she'd never have to deal with it.

The tears began to gather behind her eyes and she looked up, trying her best to swallow them before they rolled down her cheeks. The truth of the matter was, she wanted him back and she didn't want him back. She was glad they didn't get married and she was angry with herself for ruining everything. The war in her head raged almost every day, and she was so tired of the battle.

She just wanted it to be over already.

"Give me your pain..."

Lauren heard the voice again and this time stood up, and looked around. Everyone was still out to lunch, and she was the only one in this corner of the office, though she could hear the mumbled conversations of others nearby. Hastily, she wiped away her tears, hoping her face wasn't too red. She didn't want anyone at work to know she'd been crying; she didn't want to bother them with her problems. Hearts were broken every day, as the song went, and what she was going through was nothing compared to the woes of the world. Her mom had taught her to temper her emotions, to keep everything in check. "Is this a one or a ten?" she'd ask whenever Lauren got too emotional over something.

"Suck it up, Dailey," she whispered to herself, scraping around her consciousness for the strength to get past this. She knew in two months, she'd be just fine. She'd be out, dating someone else, maybe the guy she was really supposed to be with. Perhaps she'd join one of those dating sites.

Josh's voice floated into her head, voicing his opinion about online dating.

She became angry with her mind for betraying her like this. Why couldn't it just play along and do as she wished? Why was it always bringing up memories or dragging her down a path of sadness?

Again, she wished he would just disappear from her mind.

"I will ease your pain...Let me take you away...There will be no more pain..."

Closing her eyes, a tear rolled down her cheek. The voice in her head was no longer startling. Somehow, it made her feel like it had been there all along. And the idea that someone could just take away her pain...sounded lovely.

"Will you let me take you away?"

"Yes..."

Something changed in the air.

Her desk trembled under her fingertips, and for a moment, she thought it was a truck rumbling by. But it grew more intense, and things began falling from her desk shelf. Someone in the office screamed, "EARTHQUAKE!"

The room darkened as the lights went out and the shaking grew to terrifying ferocity. Lauren gripped her desk, and looked up as ceiling tiles began falling around her. She ducked under her desk and held on, praying that the cheap plastic material would hold.

From beneath the desk, she locked onto a pair of gleaming ruby eyes staring back at her.

Then the world went black.

chapter two

Lauren immediately knew something was wrong.

Everything was dark and dusty, and she could barely breathe.

There was something very heavy on top of her, on the side of her, surrounding her.

Everything rushed back to her as her brain re-calibrated.

There was an earthquake, and she was at work, and she must have gotten knocked out by something. She was buried under a pile of rubble and concrete. When she realized she couldn't move, she began to panic. She imagined herself beneath ten stories of collapsed building and could already see the headline when they dug her out in ten months.

"HELP!" she screamed, her throat closing up in fear. She struggled against the rocks that surrounded her, realizing that she was unable to budge them an inch.

"IS SOMEONE THERE?!" She tried to get a grip on herself. Maybe firefighters had already arrived; maybe everything was going to be all right. She remembered a TV show or movie that said panicking used up more oxygen, but if she didn't breathe, she was going to die. She pushed and clawed and scraped at whatever she could get her hands on, but nothing moved. She cursed herself for being so weak, for never going to the gym when she should have.

"HELP ME!" she tried again, but this one came out as a sob.

She was helpless, weak, and going to die under this rubble. She would never see her mom or dad or Josh again. She began to cry more, thinking about how distraught her mom would be when they found her body.

"P-please," she sobbed. "Somebody please help me...I don't want to die..."

Her breath caught when she heard the sound of rocks moving.

"HELP!" Lauren screamed. "IS SOMEONE THERE!"

"I'm here!" someone replied to her. "Hold on, I'll get you out!"

Relief—glorious, beautiful, agonizing relief washed over her as a beam of light fell onto her face. The person was pulling the rocks off of her as fast as he could. With a heave, the last of the rocks disappeared from her vision. Cool air touched her face and she took a long breath in, as if it were the very first one she ever took.

When she opened her eyes, that breath was sucked right back out of her when she came face to face with one of the most handsome men she'd ever laid eyes on.

"You're all right," he said, with a thousand-watt smile. "I'll get you out of here. You're a very lucky woman."

Lauren wondered for a moment if she'd died and gone to heaven, but the pain in her body told her otherwise. She watched as he used his—dare she say—*rippling* muscles to pull the rocks off of her. Even though she had just nearly died, she couldn't quite look at him without feeling a blush rising to her face.

"Silly girl, what were you doing up here anyway?" His voice sounded to Lauren like the laughter of angels. With a heave, the pressure on her legs lifted, and Lauren snuck a peak downward.

Big mistake.

When she saw how badly she was injured, pain shot up her

mangled leg, and she whimpered, feeling sick.

"We'll get you to a healer," Angel-man said, slipping his Herculean arms under her head and gently under her legs, lifting her out of the rubble.

Who is this girl, and why is she up here—

He laid her on the ground and disappeared from her vision for a moment. In her delirium, she wondered if she had misheard *healer* instead of doctor, because that would just be silly...

She felt his hands slide underneath her, and she was suddenly wrapped up in thoughts that were not her own.

She could have been killed by the Anghenfil. Why is she here?

The panic and the adrenaline from nearly dying was too much, and Lauren felt dizzy, like the world was falling out of her hands.

She seems to be convulsing. What if she's dying? I need to get her down to the village now.

Down she fell, the voice in her head growing faint. Before she succumbed completely, she saw a pair of gleaming ruby red eyes staring down at her, and a hiss of anger.

"It will be mine soon enough..."

***

The pain was the first thing to register, followed by the smell of dust. She cracked her eyes and focused in the light, becoming aware of her surroundings.

And aware that she was no longer in California.

In fact, she was aware that she might no longer be in the twenty-first century.

The walls were mud or something of that kind—definitely not drywall. The bed smelled and felt like it was stuffed with hay, not at all like her double-plush mattress in her bedroom. The floors were filthy, or maybe they were just *dirt*, and—

She looked to the door, or rather the rag that was hanging in the opening of the room, as a small form walked through the door. Fire-red hair was the first thing Lauren noticed, followed by a pale face full of freckles, and a wool dress.

"AY MA'M!" the girl called, sounding like she was Scottish or Irish or something definitely not American. "SHE'S AWAKE!"

The shrill scream from the child made Lauren wince. Her leg throbbed, and she shifted to see if she could move it—

A sharp pain shot through her and she cried out.

"There'll be none of that now." A woman with waist-length dark red hair came bustling in through the rag on the door, carrying a bucket. "Your leg will need some time to heal."

"Where am I?" Lauren choked out, looking up to see the woman squeezing water out of a washcloth and placing it on Lauren's head. The coolness was refreshing, and Lauren suddenly wondered when she'd see a shower again.

"Our village," the older woman said, as if it were common knowledge. "What were you doing in the caves anyways?"

"Caves?" Lauren said, as another cold wipe went across her face. "What caves?"

"The ones in the mountain," the woman replied, again, as plain as if she were answering what day it was. "There was a cave-in. It's a good thing the watcher was up there chasing after a wayward goat or else we wouldn't have found you."

The words made little sense to Lauren. "I wasn't in a *cave*, I was in my office, and there was an earthquake, and I woke up... buried under all that rock..."

The woman paused in her ministrations and looked down at Lauren like she had three heads.

"I'm not crazy," Lauren insisted, though she wondered if she might be. After all, she appeared to be hallucinating about a woman wearing medieval clothing in a mud hut.

"Your leg had a nasty infection," the woman said as she put

away the cloth. "Feverish. It just now broke." She placed her hand atop Lauren's head.

I'm afraid of this stranger. Why is she saying such odd thing? What is an office and what is an earthquake? Cefin asked me to watch over her, but how long—

The woman lifted her hand and Lauren let out a gasping breath, feeling like she'd just walked up a flight of stairs.

"Something the matter?" the woman said.

"You didn't just feel that?" Lauren asked, wondering if it was a smart thing to ask such a thing to a woman who already thought she was crazy. How did Lauren know that the woman thought she was crazy?

Maybe Lauren was crazy. Oh God, what was happening to her?

"You rest. I shall see about finding some more sleeping draft," the woman said, the nerves evident in her voice. She scurried out of the room as fast as she could, making sure to close the rags behind her.

Lauren leaned back into the hay-covered bed and looked at the muddy ceiling. She had *felt* what the woman was feeling, or at least that's what it seemed like to Lauren. It was as if she were siphoning the woman's emotions.

"Oh come on, Dailey, that's insanity," Lauren mumbled to herself. She was delirious probably. Most likely, she was in a coma in a hospital in California. This was nothing more than a coma-dream.

"Ooooow," she whined, trying to move her leg again. If it were a drug-induced fantasy, it was a doozy of a hallucination, because she definitely felt *that* pain. She pushed herself upright and tossed off the covers, noticing that she was still in her dress pants and silk shirt she'd gone to work in, although they were dirty and ripped in places. It certainly looked like she had been buried in the rubble.

Her left pant leg had been ripped clean off, and her leg was wrapped in thick bandages, covered in some kind of foul-smelling goop. Lauren poked at it, wishing suddenly that she had a Z-pak and a bottle of isopropyl alcohol to clean her wounds. She paid attention in history; she knew how many people died from infections in the old days.

"You'd better not touch that." The fire-headed impish child was back, or wait...Lauren blinked. Now it was a boy. But the same face, same mop of curly red hair.

"Er..." Lauren said, unsure if it would be rude to ask the kid if he/she was a he or a she. "What is this stuff?"

"Healers put it on ya," he/she replied, circling the room. "Ma'm says you're a bit loopy; is that right?"

"Sure," Lauren said. "When can I walk again?"

"I danno. Ask the healers," he/she said, standing next to the table and poking at the water bucket his mother (Lauren guessed) had left behind.

"Where are the doctors?" Lauren asked.

"What's a doctor?"

"Whoever did this," Lauren said, pointing at her leg.

"Siors, he's out tending to some other folks," he said, leaning against the bed frame. "So...is it true yer a loon?"

"EDWARD!"

The imp straightened like a board and scurried out of the room as if the table he'd been leaning on had burst into flames. No sooner had he disappeared behind the curtain, than the mother walked back in, her eyes searching the room for her wayward son.

"He just left," Lauren replied, still sitting up.

The woman sniffed and walked over to check Lauren's bandages.

"So...what's this stuff?" Lauren asked nervously.

"Mud," the woman replied. "It will heal the bone and then the skin. It was blessed with magical properties."

"Oh, well, of course," Lauren said, sounding a bit hysterical. Her broken leg was covered in bacteria-infested mud. If she didn't have an infection before, she sure was going to have one now.

"Siors should be 'round in a bit." The woman patted her bandages. "He'll reapply the mud. Be a dear and try not to scream. Near woke the village last night."

Lauren nodded and looked down at her leg, wondering how she'd look as an amputee—if she even survived. She desperately craved a shower. Was she far enough back in time when they believed baths were unhygienic? Because they could forget that mess. She *was* going to be clean, even if she had to dunk herself in the river.

"I'm sorry about the twins," the woman said, after a moment.

"I...wait...twins?" Lauren blinked.

"Yes, Eddy and Mairwan," she tutted, bustling around the room. "They don't have anyone to play with but each other and they do get into mischief. And you, I'm afraid, they are quite curious about."

"I'm curious about me too," Lauren muttered. "How did I even get here?"

"Cefin brought you down."

"Who?"

"Ay, she's awake!" Angel-man was back and looking more handsome than ever. Lauren blushed as she took him in fully. He was tall, with a smooth handsome face and dark hair that was pulled into a low ponytail. His arms which had moved the rocks so easily were covered by a tunic-looking thing, which stretched across his broad chest. He resembled a male model and it kind of hurt to look at him.

Lauren desperately wished to disappear or run away, but she was stuck on the bed in her ratty, dirty shirt and her torn pant leg and her smelly leg.

"Cefin, Siors will be here soon. Don't be making too much of a fuss," the woman said as she bustled out of the room. She leaned into whisper something to him, and Lauren caught the words "hysterical" and "loony." He nodded, coming to sit on the bed next to her. The woman left the room, although Lauren rather wished she would stay so the handsome man wouldn't have her in his sights.

"So..." Lauren mumbled like an idiot. "Thank you for... saving my life..."

"Yes," he said, tilting his head to look at her. "And why were you up in the mountains anyway? How did you get past the watcher?"

"I didn't...I mean...I don't know." Lauren shook her head.

"Do you not remember?" he asked, reaching his hand to touch her forehead.

No one should have passed me, and if Graves missed another shift, I'll kill him. We have a duty—

Lauren heard herself suck in breath again and realized Cefin was staring at her.

"Did I hurt you?" he asked.

"No, I just..." Lauren swallowed, realizing that she must be going insane. But if she knew she was going insane, did that mean she was going insane? Was it possible to watch oneself go insane?

He peered at her with his beautiful face and she had to look away. "You must still be a little faint from the fever. You were murmuring when I pulled you out of the cave."

"Yeah, what is this cave thing everyone keeps talking about?"

Lauren said, finding her tongue. "And where *am* I?"

"You are in the village of Rhianu," he said, the foreign word slipping off his tongue beautifully and unhelpfully. "I was up in the mountains and I heard you buried in the rubble, so I pulled you out."

Lauren still couldn't register his words. "I was never *in* any cave. I was sitting in my office. An earthquake happened, and now I'm in the freaking *Hobbit*."

"What's a hobbit?"

Lauren let out a long breath between her pursed lips.

"At least tell me your name," he said gently, as if she were a certifiable crazy person.

"Lauren Dailey."

"I'm Cefin."

"Kevin?"

"Keh-fin," he enunciated. "Cefin Vaughan. I'm the village watcher."

"What's that?"

"I protect the village," he said, "from the Anghenfil."

"What's an—"

Her question was silenced when an old man walked into the room, followed by the woman who had been tending to her. She wasn't sure why, but she had seen the old man in her dreams, and the thought was unnerving. He wore a dusty red robe, his white beard cut short to his face, and some liver spots dotting his bald head. He seemed pleased that she was awake.

"Cefin, lad, we need to change her bandages," the old man said. The woman had a bucket in her hands filled with the same goop currently on Lauren's leg.

"You know, I think I'll be fine." Lauren waved them off, not wishing to add fresh bacteria to her legs.

"Nonsense," the woman said, placing the foul-smelling

bucket next to Lauren.

"Oh, sure the stench is bad, but it'll do the trick," Cefin said, shouldering a giant spear that he'd brought into the room.

"Aerona, please hold her for me, she does like to thrash," the healer said, placing the bucket on the ground. The woman walked over to sit next to Lauren. When she placed her hands on Lauren's arm, she felt a rush of warm air enter her body again.

Who is this girl? Why was she in the mountains? Why is she convulsing like this? She looks possessed. Are the children safe?

Like a sharp turn from a steering wheel, another feeling came over Lauren, mixing in with the first in a loud, simultaneous two-person monologue.

She must be in shock. This leg injury isn't that bad. Where did she come from—

Where are the children now? I don't think I can keep her here, especially if she's a danger—

A screaming voice joined the off-key chorus of conversations.

She appears to be having a fit now, but...is she one of them?

Lauren plunged back into herself, and realized that the person screaming was her. She gasped for breath and her brain felt like someone had just played ping-pong with it. As she stared at the ceiling, she gripped the wool sheets on the bed so hard her knuckles were white.

"What the hell just happened to me?" she whispered, looking at the old man, Siors was his name. She knew him as well as her own grandfather, even though they had just met.

"You don't know?" Siors replied, sounding as shocked as Lauren did. Aerona (again, the familiarity of the name and the person was unnervingly new and old at the same time) was similarly shocked, not even bothering to remove the two red-headed children from the room. Eddy, who was always getting into trouble, and Mairwan, sweet Mairwan who wouldn't hurt a fly, were against the wall. And Cefin, handsome Cefin had his hand on his sword, looking ready to slay some fantastic beast.

"No." Lauren replied, her eyes dancing from one person to another.

"You are an empath," the old man whispered.

"A what?" Lauren pushed herself up right. She was dizzy and weak from whatever just occurred, but she was quite sure it had nothing to do with the fact that her leg was now covered in fresh magic mud.

"Eddy, Mairwen, out," Aerona ordered to the twins. When they didn't move, Aerona walked over and hitched them by their arms, shoving them outside. Once they were out of the house, Lauren turned to look at Siors.

"A *what*?" she repeated.

"An empath, a reader of feelings." Siors was smiling like a young boy discovering the night sky for the first time. "You felt it just now, did you not?"

"What was that?" Lauren said, pleased and horrified that she was not crazy.

"When an empath touches another person, they absorb their feelings," Siors said. "Or at the very least, they can read them."

"I just...it was like I was...you," Lauren sputtered, looking at Aerona, not even caring if she sounded crazy. She felt like Dorothy in Oz. "And then I was *you*," she pointed to Siors. "And then I was back, and it was too much and—"

"This is incredible," Siors said, sitting back and stroking his white beard. "Where did you come from?"

"My cubicle."

"Mi-cubical," the old man repeated, looking to be wracking his brain. "I have not heard of this land—"

"AARG!" Lauren cried out, laying back down. "This is a fever dream. I'm having a fever dream. Maybe if I fall asleep, I'll wake back up."

empath

She squeezed her eyes closed and wished. A twitch in her leg and a jolt of pain reminded her she wasn't dreaming.

"My child, you have a gift," the old man said. "Even in this land, empaths are rare and highly valued."

"But why do I suddenly have these powers now? I'm...I was...normal.... And why am I here? Are there other empaths I can talk to?"

"The last empath to visit this land arrived over fifty years ago," Siors said. "I was a young man, but I remember when she came to the king's castle in Traegaron. She was the first empath in some time, too."

Lauren looked up at him, hope filling her from top to bottom. "What? Really? Can I talk to her?"

"The Anghenfil took her."

"I'm sorry, the what?" Lauren said, after a moment. Cefin had used the same word as well, and somewhere in the back of her mind, she felt a drip of dread.

"*Ang-hen-fil*," he said slower. "A monster, made of fire and smoke. It lives in the mountains, in the very caves where we found you."

"Oh." Lauren nodded. "When you say it *took* her..."

"The beast appeared in the kingdom and took her back to the mountains that surround the village. No one has seen her since."

"Fantastic. And you said this...monster...inhabits the same caves where you found me?"

The old man nodded.

"No, I'm not—I'm normal, I'm feverish or something, I'm having a coma dream, but I'm not....NO!"

She surprised herself with the ferocity of her words and tears welled up from a place deep within her. She was so tired of crying, but now she felt like her tears were worth it.

"I wanna go home," she whimpered. She didn't care that she

was twenty-four years old. She wanted her mom, she wanted her bed. She didn't want to be an empath or be eaten by a giant smoke monster or lose her leg to a bacterial infection or any of this.

Aerona sat down next to her but didn't move to touch her.

"You need your rest," Siors said gently. "You have endured quite a shock, and need some time. Aerona, Cefin, let's give her a moment."

Lauren lay in the quiet room and felt the tug of sleep pulling at her. Maybe she was dreaming, and if she fell *back* asleep, she'd wake up in the hospital.

She hoped.

chapter three

Unfortunately, when Lauren awoke to the smell of hay and mud, she realized that she was not, in fact, having a coma dream.

This was really happening.

She rolled over and stopped, not from pain but from a lack of it. She looked down at her leg, which was still covered in the goop, and moved it gingerly. When it didn't explode in pain, she moved it more, testing it.

"Well I'll be damned, it is magic goop," Lauren said, as if this were perfectly acceptable. Because why not; she'd already been transported to a brand new world. Of course, the mud was magic. Next there would be flying unicorns.

She slid her leg off the bed, testing it out and watching as the bandages and goop slid off, and her leg was, indeed, healed. She tested her weight; it hurt, but not so much that she could not stand. On the edge of the bed, she saw of two folded pieces of cloth—one that resembled burlap and the other a dull white. She picked up the white cloth and it unfurled as a long white dress with sleeves. She assumed the burlap was another dress; she vaguely recalled Aerona wearing something similar. And together, they looked like something out of a fantasy novel.

In which she was now living, she reminded herself. Magic goop and flying unicorns and such utter nonsense.

She supposed she couldn't wander around in half-torn pants

and a filthy silk shirt, so she peeled them off and put them on the ground. As her shirt went over her head, the cool backing of her new, expensive ruby necklace hit against her skin. The light reflected off the red stone, and she could have sworn it was alive. She almost pulled it off to stick it with the rest of her clothes, but something stopped her. Instead, she started peeling off her dirty underwear and bra, poking around on the bed for something to replace them. When she came up empty, she realized she was going to have to go commando until she could find a washing machine.

Or, she realized with a terrible scowl, a river.

God, she was in real shit now.

Longing for her shower, she slid the long white cotton dress on, and it fell all the way to her ankles. She pulled on the burlap-looking dress over the cotton dress, the material itching at her arms. Although she missed her sweatpants, there was a draft in the room. But with this dress on, she was at least a little warmer.

There was only one room in this small little house, with one bed corner, presumably where the entire family slept. Lauren had slept in another corner on a pile of hay with a single sheet thrown over it. No wonder she'd felt like something was poking her all night.

There wasn't much else in this one room, a cold hearth where an iron pot hung, and a small wooden table. Lauren was playing with the rusted metal spoons when the rags to the outside rustled and Aerona came walking in, carrying a bucket of water.

"Oh goodness, you're up," she said, a small smile on her face. "Glad to see Siors' healing has worked on you."

"Yeah," Lauren said, putting the spoon down. "Um...thank you for letting me stay with you."

"Think nothing of it," Aerona said, placing the water next to the fire. Lauren suddenly realized that she was perhaps a few years older than Lauren herself. Lauren still felt sixteen most of the time, a kid, but this woman couldn't have been older than twenty-seven with two young children.

Aerona grunted as she lifted the water to pour into the cast iron pot over the fire.

"Oh, geez, sorry!" Lauren hurried over to help, realizing that she was standing around like an idiot.

"Thank you, dear." Aerona said, allowing Lauren to take the other side of the bucket. Even between the two of them, it was heavy, and Lauren realized she hadn't seen Aerona's husband—

Aerona's husband was gone.

She shook her head, the memory washing over her like it was her own. She wasn't sure where it came from, but she knew that however it happened still caused Aerona great pain.

"Lauren?" Aerona asked, placing a hand on Lauren's arm.

She is so strange, this empath. I'm still worried for the children, but Siors thinks it is best to keep her in the village, perhaps she can be
—

Lauren gasped and registered that water bucket had fallen, dousing the bottom half of her dress in water. She couldn't remember the past few seconds and was still feeling the aftershocks of Aerona's thoughts. Thoughts about *her.*

"My dear, are you all right?" Aerona asked, looking both concerned and afraid at once.

"Y-yes," Lauren croaked out, sitting down at the table and rubbing her face in her hands. She was dizzy and couldn't shake Aerona's concerns from her head.

"That's right, we can't touch you." Aerona opened and closed her hands, and Lauren caught the hint of pity in her face. "Siors says that you read others through touch."

"I..." Lauren looked up at her, nervous that Aerona was going to throw her out of the house for being a freak, or worse, for invading her privacy. The idea of someone knowing Lauren's deepest darkest secrets was enough to make her skin crawl.

"Oh my dear, don't worry!" Aerona hurried over to the table and knelt in front of Lauren, but did not touch her. "I know this must all be very..."

"Overwhelming," Lauren mumbled. "I'm sorry that I read your...I mean...I..." She couldn't keep it in another moment. "Please don't kick me out!"

To her surprise, Aerona just laughed.

"I most certainly will not 'kick you out,' dear." She stood and walked over to the overturned bucket. "We have too few people in the village as it is, and we always need help with things. We are glad to have you."

Lauren suddenly realized the full scope of her predicament and she found it hard to breathe. She was *stuck* somewhere that was definitely not home. She had no idea where she even was—a different time, a different dimension? And without knowing *where* she was, she had no way to figure out how to get back home.

"That reminds me," Aerona said, ignorant of Lauren's inner turmoil. "Siors wanted you to come visit him today. He's very interested in hearing about where you came from. And"—she smiled lovingly—"I'm sure that if there is a way for you to get back home, he would know it."

***

Lauren stepped outside of Aerona's small one-room hut and took in this new village. It definitely looked like something from *Lord of the Rings*, tiny houses like Aerona's nestled along a gravel and stone path. Snowcapped mountain peaks rose all around them—the air was chilly and a little thin. She counted maybe twenty houses that she could see, each one looking like they had sprung from the land organically.

She heard hushed whispering and saw two women talking in the front yard of a nearby house. They were looking at her and pointing. She waved to them, and they hurried inside their house.

"Whatever."

She wrapped her arms around herself and began walking along the main road in the village, lined by the ramshackle fences in front of the houses. Aerona had described Siors' house as the oldest of the bunch, one that she would find on the edge of town. She stopped in front of the last house on the street, the nearby trees dangling branches into the overgrown grass and vines that covered the front of the house. Smoke poured from the leaning chimney atop the roof. It certainly looked like a house the old man would live in, so she walked up to the door and knocked.

"Hello?" she called. "Siors?"

After a few moments, she pushed the door open and poked her head into the room. It was heavily perfumed with spices, smoke, and old books, which seemed to be stuffed into every nook and cranny of the small house. A small table stood in the center of the room, the only surface not covered by books. Lauren looked around for a sign of the old man, but didn't see any movement.

"Siors, are you here?" Lauren called out again.

"Oh, the empath!" Siors emerged through an open door on the other side of the room, a kind smile on his old face. "My dear, to what do I owe the pleasure of your visit?"

"Well," Lauren said, "I have a lot of questions...such as how the hell I got here in the first place."

"I'm sure you do," Siors said, pulling out an old book from the stack. "I've been looking through my own library here to see if I can find any mention of the girl who came here when I was a boy, but so far, no luck. All I know is the last empath arrived in much the same manner as you did."

"Do people suddenly appear out of thin air normally here?" Lauren asked.

Siors smiled. "I'm afraid not"

"What about this empath stuff?" Lauren asked. "Is that normal? I didn't have any of these kinds of powers in my world." Even saying the word powers was strange for her.

"Empaths have been legend for centuries," Siors said. "Some of the old texts say that an empath can read emotions, and others say that an empath is really connecting with the other person's soul."

Lauren grimaced; she wasn't sure she liked the sound of that.

"So, there aren't any other empaths I can talk to?" she asked.

"No, the only other one I am aware of was taken by the Anghenfil."

"So this....Anghenfil." Lauren swallowed nervously. "You said that you found me near the caves where it lives? What...*is it* exactly?"

Siors placed a thick and dusty book on the table, flipping it open and turning the dusty pages. He paused and turned it around, showing Lauren a painting of a winged red dragon looming over a flaming city. Bright red eyes and gleaming white teeth rounded out the frightening image.

"Beautiful," Lauren pushed the book away before she had a full-blown panic attack. "And it ate the last empath, you say?"

"The empath had been summoned by the king to the castle in Traegaron. The beast itself had not been seen in centuries. Most thought it was just a myth. And then it appeared and destroyed half the castle as it hunted for her. Those who were there say it wrapped her up in its fearsome tail and carried her to these very mountains."

Lauren caught the vision of the beast in the book again and wondered if *it* was the reason why she was here. She remembered that odd voice that she heard in her office moments before the earthquake—

She quickly squashed that train of thought to refocus her attention on Siors, and she began to play with her necklace anxiously.

"The beast has been seen every few years since that day," Siors said. "But I'm afraid we do not know what powers the beast may have; just the fire and the claws are enough to be getting on with."

"Do you have any more books about the Anghenfil?" Lauren asked.

"This is the end of my compendium on the subject," Siors smiled. "But I shall send word to my scholar-brother. He is the keeper of the great library in Traegaron and one of the wisest men in the entire kingdom. If there is more to be known—about the Anghenfil, or about yourself—then he will know it."

***

Not quite ready to face the villagers and their pointing and whispering, Lauren shuffled down the gravel path away from the village. Her head was spinning from all the new information, being in this new place, with these new people, and these new powers. She was in strange clothes and no underwear. She began to play with the stone around her neck, the rough edges of the ruby giving her some kind of salve to her anxiety, like a pacifier to a crying baby.

Her thoughts floated back to the reason why she bought the item in the first place: to replace the necklace that Josh had given her on their first anniversary. And with a small smile, she realized that in the disarray of the past day and a half—finding herself in a fantasy world with strange powers she didn't understand—she hadn't *once* thought about Josh.

And yet, she suddenly wondered if he was okay back in California. He worked in a different building, but the thought of him lying somewhere hurt terrified her. She half wished that he'd been transported to this world too, so they would have no other choice but to get back together.

She laughed at herself. Such a silly thought. Why on Earth (or wherever she was now) was she so damned melodramatic?

She slowed her gait further and began to dwell on this idea for a moment. She had always felt things deeply and always seemed to have an inner sense of peoples' motivations. Here, though, that sense was magnified to the point where she couldn't even shake someone's hand without getting an inside glimpse of their emotional current.

Was there something about this land that gave her these powers?

Was it the reason she had been brought to this place?

And did it have anything to do with that Anghenfil monster?

The terrifying thought of that snake-like voice threatened to break free from the box she had shoved it into, and she shook her head to push it back.

Her hand clasped around the ruby necklace and she rubbed her thumb along the ridges on the casing. *This* was real. This was proof that she had come from a different world, that she was really Lauren Dailey, twenty-four years old from Santa Rosa, California, who worked as a data entry clerk for an insurance company. This was proof that she was once a normal person with normal hopes and dreams and normal problems.

"I'm *not* going to be stuck here," she said to the forest around her, and she meant it. If some magic portal opened and brought her to this strange land, there *had* to be a way to re-open it.

She paused for a minute, and clicked her heels together three times. "There's no place like home?" she tried, but remained firmly in place.

Her mind wandered again to the beast Siors had told her about. It sounded like something out of a movie, and she envisioned a fire-breathing dragon. Anxiety awakened in her chest and she spoke aloud to shut it down.

"I'm sure it doesn't really exist, either, that ang-whatever." She hoped that if she said it out loud it would be true. A fire-breathing monster couldn't exist. That was just silly.

She turned to look up at the mountains above the village. Aerona had said that was where Lauren had been found, buried in a cave-in.

Right about where the Anghenfil—

"NOPE," she said out loud, stopping the thought before it could complete itself.

That thought-she-was-not-thinking aside, perhaps if she returned to the place where she'd been found, she could find some clue to get her home. She spun on her heel and marched up the mountainside, hoping if she walked up far enough, she'd stumble across the cave-in.

Siors' house was on the edge of the village, so she continued on that path that had been cut through the trees. It led her to a stonier path, one which dropped of steeply on one side. She knew she must be climbing up the mountain and picked up her speed as the slope increased.

She turned a corner and stopped short at the view before her. The edge of the path dropped off steeply, revealing the beauty of the valley and the world beyond the small village. The mountains rose in snowy peaks that stretched around her. Below her feet, the sleepy village looked small and contained between the green trees and boulders. If she kept looking out, she spotted another village at the bottom of the mountain, and, even farther, a large green plain that spanned all the way to the horizon.

The view was so pretty that she didn't even notice Cefin sitting on the edge, his spear beside him.

"Get back to the village," Cefin said without turning around.

"I-what?" Lauren was taken aback by the harshness of his tone.

Cefin spun around, and she saw him flush just slightly. "Oh, it's you!"

"Yeah, it's me," Lauren said lamely.

He hopped to his feet, his face still red. "Sorry, I thought you were the twins. They like to sneak up on me."

"Really?" Lauren peered over the edge of the cliff. She worried that the kids would scare him right off.

She noticed Cefin watching her. "How are you feeling?"

"Much better, thank you," Lauren said, coming to join him at the edge to take in the view. "It's gorgeous up here."

"Sometimes on a very clear day you can see all the way to Traegaron." He pointed to an unseeable place in the distance. "It's a day's journey from here."

Lauren nodded, wrapping her arms around herself. It was chillier up here now that she wasn't moving, and she noticed Cefin wasn't wearing anything but a thin shirt. She also happened to notice how it clung to him and tore her eyes away, not wanting to seem like an idiot for gawking at him. She cleared her throat and tried to be conversational. "So what are you doing all the way up here?"

"This is my place as watcher," Cefin said. "I protect the village from the Anghenfil."

"All by yourself?" Lauren asked. The monster couldn't have been that fearsome if they sent this guy to stand watch all by himself. He seemed to know his way around his weaponry, but he was still one man. One very handsome man.

"The Anghenfil caused many to leave our village. Most men did not wish to stay and fight when it last appeared. I am the only one who answered the call."

"So why do you?"

"Because if no one else did, it would wreak havoc on the kingdom. Men in my family have always been watchers. One day, Eddy will join me, when he's old enough."

"That's right, Aerona is your aunt," Lauren said without thinking. To Cefin's surprised face, she blushed. "I mean...I felt it...when I was...whatever yesterday." She winced. "Empathing...?"

"So it's true then," he said, leaning on his spear. "You are an empath."

"I guess." She blew air between her lips. If it wasn't for this morning and the lucid way she read Aerona's thoughts, she would have considered everything to be just a bad dream. She inched away from him, not wanting to read Cefin's mind to find out how strange he thought her.

"Siors says that you came from a different land. I wondered why such a pretty girl decided to tempt fate at the hands of the Anghenfil in the mountains." He grinned, and she was amazed at how her heart began to pound at his compliment.

She hadn't flirted—really flirted—with anyone in ages, and she was very rusty at it. But it also felt kind of...nice. "Well, you know, my middle name is Danger."

"Is it really?" Cefin asked with all the innocence of a man who had never heard that joke before.

"No, it's...anyway..." She supposed her normal brand of pop culture-inspired humor wouldn't fly here, and she suddenly and violently missed Josh and the back-and-forth banter they shared. She wondered what he would think about her here in this strange land. An empath of all things. Did he even know she was gone?

"You're an interesting woman, Lauren," Cefin said, his voice pulling her from her miserable thoughts.

"That's what they tell me," Lauren said, having lost her desire to flirt more with Cefin after the unwelcome reminder of her ex. "Well, I'll see you around."

"Where are you going?" he asked after her.

"Oh," Lauren said, spinning around. "I'm going to check out where I landed here, you know, to see if there's anything that could help me get home."

She got three steps before Cefin was standing in front of her (how did he move that fast?), blocking her path. "I cannot let you do that."

"Why not?" Lauren asked, folding her arms across her chest. She tried to step around him, but he moved with her to block her path.

"My job as watcher is to protect the village from the Anghenfil," Cefin said. "And also to prevent foolhardy children from wandering up the mountainside to bother it."

"First of all, I am not a child," Lauren insisted, knowing that she sounded very much like a child as she said it. "And second of all, I can go up there if I damn well want to."

In response, Cefin unsheathed his sword at his hip and pointed it at her. Her eyes ran over the sharp point and the edges, and then back to Cefin's face, which was surprisingly taut and tense.

"Go back to the village."

"No." She couldn't understand why he was being such a dill weed about this. How did he not get that she didn't belong here? That she wanted to go home?

"Go back to the village," he repeated, holding his sword steady.

She returned his steely gaze for a few moments, locked in a silent battle of wills. After a moment, she let out a frustrated growl.

"Fine," she said, stepping back. "You win."

"Thank you," Cefin said, lowering his sword. "I don't mean to be harsh, but—"

In the moment that he was distracted by sheathing his sword, Lauren darted around him as fast as she could. She got four steps before she was plunged in emotion.

Gods above, she is going to get herself killed by going up that mountain—

The glimpse into his mind was short-lived as she landed hard on her hands, which stung from the rocks and the sand. She turned around to glare at Cefin, who was smirking for someone who was so nervous on the inside.

"Do you know how many times the twins try to get up the mountain?" Cefin said. "I've had plenty of practice."

"I can tell," Lauren huffed, rubbing the heels of her hands that were raw from where she landed. She looked up at him, his fear and annoyance still swimming in her brain and clouding her initial desire to wander up the mountain. She reached a hand to her necklace, and it reminded her of her mission.

Perhaps she'd try a different tactic.

She offered her hands to him. "You hurt me."

"The Anghenfil will do much worse, I promise you," he said without pity.

Her eyes grew large and she gave him the most adorable, simpering face she could muster. If she couldn't win him over with sneakiness or brute strength, perhaps with sugar. He already seemed to like her, calling her beautiful; maybe this would work.

"I thought you said you weren't a child," he replied,

impervious to her charms. "These are the same tricks the twins use on me thrice a week."

"GOD DAMN IT," Lauren huffed, losing her patience. "I just want to go *home*, Cefin!"

"Then talk to Siors."

"He doesn't know how I got here either and I just...damn it. If there's something up on that mountain that would get me home, I have to know."

"The only thing that will greet you on that mountain is death."

"You went up there before to dig me out of the cave. Why are you afraid now?"

"I am not afraid," he replied but she could feel his fear from two feet away. "But I value my life *and* yours—"

"You don't even *know* me!" Lauren replied.

"ENOUGH!" he bellowed, his words echoing in the valley. He walked up to Lauren and unsheathed his sword. "You *will* go down to the village or I will kill you myself."

"*This isn't over*," Lauren huffed, picking up the hem of her dress and storming down to the village.

chapter four

Lauren was so angry at Cefin for his interference that she spent all dinner glaring at him across the table when he showed up to share in the meal Aerona had cooked. She had hoped to slip out after dinner, when Cefin disappeared towards his own little hut, but Aerona asked her to help with the dishes and by the time they had finished with *that*, sleep was calling.

But no sooner had she closed her eyes than she could hear the quiet *Wake up, Lauren* of Aerona's hand shaking her. Lauren's half-asleep brain was still buzzing with sensations of Aerona's morning worries—having to get water, having to wake the children—and it was unpleasant to say the least.

"That could never happen again and it would be too soon," Lauren moaned, sitting up in the dark room. The shock of the empathy wore off and she leaned back into the makeshift bed, yawning and rubbing her face. She would have killed for a cup of coffee right about now, but instead looked over to Aerona who was leaning over the hearth.

"What are you doing?"

"Breakfast," Aerona said, lighting a small fire in the hearth. "I've already gone to the river to get the water, but I need you to help me tend to the fire."

Lauren pulled herself out of bed and sauntered over to the fireplace. She plopped down on the floor and poked the small flame with the poker. "I don't suppose we've got waffles, do we?"

"Waffles?" Aerona looked puzzled, but then shook her head. "Porridge."

Lauren couldn't help the face she made but did her best to hide it from Aerona. Porridge did not sound appetizing, but she was hungry and was fairly sure the other woman would kick her out at the first sign of ungratefulness. Especially considering Lauren hadn't done anything but sleep and eat since she arrived the day before.

"You've got a busy day today," Aerona said, walking over to pour the bucket of water into the pot on top of the fire. She added meal from a bag next to the fireplace and began stirring with a wooden spoon. "You'll be taking the laundry down to the river for a good cleaning."

"Laundry?" Lauren said, her face falling. She'd pondered all night on a good plan, settling for knocking Cefin on the head with a shovel. But doing laundry put a damper on those plans.

"Yes, I normally have Mairwan tend to it, but I thought it would be a good chore for you today." There was something hidden behind Aerona's smile, but Lauren couldn't place it.

The twins woke up just as the porridge, or what she was calling the white goop in the cast iron pot, began to boil. Lauren helped Mairwan set the table with the wooden bowls and utensils they had used for dinner the night before.

"Oi, munchkins," Lauren said, breaking up the small sibling spat that had broken out between Mairwan and Eddy as they fussed at the table. She tossed a look to Aerona, who was leaning over the fire, before leaning in closer to them. "Cefin said you two try to go up the mountain all the time."

"Aye," Eddy nodded solemnly, leaning forward. "Ya wanna know how?"

Lauren nodded, leaning in closer to ask, but before she could, a bowl of steaming porridge was placed in front of her.

"What are you three whispering about?" Aerona said, sternly placing the other bowl in front of Eddy. She returned to the hearth and Lauren leaned in again to talk with Eddy.

"Ya gotta wait until it's old man Graves up on the mountain," Eddy continued, his freckles dancing in the low light of the fire. "He falls asleep—"

"You leave that mountain alone, Lauren," Aerona interrupted, placing another bowl on the table in front of Mairwan and one at the head of the table for herself. "Didn't Cefin already tell you what would happen?"

"I don't understand why I can't go up there," Lauren said, swallowing the goopy and tasteless porridge and forcing herself not to look disgusted. "I'm perfectly capable of handling myself."

"There's things up there that we don't wake," Aerona said sternly. "And Edward, you should still have them scars on your back from the last time Cefin caught you up there. I would hope they'd be a reminder against anymore foolishness."

Eddy blushed as red as his hair and quietly ate his porridge.

"And don't think because you're a grown woman I won't flay you as well if I catch you up that ways," Aerona said to Lauren.

The children left for their chores right after breakfast, and Lauren offered to help with cleaning up, hoping that maybe she could sweet talk her way out of laundry.

"So, this laundry, does it have to be done right now?" Lauren asked, with a laugh.

"Right now." Aerona nodded to a woven basket next to the door. "Take that and the rest of it down to the river." She handed Lauren a washboard and a bar of soap. "Make sure you hang it up to dry before you bring it back."

Lauren nodded and went to pick up the basket, huffing at the weight. She nodded to Aerona, who looked pleased with herself, and began shuffling towards the door. Lauren calculated how long it would take her to finish the laundry and hang it up. If she were lucky, she'd be done by...

Her thoughts stopped when she saw ten more baskets in front of Aerona's house, all overflowing with dresses and shirts and sheets. Lauren let the basket fall to the ground with a loud thump.

"We do laundry for a few others as well," Aerona said, appearing in the doorway and ignoring Lauren's glower. "As I said, we all help each other in the village, since there's so few of us." She smirked at Lauren and then disappeared into the house.

"Son of a bitch," Lauren grumbled, picking back up Aerona's basket and trying to find a good way to hold it. Her arms protested, but she found a balance for a few steps and stumbled out of the house. The sun was barely over the ridge, yet the quiet village was already awake. Some of the same women who had pointed and gossiped about her the day before were out and about. They twittered with laughter as Lauren shuffled toward the river, a light sheen of sweat on her head from the effort.

After an eternity, she finally made it to the river, the basket falling to the ground with a thump. Lauren sat on top of the clothes for a moment, huffing and puffing and remembering with a groan she had ten more baskets to bring out there. She rubbed her sore arms and tried to look on the bright side—at least she would be buff living there.

No, she reminded herself, she was going to get home soon.

She looked up at the mountain again, narrowing her eyes to where Cefin was most likely standing watch. That asshole probably told Aerona to put her to work.

Lauren very well could have told Aerona to go to hell and gone up the mountain anyway, but then again, what if she found nothing up there? Aerona might throw her out of the house, and Lauren was quite sure that a place to live and square meals were hard to come by in this place. As it was, she needed to suck it up and do what Aerona asked, at least for a little while.

The sun was high in the sky by the time she finished bringing all of the laundry baskets to the river. The heat beat down on her mercilessly, making an already difficult task even more so. She paused on the banks of the stream with the last basket and collapsed next to the rushing water. It was actually quite beautiful, with clear water rushing over well-worn rocks. She dipped her hands into the chilly water and took a long, luxurious sip.

She turned to look up at the mountain. If she didn't get started soon, she'd never make it up there.

Her arms were still protesting when she turned to grab the first shirt from the nearest basket. She dipped it into the stream, letting the running water dampen it before pulling it out and grabbing the washboard and soap. She wasn't a hundred percent sure what she was doing here but could make an educated guess. She rubbed the bar of soap inside of the shirt and then ran the shirt up and down on the washboard in the stream. As she worked, she became lost in the methodical movements, not stopping until the water ran clear of soap bubbles.

She held the cold, wet shirt in her hands and was unsure of where to put it. She stood there with the shirt dripping down the front of her dress for a few moments before deciding to just lay the clean clothes out on the riverbed. Shrugging, she worked on two more men's shirts.

She wondered if she was washing Cefin's clothes, and she supposed his was probably mixed in there somewhere. After all, with him up on the mountain all day protecting the village from a stupid, not-real monster, he probably had no time to worry about trivial things like cleaning his own damned shirts.

She laid the clean shirt next to the other damp one, and pulled the next thing her fingers landed on out of the basket, a bed sheet. It became heavy when she dunked it in the water, sopping her with more water.

She worked and thought about bedsheets, and things people do on sheets, and suddenly she was remembering the last time she and Josh slept together, a few days before they broke up. With an annoyed growl, she tried to banish the thought from her head, but it played over and over. She paused in her ministrations over the sheet and sat back, hating herself for the way she still thought about him.

"Think about something else, Dailey," she whispered to herself. She had more control over her tongue than her mind. "Stupid Cefin and his stupid mountain. Aerona and this stupid laundry."

"She's talking to herself!"

Lauren nearly dropped the sheet in the river as the two red-headed imps appeared out of nowhere, bouncing and bobbing along the riverbank. Their faces and hands were dirty, presumably from working with the farmer all morning.

"What are you two doing here?" Lauren asked, placing the sopping wet sheet on the ground next to Cefin's dripping shirt.

"Baltes told us to go," Eddy said, dipping his hands into the river and taking a long sip of the water. "Said we's causing more trouble than help!"

Lauren chuckled; Eddy seemed to have mastered the art of not working. Mairwan, however, promptly plucked the next cloth out of the basket and, with a sisterly smile, began washing it in the stream next to Lauren.

"Where's the line?" Mairwan asked, looking around.

"What line?" Lauren asked.

"The drying line?" Mairwan grinned. "Where are you..." she spotted the shirts lining the ground and began to giggle. "Why are they on the ground?"

"Where else am I supposed to put them?"

"You've never done laundry before?"

"Yes, but in my Maytag," Lauren muttered under her breath.

"Where's the string?" Mairwan said, digging through the baskets. She procured a ball of twine from one of the baskets and set to stringing it across two nearby trees. Scampering over to the clothes on the ground, she dipped them into the river again, scrubbing them in a matter of seconds, and brought them over to the line.

"Thanks," Lauren said stupidly. She was being shown up by an eight-year-old and it was a bit embarrassing. Even though she was new to this world, she should have known how to do laundry, at least.

"You're taking too long," Mairwan said, scrubbing another shirt fast and quick, before standing up and wringing out the suds and dipping it in again. "You'll be here until nightfall!"

Lauren watched her pick up another cloth with an expertise strange to someone so young. "Do you do this by yourself often?"

"Aye." She nodded. "But Cefin brings the laundry basket down to the river for me on his way up the mountain." She paused thoughtfully. "I wonder why he didn't bring it for you?"

"Because he's a son of a bitch," Lauren muttered darkly. "And he's trying to keep me from going up the mountain."

"Why d'ya want to go up the mountain?" Eddy asked, not helping either of them, but choosing instead to hop on the rocks by the river.

"Because if I go up there, I might be able to find a way to get home," Lauren said, adding under her breath, "where there are things like washing machines and dryers."

"Wha's that?" Mairwan asked.

"Don't worry about it," Lauren didn't want the little girl to know that there existed such a land where shirts could be tossed into a box and cleaned automatically.

"Cefin's got a good heart," Mairwan said, putting her fifth shirt up on the line, while Lauren still worked on her third garment, a wool dress resembling the one she wore now. "He's just worried about the Anghenfil."

"Well, it's not like I'm going to go bother it or anything," Lauren replied. "Have you ever seen it?"

"Nah," Eddy said. "Never got far enough up before Cefin found me."

"EDWARD!" Aerona's voice echoed across the valley and Eddy nearly slipped into the stream. He turned to face Aerona, who was storming down the road with another basket of laundry against her hip. Lauren was impressed at the ease with which she carried it as she thumped it down next to the other piles.

"I just had a nice visit with Baltes," Aerona seethed dangerously towards the boy, who had shrunk down to the size of a mouse. "Says that you left to gather water for the potatoes an hour ago and never returned. Says you do this a lot."

"Aye, Ma," Eddy said, rubbing his hands. "Mairwan wanted to help Lauren—"

"Mairwan, stay here with Lauren," Aerona ordered. "And these clothes are filthy, do them again."

Lauren realized with a sour face that Aerona was looking at the ones she had washed.

"Edward, with *me*," Aerona said, grabbing the young boy by the arm and dragging him down the path.

"Here." Mairwan said as she gently helped Lauren scrub the

dress. "You gotta scrub harder to get the dirt out of it."

***

If Lauren thought that Aerona was done giving her tasks to do, she was sorely (literally) mistaken the next morning, when she was poked awake by a broomstick, and ordered to help Eddy and Mairwan at Baltes' farm. Lauren saw the look that Aerona gave Eddy and knew this was as much about keeping an eye the little boy as it was about Baltes keeping an eye on her. After sucking down another goopy breakfast of porridge again, she followed the two sleepy children down to the other side of the village, where they were met by the jolly face of the farmer.

Baltes was middle aged, with skin darkened and leathery from too much sun exposure, and straw-colored hair that was turning gray. He seemed to be a nice man, greeting Eddy with a hearty clap on the shoulder and giving him a good-natured wink about his escaping the day before.

"And you'll be the empath, yes?" Baltes grinned to Lauren, who yawned and rubbed her sore arms. "Cefin says you've got a mind to head up to the mountain."

She grimaced and cursed his handsome name.

"It'll be best to keep that thought out of your head." Baltes smiled at her, clapping her on the back as he had Eddy—

It's a beautiful morning, and the children better get to the yams now before the sun gets too hot—

Lauren heard herself take a deep gasp in as she came back into herself. She also realized she was on the ground, looking up at Baltes and the two kids.

"Ya can't touch her," Mairwan said plainly.

"Sorry about that, then..." Baltes held out his hand to help her up. After Lauren gave him a look, he retracted it, mumbling something about being thickheaded. She pushed herself to her feet and dusted the dirt off of her dress.

"So, to the yams?" Lauren asked, ignoring the look of surprise on his face.

Unfortunately, gardening was about as physically intense as laundry had been the day before. Lauren and the twins crept through the rows of small plants, Baltes pointing out which of the sprouts were the beans or the potatoes and which were the weeds. Lauren's back, still protesting from laundry, was nearly screaming in agony every time she sat up.

The sun was high overhead when Baltes called them out of the garden to help feed the livestock. The twins seemed unaffected by the work of the morning and raced over to the paddock where an old brown horse was swatting flies with its tail.

"That's Bessie," Baltes said, patting the horse on the side as he brushed it. "She's an old one but still good enough for farm work."

"I see," Lauren said. She hadn't actually seen a real horse since she was a kid—and even that was a sad-looking pony at a friend's birthday party. She walked up to the animal and out of habit placed her hand on its hindquarters.

There is a rock in my foot.

She lifted her hand, coming back into herself with a quiet sigh. She had almost become used to the way it felt when she touched another living thing, but this...was different. Reading someone like Aerona, or even the children was like diving into a hurricane of thoughts and dreams and feelings. Lauren could barely even remember her own name until she lifted her hand.

Reading the horse was more akin to sliding into a warm pool. Very matter of fact, very unemotional.

Lauren touched the horse again to test it out.

There is a rock in my foot.

She still had control of her body, she realized, and slowly

bent down to the left back leg. The horse lifted its leg showing a rather large pebble wedged in its hoof.

"Oy! Bet that's hurting!" Baltes said, although she heard him more through the horse than through her own ears. Baltes pulled the rock out with little effort, and relief washed over the horse and filtered into Lauren as well.

Lauren lifted her hand again, still in a trancelike state from feeling a non-human's thoughts.

"I've never seen Bessie take a liking to anyone so quickly," Baltes said, tossing the rock away. "You wanna ride her?"

"Oh, no," Lauren laughed. It was enough to just touch it; she wasn't sure if she could handle reading the horse and riding it at the same time.

"Mairwan can teach you, can't ya?" Baltes patted the young girl on her strawberry head. "She's the best horse-woman in Rhianu."

"That's cause I'm the only horse woman in Rhianu." Mairwan stuck her tongue out. But to prove her point, she let Baltes hoist her on top of Bessie. The young girl grabbed onto the mane and kicked at the barrel, pushing the old horse into moving forward.

"Wow." Lauren smiled, leaning back. "You sure know how to ride that horse, don't you?"

"I can teach ya!" Mairwan grinned, kicking Bessie into a trot.

"No, I think I'm okay."

A voice echoed across the open air. "Don't tell me you're brave enough to face the Anghenfil, but not brave enough to ride Bessie?"

Lauren looked to the other side of the paddock to see Cefin leaning against the fence. He smirked happily, his spear slung around his back. He waved to Baltes, who was following behind Mairwan and Bessie.

"What do *you* want?" Lauren snapped.

"Checking to see if Aerona and Baltes have worked you long enough that you've forgotten about your foolhardy quest," Cefin said. "Appears so."

"Aye, dear," Baltes said, patting Bessie on the side. "You'd be best staying here in the village where it's safe."

But Lauren wasn't listening to the old farmer. Cefin's words were bouncing around in her head, mixing in the soup of too little sleep and too much hard work. Without another word, she marched up to his smug face and slapped him, enjoying the jolt of his shock when their skin touched for a moment.

"Ow," he said, rubbing his chin. "What was that for?"

"For being an insufferable *dick*." She turned on her heel and walked out of the paddock toward the village. She couldn't stand the sight of Cefin any longer, she couldn't stand to be *here* anymore. She was becoming emotional, all of her anger from the past few days bubbling to the surface. She was halfway back to the village when she heard Cefin running after her.

"Now hold on a second," he said, stepping in front of her. "There's no need to be angry with me, I'm just trying—"

"Do you not understand what it's like for me here?" she cried. "I don't belong here! I have a mom and a dad who are probably worried sick about me! I have people who care about me! And all I want to do is see if there is a chance—a *small chance that I could go home*. Why is that so hard to understand?"

Pushed to her limit, the tears burst forth and she began crying into her hands.

"I just want to go home, Cefin," she sobbed.

She heard him sigh loudly. "If I take you up the mountain, to where I found you, will it satisfy you and you won't try to go up there alone?"

Lauren looked up at him, knowing that she must have

looked a mess.

"Yes," she nodded.

"And if I take you," Cefin said, stepping towards her. He was staring at her with such fierce intensity that she suddenly remembered how damned handsome he was. "And it becomes too dangerous, will you listen to me and return to the village? And you will never speak of it again?"

Lauren nodded.

"Then I will take you," he said heavily.

Relief washed over her as a grin replaced her tears. She couldn't help herself and flung herself at him, wrapping her arms tight.

She is an idiot, and I'm an idiot for agreeing to go with her. The Anghenfil will kill the both of us. This is going to end badly, I just know it, but she looks so sad—

"Lauren?" Cefin's voice was far away, but she came back into herself, swaying slightly.

"Damn this stupid empath thing," Lauren hissed, shaking her head, but unable to shake the uneasiness that Cefin had left in her soul.

chapter five

Cefin's disquiet was a seed that grew unchecked as the hours passed. Lauren was caught between excitement about the idea and sheer panic about what lay at the top of the mountain. She barely said two words during a raucous dinner with Aerona and the twins, who argued over who pushed who into the river earlier that day. Aerona asked once or twice if Lauren was feeling all right, but Lauren forced a smile and said she was simply tired from working all day. Her old excuse worked on Aerona as well as it had back in Lauren's old world with her friends, and no more was said on the matter.

The activity quieted down as everyone took to their beds. But Lauren lay awake in the darkness, listening to the rustling of the twins stirring next to their mother while they tried to fall asleep. After a while, everything was quiet—except within her head.

She'd been so gung-ho about wanting to get up the mountain, that it was the right thing to do. She just *knew* she'd find something that would help her get home. Cefin's initial reservations about the idea only served to make her *more* determined and surer of her own plan out of pure stubbornness. But now that all the barriers were down and she was faced with the prospect of *actually* going up there, she was gripped with a panic that would not subside.

But after making such a fuss about it all, backing out wasn't really an option.

She touched the necklace at her chest, the texture of the stone now a source of comfort. She reminded herself why she was doing this, and imagined the sights and sounds of her home and her family. She wanted to sleep in her own bed, she wanted to take a long, hot shower.

She even told herself that if she made it home, she'd call Josh. The idea made her chest flutter with nerves nearly as bad as thinking about the next day's journey, so she rolled over to try and get some sleep.

She wasn't sure how late (or early) it was when a sound outside awoke her from her light slumber. She sat up just as a shadow appeared in the doorway—Cefin. He put his finger to his lips, looking over to the bed on the other side of the room. Lauren kicked the blanket off of herself and followed him outside.

"Now?" she whispered, looking up at the bright moon still overhead. "Why so early?"

"I don't want anyone to know what we're doing," he said simply, walking towards the edge of the village.

Lauren didn't argue with him, but she still thought it was odd that he didn't at least want to tell Aerona. Then again, Aerona might try to talk them out of it, so it was probably for the best.

Lauren walked faster to catch up with him. "Thank you for —"

"If it gets too dangerous, or if I say we turn around, we turn around. Do you remember your promise?" he snapped, cutting her off.

"Y-yes," Lauren nodded, taken aback by his gruff tone.

He grunted and walked faster as she fell behind him. She

decided that he had definitely woken up on the wrong side of the bed that morning.

They passed Cefin's watcher's post and headed higher up the mountain trail. The trees overhead blocked out whatever moonlight was offered, and Lauren found herself tripping and falling every few minutes. Cefin seemed like a panther, tackling the uneven terrain easily. He was either deaf or purposely ignoring her. She assumed it was the latter when he paused while she pulled herself back to her feet after a particularly nasty fall, leaving her palms scratched and bloody.

"Are you even going to offer to help me?" Lauren hissed to the shadowy figure up ahead.

"I don't want to cause the empath any discomfort," Cefin replied coolly.

She scowled at him, not needing her empath sense to know he was just being an asshole. She suddenly wondered why she ever thought him to be cute in the first place.

They continued walking in silence for a while, until the faint light of the sun could be seen on the edge of the mountain range. The higher they climbed, it seemed the more treacherous the path before them. They encountered a particularly rocky stretch, big boulders that they had to hoist themselves up and over. Lauren was sweating from exertion as she struggled over the first one.

"How much farther?" she panted.

"Tired already?" he replied, four rocks ahead of her. "Ready to turn around yet?"

"No, I'm just wondering," Lauren said, sliding down the side of the boulder and walking over to the next one. She grabbed the top of the rock and pulled, but her body didn't move an inch. She tried jumping and pulling herself over, but her fingers slipped and she landed in a heap on the ground. Brushing her hair out of her face, she searched for an alternative means of climbing around the rock.

"It will take some hours," Cefin replied, his voice carrying over the path as she couldn't see his face. "We are going much slower than anticipated."

"Well," Lauren grunted, wriggling her way on top of the boulder and sitting on top of it. "Perhaps if someone wasn't being such a jackass and offered to help me, this would go easier."

"As I said, I don't want to cause you any—"

"Oh, go to hell," Lauren hissed, as she tackled the next boulder.

She was now quite sure that Cefin was mad at her for dragging him all the way up here, which she didn't understand at all. *He* didn't have to come with her; he wasn't much help anyway.

The sky was turning pink as sunrise fast approached, and Lauren was grateful for the additional light. The ground was even now, with low bushes scratching them on either side of the non-existent trail. Lauren's dress was covered with the small bristles, but she said nothing, not wanting to give Cefin the satisfaction of knowing she was uncomfortable.

Movement nearby brought both of them to a halt. Cefin was concerned enough to throw his arm out, preventing Lauren from going forward. She almost ran into him, but stopped mere inches from his skin, preventing another empath intrusion.

"Stay back," Cefin said, unsheathing his sword. With a voice that oozed authority, he bellowed into the early morning, "Come out and show yourself!"

The bushes rattled again, and Lauren held her breath.

A ball of leaves and twigs emerged from the bushes. Dead, soulless eyes looked out into nothing behind heavy lids, and

Lauren realized she was staring at an old woman, mumbling wildly to herself and glancing at nothing.

"Owena," Cefin hissed, sheathing his sword again. "How did you get up here?"

The woman simply grunted, stumbling around like a child.

"What's wrong with her?" Lauren asked. The woman reminded her of a man on the streets near her office back in California. He always muttered to himself, talking to someone in the far off distance that no one else could see.

"She arrived in the village this way," Cefin said. "Crazy as they come. Baltes has her tending to the sheep sometimes, but sometimes she wanders. This is the fifth time this month I've caught her in the mountain."

Owena looked at Lauren and for the briefest of moments, Lauren saw a flash of recognition. But Lauren thought perhaps she had imagined it, as the woman began humming to herself and picking the leaves.

"Come on. She never causes any trouble. She'll venture back down to the village when she's hungry."

Lauren paused, staring at the woman. "How did she get all the way up here? We've been walking for hours over rocks and boulders."

"Who knows? Shall we get a move on?"

"No," Lauren said, walking over to Owena. "How did you get up here?"

"You. Empath," the woman muttered, stepping back from her.

"Where's the village?" Lauren asked.

"Village." Owena pointed to her left—the completely opposite way she and Cefin had come.

"That way, huh?" Lauren said, turning on her heel and glowering at Cefin. "That way?"

65

"She's insane." Cefin shook his head. "I wouldn't—"

"And *you* are an unbelievable asshole," Lauren seethed. "You've been dragging me around the mountain, but not towards the caves where you found me!"

"That's not true," Cefin said unconvincingly.

"Oh yeah? Then tell me this: you said you carried me all the way down the mountain when you found me? How did you climb over rocks and boulders and all the other crap you've pulled me through?"

Cefin swallowed.

"For that matter," Lauren continued, her voice rising in anger. "You said you were chasing a goat up the mountain? How the hell did a *goat* get all the way up the mountain?"

"Goats are—"

"I've got a pretty good lie detector right here," Lauren hissed, holding up her hand. "But I don't need to touch you to know that you, my friend, are full of shit."

"You think this is some kind of a lark?" he growled, realizing that she had him. "You have *no idea* what you're asking for by going up there."

"You didn't have to come with me—"

"And when you wake the Anghenfil and are devoured, who will protect the village? Don't misunderstand me: I am only here to keep the monster out of Rhianu."

"It's gonna be hard to wake it up if you never take me there, now isn't it? Now you have a choice, spear-boy: either you take me up there *right now* or *get out of my way*."

Cefin grunted in frustration, tearing his eyes away from her. Without speaking, he turned and marched into the forest. Lauren turned to follow him, but stopped when the old woman was babbling to a nearby rock. Lauren felt guilty leaving the poor dear up here all alone.

"Hey, go back to the village," Lauren whispered to her.

Owena looked up at her and pointed at Lauren's necklace. "Empath."

"Yes," Lauren nodded, watching Cefin's disappearing form. "Look, I gotta go. But get back to the village, okay?"

"Empath," Owena mumbled, grasping at her own chest.

"Get back to the village," Lauren repeated, turning to run after Cefin, who had stopped to wait for her with a sour look on his face.

"There's no use in talking with her; she's insane," he snapped.

"Pardon me for being a decent human being," Lauren growled back. "You could take a lesson, you know?"

They spent the next hour in silence, climbing over rocks as the forest thinned around them. It was difficult, but not nearly as difficult as the pre-dawn jaunt Cefin had taken her on. The air was thinner, and her legs were screaming in pain, but she was determined. And she didn't want to give Cefin the satisfaction of knowing she was miserable.

"We're getting close," he muttered, pointing to a rock on the ground that seemed to have tumbled there recently. They crested another hill and Cefin stopped.

"There," he said, pointing to a pile of rocks that leaned against the side of the mountain. "That is where I found you."

"I was under *there*?" Lauren breathed. It was obviously a cave-in, and the boulders were thick and heavy. If any of them had fallen in the wrong place, she would have been crushed.

It was a miracle she *wasn't* crushed.

She approached the pile and saw where Cefin must have dug her out. Seeing the size of the rocks, knowing how close she had come to almost certain death, she felt a little sorry for being so angry with him.

67

"Hey," Lauren said, tossing him a sideways glance. "Thanks for digging me out."

"Just hurry up," he huffed, pulling his spear off of his back. "The Anghenfil could be in any one of these caves."

"The right response is 'you're welcome'..."

She walked up to the pile and began pushing aside smaller rocks, looking for anything strange. To be honest, she wasn't quite sure *what* she was looking for, but she hoped she'd know when she saw it.

She pushed aside a rather large rock, revealing the darkness of a cave, and her heartbeat quickened.

"Hey Cefin," she said. "There's something here."

She began digging faster, pushing rocks into the cave to widen the hole. She covered the tops of her eyes and peered inside, but couldn't see anything other than blackness. She tossed a look back to Cefin, who was standing with his spear in his hand and not helping her whatsoever.

She began tugging at a big rock, hoping that if she could move it a little bit, it would dislodge other ones and create a hole big enough for her to crawl through. She pulled and pushed at it, feeling it move just a little bit. With a mighty heave, it broke free, tumbling down into the blackness and taking Lauren with it.

She landed in a heap in the dark, cool cave, coughing up dust and other particles. A small halo of light formed a circle on the ground but didn't offer any other illumination. Pushing herself to her feet, she walked over to the hole and peered out, spying Cefin standing at attention on the other side.

"I'm fine. Thanks for asking."

"Hurry up," Cefin snapped, his eyes glued to the skies.

"Yeah, yeah." Lauren rolled her eyes and disappeared into the darkness.

She stumbled around for a moment, feeling at the floor with her feet for anything that would give her a clue as to how she got here. Maybe she just needed to walk to the end of the cave and she'd wake up back in her own bed. She kicked the ground until she found the wall, placing her hands on the chilly stone to guide her.

Her foot caught on something and she fell, but not onto the hard ground, onto something firm...

And scaly.

Alarm bells went off in her head.

"Oh shit," she whispered, scrambling backwards.

In the darkness, a gigantic red eye opened.

"*Fuck* me," she gasped, fear gripping her as she scrambled for the small pinhole in the distance that was the edge of the cave. "CEFIN!" she screamed, her voice echoing in the cave.

The monster was moving, and Lauren saw a flash of bright fire, illuminating a black body the size of an elephant.

She screamed and ran faster, hating herself for ever coming up here. She flung herself at the small hole, wriggling out as fast as she could. Cefin's spear was out, concern on his face.

"Lauren, quiet down, you'll wake the—"

"TOO LATE!" she screamed, pulling herself out of the cave and running past him as fast as her feet could carry her. "RUN!"

BOOM.

The rocks in front of the cave exploded around them, spewing rocks and dust. Cefin grabbed Lauren by the dress sleeve and yanked her forward, putting on a burst of speed as they clattered down the rocky pathway. A loud screeching roar echoed between the mountains, and a beating of wings thumped above them.

It landed in their path and Lauren's heart stopped as she took in the sight of the living, breathing dragon before her. The

Anghenfil was the biggest living thing she'd ever seen in her life, scarier than any painting in any book. Its body was a deep red, with a orangish, scaled belly. Black hair-looking scales lined the back of its head. Fangs that looked longer than her legs gleamed in the sunlight, and the eyes—ruby red eyes that somehow looked familiar, were trained on her and Cefin.

She whimpered and stepped behind Cefin, careful not to touch him. She needed to keep all of her wits about her when facing this monster.

"Stay back," Cefin growled, facing the monster with all of the strength and courage expected of him.

Lauren, who had never thought in her entire adult life she would ever face a dragon, happily complied and wilted behind him.

"Go back to your cave, beast," Cefin bellowed, pulling the spear from behind his back. "Leave us in peace!"

The Anghenfil lifted its huge head to the sky and roared so loud the rocks shook.

Lauren prayed that maybe she'd finally wake up from this dream, and be back in her bed, safe and sound, and not about to be eaten by a dragon. As Cefin lunged at the beast with a roar, she pressed herself against the side of the mountain, crouching down low and hoping that the monster would forget she was there.

She saw the tail, much less like a dragon's tail and more like a snake's, wriggling and curling behind it.

"Cefin, look out!" she cried, as he jumped out of the way mere moments before the tail whipped by.

The dragon opened its mouth, and a fire-laced roar echoed across the land. Cefin adjusted the sword in his hand, his eyes moving between her and the Anghenfil.

"Lauren, go back to the village," he called to her. She heard the fear in his voice, even as he turned to face the dragon again. "I'll deal with the beast now."

"No way!" Lauren shook her head.

"*Go!*"

The Anghenfil tilted its head back and roared, flapping its great big wings and sending bursts of wind towards the two of them. Lauren lost her footing and fell to the ground, looking over to see Cefin on the ground as well.

"CEFIN!" she called.

"LAUREN LOOK OUT!" Cefin screamed back at her.

Lauren looked up just as the black serpentine tail landed on top of her. It wrapped around her body. And then everything went black.

***

She sat beside him in the car, filled with trepidation and anxiety. Somehow, she'd woken up this morning and just knew that today was the day.

To be honest, she'd known for months that this was inevitable, but she'd tried to convince herself that she was wrong. She'd spent weeks on edge, wondering when he was going to surprise her with a diamond ring. She knew there would be parades and fireworks, and all would be right in the world just as soon as he figured out what he had. And she'd done a good job of shoving any thoughts about leaving him deep down into the section of her mind reserved for forbidden thoughts, the things she was afraid to even think.

But it had broken free that morning, and during a particularly teary shower, anxious resolution was all she felt.

Today was the day.

He pulled into her driveway and her heartbeat raced. He asked if he could come inside to hang out, but she heard herself say the dreaded words as if someone else were controlling her.

empath

"We should talk..."

"Ugh," he said, sitting back. "What do you want to talk about?"

"Do you even want to marry me?"

He was silent, and she saw the wheels turning in his head. She had known him long enough to know what he was thinking. When he didn't speak, her heart began to break.

"I think...I think it's just time for us to cut our losses and move on," she whispered.

Tears fell down her face, and she looked out the car window. It was a gorgeous day, everything was green and bright in the late spring around them. She felt like it should be dark and gloomy, that the world should come to an end right then and there.

The memory became hazy, as their relationship dissolved right before their eyes.

"You're the best person I've ever known," he said.

She nodded, unable to look at him. She went to get out of the car, but he stopped her.

"Can I at least get a kiss goodbye?" he asked, his voice thick.

She turned to look at him and gently pressed her lips to his. As the full weight of the situation fell down on her—this was their *last kiss*—she sobbed harder, needing to get free of him and get inside the house.

She tore out of the car and ran into the house. She stood in her living room with wet cheeks, and watched him sit in his car.

And she waited.

Waited for him to get out of the car and come tell her it wasn't true and he wanted her.

Waited for herself to wake up from this nightmare.

But he put his car in reverse and drove away.

She sat down on the couch, in shock.

Did that just happen? Did they just break up?

Five years up in smoke, like that?

Lauren and Josh, they were inseparable.

And now separated.

She felt sick and ran upstairs to empty the contents of her stomach in the toilet. She sat against the toilet, and her first instinct was to text Josh and tell him she'd just thrown up, wanting him to text back, "Aw, poor puppy."

But he wasn't hers anymore. He no longer cared about her.

The reality crashed down on her and she collapsed on the floor, curling into a ball.

She couldn't breathe; she couldn't think; she couldn't even *move*.

Hurting. She was hurting so badly.

Everything was just painful now.

Why was everyone happy except for her?

When the hell was she going to feel normal again?

"Would you like it to go away?"

"Yes," she whispered.

A black tail slithered tighter around her—maybe that was why she couldn't breathe—and she saw the tip of the tail slip inside of her chest, tightening around her heart.

***

She heard a roar in the distance and took a large gulp of precious, sweet air. She opened her eyes for a moment, spotting nothing but Cefin and his sword covered in green blood. She saw the great beast take flight, the stub of a tail dripping behind it.

Cefin's face was in her line of sight, but his voice was far away. She was sinking lower and lower into the darkness.

"LAUREN!"

chapter six

Lauren awoke, and for a moment, she was terrified she was back in the monster's thoughts—or worse, the monster had taken her. But she was in the quiet darkness, leaning against a very uncomfortable tree. She sat up and looked around, groggy and despondent, until she realized Cefin was nowhere to be found.

Fear shot through her. Had he been killed?

"Cefin?" she called, noticing the feeble sound of her own voice.

"I'm here," he said, appearing in the darkness next to her. Relief was immediate at the sight of his uninjured face, and she sunk back into the tree.

"Thank God," she whispered into her hands as she rubbed her face. She paused in her movements and looked around. "Where is here?"

"Outside of town, at the watcher's post," Cefin replied, looking around them before settling his eyes on her again. "Are you hurt?"

"I feel like death. I remember..."

The fear was back, a sharp coldness that settled in her chest. The Anghenfil had put her back in the worst moment of her short life—the day that she and Josh ended things. When she first fell into the deep darkness that had lasted the past four months.

She was at her lowest, miserable and hurting, and she had told the monster to take her pain.

The monster wanted her miserable, sad heart. That's why it brought her here.

It was suddenly hard to breathe again.

"The Anghenfil tried to take you," Cefin said, unaware of her inner turmoil. "It wrapped its tail around you and...I thought it had killed you. You were so pale and barely breathing."

Lauren swallowed and stared at the ground, forcing all of the thoughts about the Anghenfil into the space reserved for forbidden things. It was over now, no need to worry about it, and there was no need to tell Cefin that the monster was not only after her, but was the reason she had been brought here.

She could only imagine what he would say if he knew.

"It was unmoving when it had you in its grip, and I was able to sever the tail," Cefin continued. "It took to the skies and I brought you here..."

"I'm sorry I made you go up there," Lauren cried, trying to salvage the situation. "You were right, and I know now that—"

He stood up suddenly, his face unreadable.

"Cefin?" she whispered, his silence worrying her.

"We need to get back to the village. "

Lauren wished she could crawl into a hole and die as she followed Cefin back into the village. How could she be so stupid? Why hadn't she just *listened* to him when he told her it was a bad idea? She'd always prided herself on knowing the right thing to do, and she'd been so sure that it was the *right* thing to do. But now, she was left more confused than ever.

She slipped inside Aerona's house without so much as a goodbye and was thankful that Aerona and the kids were fast asleep. Lauren crawled onto her pile of hay and bedsheets, and let the tears silently fall as her thoughts ran unabated.

empath

She thought about her and Josh, their final day together, punctuated by the voice of the Anghenfil and the snide inner voice telling her that she *knew* why she was brought here. In the moments she let the thought escape, it pointed out the indisputable evidence—where she'd been found, the last empath being taken by the Anghenfil, and even the monster's voice—and she knew she was too afraid of the truth to face it head on. So, as usual, she buried the truth and pretended to be ignorant of reality.

The same way she'd pretended for three months that Josh was going to propose "any day now" instead of seeing the writing on the wall.

Lauren Dailey, master denier.

Only this time, her denial was almost responsible for not only her death, but the death of poor, innocent Cefin. He had warned her, hadn't he? And she stupidly chose to ignore him.

For what?

To go home, her mind answered. She wanted to go home.

She began to sob silently, realizing that she was never going to see home again. She was never going to walk into her parents' house, never going to see her mom and dad, feel the warmth of the small town where she had grown up. Everyone was probably worried sick about her, and they would never know what happened to her. Was her body even back in her old world?

Did Josh even miss her?

She bit her lip to prevent any sound from coming out as she sobbed harder. She missed him so much right then it hurt. The irrational desire for his comforting presence was overwhelming. He was the entirety of her support system, and without her security blanket, she felt lost and alone.

She quietly took a breath, careful not to make any noise and wake Aerona or the twins. Part of her wanted someone to talk to, but she knew no one would understand. Even more, no one would care. These people were too busy worrying about their own lives and problems; why would they care about her?

And what would they say if they knew she was the target of the monster's hunger?

That thought was squashed as Aerona stirred in the corner. Lauren hastily wiped her face and hoped the darkness would hide her puffy eyes. Aerona pulled herself out of the bed carefully so as to not wake the children, and recovered them with the blankets. She seemed surprised to see Lauren awake.

"Oh, I didn't hear you come in."

"Yeah, well, we had a late day," Lauren whispered.

"And yet you survived the Anghenfil," Aerona said, walking over to the hearth and lighting it. She sounded neither upset nor surprised by this fact. "Are you satisfied? Did you find what you were looking for?"

"Yes," Lauren whispered. And more than she'd ever wanted to look for again.

"Then you won't be making any more trouble for me." Aerona smiled. "I understand that you are hurting, and that you wish to be reunited with your family. And if I could, I would do everything in my power to see you back in your own home." She sighed. "But rushing up the mountain to almost certain death is *not* the way to go about it."

"I know," Lauren said, wondering why Aerona's words sounded more violent and angry in her head.

"Everyone is safe and sound. So all is well."

"Perhaps I can learn to live here," Lauren murmured, ignoring the crushing sadness that came with the resignation that she was stuck. "I mean, I've almost gotten the hang of laundry."

Aerona laughed softly so as to not wake the children. "I'm afraid if I let you do laundry, it will never be done. Baltes seems to have more use for you. He says you've got a way with the livestock."

"That sounds nice," Lauren lied.

"Go back to sleep. You look like you've had a trying night."

"No, I think I'll help you get things ready," Lauren said, needing the distraction.

"Then run down to the river and fetch me some water." Aerona handed her a bucket. Lauren brushed her hand, getting another dose of Aerona's mild but firm annoyance at Lauren's actions the day before.

By the time Lauren returned from the river, sloshing the water in the bucket, the twins had awoken and were sleepily moving about, helping their mother with the pre-dawn chores. They said nothing about Lauren's absence the day before, choosing to poke and prod each other as young siblings do. Aerona broke up a squabble by placing a bowl in front of each of them, and then placed a third in front of Lauren and a fourth at the head of the table.

"Who's that—"

Lauren stiffened when Cefin walked in the door, looking about as ragged and sleepless as she did. He nodded his hello to Aerona, who pointed to the empty seat. He looked right through her as he sat down at the table. Wordlessly, he began shoveling porridge into his mouth.

"Ay Cefin, what's your problem this morning?" Eddy barked, his small voice cutting through the tension Lauren felt in the room.

Cefin looked up at Lauren who immediately looked down at her bowl and began quietly eating. Of course Cefin was angry with her. Aerona may have been more forgiving of her stupidity, but she had put Cefin in danger, and he had every right to hate her.

"I think I'll get a head start on work at the farm," Lauren whispered, pushing her porridge out of the way.

"But you've barely eaten?" She heard Aerona call as she disappeared quickly out the door.

***

Lauren took a deep breath in the cool morning air, grateful to be out of the uncomfortable tension in the house. She was actually looking forward to a day of getting lost in the simple emotions of animals. It was much like data entry in that way, or binge-watching Netflix. Since she could barely control her own mind, it was a nice change of pace to give it away to someone else.

But that's what the Anghenfil promised, wasn't it?

Chills ran down her spine and she thought she heard a hissing in the back of her mind.

She was so distracted that she didn't see the shadow cross in front of her until it was too late.

"OOF!" She fell backwards and landed hard on the heels of her hands. Looking up, she was surprised to see the wild, gray hair of Owena, the insane woman she and Cefin saw on their way up the mountain the day before. She looked about as insane today as she did the day before, muttering and glancing around.

"Hi there," Lauren said, pulling herself up to her feet. "Sorry about that. I wasn't watching where I was going."

Owena turned around and leaned back, giving Lauren a crazy-eyed once over. The old woman leaned forward then back, rocking in a haphazard motion that made Lauren uncomfortable.

"You, empath," Owena said after a few minutes of rocking and observing.

"Lauren," she replied gently before adding, "and yeah, I guess I am."

"You meet Anghenfil?"

"Er...yes," Lauren said, the memory of the terrifying monster fresh in her mind. "I won't do it again."

"You be careful," Owena said. "You stick with animals. Safer. No Anghenfil. No King. No pain."

"What do you mean?"

"Empath came from a land far away."

"Yes, I did." Lauren nodded, curious how Owena knew that. Perhaps the news had traveled fast, but how much comprehension did she have?

"No, empath," Owena muttered, looking confused for a moment.

"I am the—"

"NO EMPATH," Owena exclaimed. Lauren jumped at the volume of her voice, and the anger with which she spoke. Owena closed her eyes and looked like she was trying to focus. "Empath....other..."

"The other empath?" Lauren was suddenly all ears. Siors had mentioned there was a girl here some fifty years prior. Was that who this woman was talking about? She was certainly old enough to have known her, but was she mentally sound enough to remember such a thing?

"Anghenfil take Empath," Owena mumbled.

"I know," Lauren whispered and wondered if the other girl had given into temptation as she had almost done. If Cefin hadn't been there...Lauren shivered at the thought.

"King take Empath. Anghenfil take Empath," Owena cried, wrapping her arms around herself. She was looking all around her and kept glancing up to the sky. "Everything black."

"Siors said that she was in the king's castle." Lauren nodded, trying to make sense of what the woman was saying. "And that's where the Anghenfil found her—"

"NO KING!" Owena bellowed. "KING MADE BAD!

ANGHENFIL TAKE HER AWAY! ANGHENFIL BLACK!"

"Hey, it's all right," Lauren reached forward out of habit to calm the woman down.

Nothing.

With a gasp, Lauren removed her hand. It was the first time since she'd arrived in this world that she hadn't been sucked into someone else's mind. Even animals had something, but to not have any thoughts or emotions?

Lauren watched as Owena bobbled away, muttering to herself about the sky and the Anghenfil and something turning black. Lauren was curious about all of this and wanted to press the old woman further, hoping she could piece together something important about the previous empath.

Then again, the other empath was devoured by the Anghenfil who also—

She shoved that thought into the back of her mind. Turning on her heel, she hurried up the trail to Baltes' farm, eager to fill her brain with something other than reality.

***

Lauren came back to herself, dizzy and lightheaded from all of the different goat thoughts swimming in her brain. But she was no longer thinking about anything else—although thinking about things she was trying to avoid brought them back to the fold, so she was quick to jump back into the minds of the livestock.

Baltes let her wander around with his herd that day but still didn't get the concept of her empathy, as he chatted with her all day long. She heard about a tenth of what he said, making a show of nodding to him every so often before diving into another animal. It wasn't until he asked if she was going to stay all night that she finally stopped reading all the animals and noticed that the sun was setting.

"I have to say, you do like them goats, huh?" Baltes laughed, walking her to the edge of his farm. "Do they have interesting thoughts?"

"Better than what's going on in my own head," Lauren said, happily too brain-tired to be pulled back into her anxious thoughts. She was thankful that, for once, her mind played nice with her.

"I usually use whiskey for that." Baltes winked at her.

"Not as bad of a hangover in this case." Although Lauren thought a drink would have been great right then.

"See you tomorrow?" Baltes asked.

"Absolutely!" Lauren waved back at him, eager to get back to Aerona's house. She wanted nothing more than to eat a hot meal, curl up in bed, and fall into a dreamless sleep.

What she did not want was Cefin in the middle of the street, his spear slung across his back and his face still agitated. A flame lit in her chest like a gas stove, and her hands began to shake. She didn't want to talk to him, didn't want to remember the stupid thing she made him do. The scathing voice began to babble on repeat, "you knew better," and the panicked flame spread across her whole body, speeding her heartbeat and shortening her breath.

"Oh...hi," Lauren said, hoping that he was just standing there dazed and not waiting for her.

"I think we should...speak about what happened."

"Uh, I think I hear Aerona calling," Lauren said, suddenly unable to look at him. She knew he was going to berate her, and all she could think about was that she *knew better*. God, she *knew better,* and she chose to ignore it and walk ahead blindly like she was the stupidest—

She tried to rush away when the hem of her dress caught on something. Cefin's foot, as it turned out.

"Why are you avoiding me?"

"Because," Lauren's voice shook. "Because I know you're mad at me, and...I just..."

"I'm not angry with you, I'm just..." he trailed off. "My father and my uncle died because *I* went up to the mountain when I was a boy. I should have told you."

"I...what?" Lauren's train of thought came to a screeching halt, and she turned her attention to Cefin, finally seeing his face and his misery for what it was—self-inflicted. Her panic dulled to a ghost-like whisper.

"I was fifteen," Cefin whispered. "Aerona was about to give birth to the twins, and I told my father I was ready to stand guard as the watcher." He looked off into the distance. "When he refused, I went up to the mountain myself to try and slay the beast." His jaw tensed, and he swallowed hard. "My father and my uncle—Aerona's husband—came to bring me back...and they..." He trailed off and stared off into the distance.

"Oh, Cefin," Lauren said, covering her mouth with her hands. Even standing all the way over here, she could feel his guilt and his misery, and something else that she couldn't put her finger on.

"And when you were lying there, I was afraid...I had brought someone to their death again." Pain was etched on his face as he turned to stare at her intensely. "I am sorry that I put you in danger."

"It was my stupid idea!" Lauren exclaimed, taking him by surprise. She opened her mouth to say that she should have known better, but something stopped her. Instead, she said, "I should have listened to you. And for that, *I'm* sorry. You were right, it was dangerous..." She shivered again.

"The Anghenfil has taken much from me and my family," he said. "But if I thought it could get you back home, I would go face it another hundred times."

Different kind of nerves fluttered through her, accompanied by a slight blush to the face.

"You were...so pale," Cefin said, his eyes scanning her face. "I can only imagine what the monster did to you."

"Oh," Lauren scoffed, waving him off. "It was nothing. I mean..." She shrunk under his dubious stare. "The monster just forced me to relive my worst memory and—"

"Lauren, I am so sorry," Cefin said. "It must have been horrible."

"Nah," Lauren said with a lying smile. "I mean, I'm pretty lucky. It was just...a break-up."

"Break-up?" Cefin asked.

"When my boyfriend—my love, I guess— and I broke...ended our relationship," Lauren said, the words sounding stupid in her head in the context of all the other things that could have happened to her. Cefin still didn't look as if he understood, so she waved him off. "In any case, it wasn't that bad."

"But you were so pale," Cefin cried, "and barely breathing—"

"It's not something I want to do again!" Lauren laughed forcefully. "And, yeah, if it grabs me again, I've got a brand new memory for it to drudge up. I never thought I'd be facing a *dragon*."

Cefin nodded, but she could tell he didn't believe her.

"ANYWAY," she announced, hoping they could change the subject. "Walk back to Aerona's?"

"Sure," Cefin said, turning to walk beside her.

"You know, it's not so bad here after all. I think I might get used to it after a while," Lauren said, amazed at how normal she suddenly sounded. Maybe she was finally coming back to herself, after all these months.

"If you've not got a mind to bother the Anghenfil, I won't

ask Aerona to make you tend laundry." Cefin winked at her.

Lauren smiled at him playfully and realized she was flirting with him again. It was awkward but easy. After all, they'd faced the Anghenfil and survived, they must have bonded. Maybe she *could* learn to live here after all. Some wild thoughts about possibilities with him erupted unbidden, and she allowed her mind to wander. He *had* saved her, and he was definitely interested in her.

And yet, Josh's face popped up in the middle of planning her hypothetical wedding with Cefin.

"Son of a bitch," she muttered to herself, hoping Cefin wouldn't hear it.

"Who is that?" Cefin said, looking behind Lauren. She turned to follow his gaze and saw a young boy scrambling up the rocky path as fast as fast as his small legs could carry him. Cefin rushed forward to him, helping him up the final few steps until he reached the clearing.

"Please, I need help," he gasped. Lauren saw he couldn't have been older than eight or nine, with long brown hair that was wet with sweat and hung limply around his eyes. "Please, where is the empath!"

Lauren's eyes widened as Cefin's eyes snapped over to her.

"It's you! You're the one!" he said, stumbling forward. Lauren took two steps back, almost able to read this boy's emotions from the distance away. She was not interested in feeling more of it.

"Why do you need her?" Cefin asked, his hand still firmly on the boy's arm.

"Tyllwyllwch!" he gasped.

"Bless you," Lauren replied, but one look at Cefin and she knew whatever the boy had just uttered was serious.

"Are you sure, child?" Cefin said, lowering down to face him.

"What's your name?"

"Tomos, sir. Please, my village is dying. You have to come and help us."

"I'm sorry, but what the hell is this till-will-wick thing?" Lauren said to Cefin. "Please tell me it's not another fire-breathing monster."

"It's a terrible illness," Cefin said.

"My village has lost ten men this week," the boy whispered. "Please, you have to help—"

"What can I do?" Lauren said. "I'm not a doctor."

"Let's bring him to Siors." Cefin nodded. "He'll know what to do."

***

"Tyllwyllwch is a dangerous disease indeed," Siors nodded, tipping the spout of the tea kettle into the boy's cup that was almost too big for his hands before offering some to Lauren and Cefin, who were huddled on either side of the hearth. Once he put the kettle back, he turned to look through his stacks of books on the wall.

"I mean, what is it?" Lauren asked. "Is it a virus or a..." She trailed off when she realized no one knew the difference between a virus and a bacterial infection. Also, she had no treatments for either. In any case, she decided to shut up and listen to Siors.

"A darkening of the soul," he said, pulling out an old book and flipping the pages. "It seeps into a village, quietly and without warning. It passes from person to person, until the person has no energy to move, no energy to eat, and they waste away."

Lauren swallowed hard. That didn't sound like anything she wanted to be involved in.

"So what do I have to do with it?"

"An old wives' tale says the empath can cure the darkness,"

Siors said, placing the book in front of her. On the open page was a painting, one that looked like it came out of middle ages Europe (or a Monty Python cartoon). Each person had a pained look on his face and was surrounded by a thick black cartoonish smoke.

But what drew Lauren's eye was the girl on the page standing apart from the group, seemingly sucking in the darkness through a bright light at her chest.

"That's what my village elders said, too," Tomos squeaked, looking between Siors and Lauren. "They said that they'd heard a new empath had arrived and to bring her before anyone else... died."

Lauren could feel the eyes of everyone on her. It became quite toasty in the room.

"I don't know...I have no idea..." Lauren swallowed and glanced around, trying to buy herself some time. "I've only been an empath for a few days. I don't know how to...fix this."

"Please, you have to help us. Otherwise, we have no hope," Tomos cried, dropping the mug of tea and rushing towards her. She barely got a breath in before the boy's hands were around her waist.

My momma and my sister, what will happen to them? It came so fast and this girl, she's the only one who can save us. I am so afraid—

Lauren let out a gasp as she came back to herself, more relieved to be back in her own mind than in someone else's. Cefin had the boy by the arm, and Tomos was struggling against him with tears in his eyes.

"Are you all right?" Cefin asked Lauren.

"Yeah." Lauren nodded, rubbing her face. The boy's terror surged through her, until it became her own, and every fiber of her being was demanding she accompany him. She hated this feeling; she hated not being in control, but she knew if she walked away now, she would be haunted by this little boy's fear for a long time.

"Okay, I'll go," she said quietly.

"You will?" the boy cried.

"Yeah, I don't know what I'm doing, but...yeah, I'll try."

chapter seven

Cefin insisted on going with her, and regardless of her protests, the three of them—Lauren, Cefin, and Tomos—set off down the mountainside to the village of Heulog. Tomos scurried out in front of them, throwing a look back every few moments to make sure they were still following him. Each time, she'd give him an affirming smile, even as she, herself, slipped and slid on the rocks.

"I'm getting *really* tired of this," Lauren hissed, pushing herself upright. "Really wish there were some stairs or something on this mountain." Cefin trotted back over to her and reached out a hand. Lauren took it without thinking—

She's quite pretty when she's frustrated.

"Gods, sorry," Cefin said, pulling his hand back like she had burnt him. Lauren fell back to the ground in a heap, suddenly realizing what this whole can't-touch-anyone thing really meant for her. Especially now, considering she and Cefin had just come to a good place.

And also, he was attracted to her.

"What are you waiting for? It's just up ahead," Tomos said, appearing over a ridge.

"I...sorry..." Cefin said. He opened and closed his hand like he wanted to hold onto her again, but then clamped his arms down by his side.

Lauren pulled herself up to stand and tossed a smile at Cefin. "No worries," she said, marching beside him. She had to remain normal; she didn't want to torture herself by pining after someone she couldn't be with. Suddenly, her hypothetical wedding disappeared just as quickly as the one she'd made on Pinterest for her and Josh.

"There it is!" Tomos cried, pointing out the distance and taking off at a run.

"Whoa," she whispered, stopping in her tracks.

She could barely see the village through a dark gray and very thick fog. For a moment, she thought it was smoke from a fire or from a morning mist. But she saw no fire; in fact, it chilled her to the bone just looking at it.

"What is it?" Cefin asked.

"There's something over that village," Lauren replied. "It's... don't you see it?"

"No." Cefin shook his head. "Looks like a normal village to me?"

Lauren, no longer surprised that she could see things others could not, was still concerned about the ominous sight. With every step closer to the darkness, the temperature seemed to fall another two degrees until she could even see her breath in front of her. Lauren turned behind her and realized they'd been walking through the darkness for some time now. A small shape wandered up to her in the darkness, forming into the shape of Tomos.

"Come!" he said, disappearing into the mist again.

Lauren hurried off into the direction he came from but soon lost him. Another dark shape was moving next to her, coming close enough for Lauren to see it was an old man. He seemed to be emanating a dark aura—the same blackness that surrounded them. Lauren would have thought him the source of the darkness, but for another woman that walked by covered in the dark mist.

"So you're not seeing this?" Lauren whispered to Cefin, the only non-dark thing she could see in this village.

"Seeing what?" Cefin said.

"Over here!" Tomos was back, appearing through the dark like a ghost. Lauren followed behind Cefin, who could obviously still see the boy. She wondered if this darkness was the tyllwyllwch. If so, there was so much of it, she wasn't sure how she'd be able to get rid of it. She had visions of a giant room fan, but dismissed the notion.

A man wheeled a cart with two burlap bags on it.

"Are they?" she asked.

"Taken by the tyllwyllwch," he said sadly, continuing to move forward, unaware that he too was surrounded by the darkness.

"Lauren." Cefin stood close to her, but he didn't touch her.

She nodded and followed him into a hut not unlike those in Rhianu. She passed over the threshold and let out a hot breath that fogged in front of her. It was *ice cold*, as cold as the dead of winter. Her body shook involuntarily, trying to get warm. The blackness was thick in here too, almost too thick for her to see. She felt weighed down, and it was hard to breathe.

"Mamma!" Tomos was crying out in the corner, and Lauren didn't need her eyes to know where his mother lay. Rather, she could sense the cold darkness coming from the corner. She took several tentative steps before kneeling next to a bed, where a woman lay on the bed.

She was young, not older than Lauren herself, and already with a little boy who was eight or nine. The darkness poured from her like a frigid steam, her shallow breaths the only sign that the woman was not dead.

"Can you help her?" Tomos asked.

"I don't know," Lauren said, hesitating. She wasn't sure what would happen if she placed her hands on this woman, if she'd be contaminated as well. More than that, something about this darkness told her that it was going to hurt like hell.

She turned to the boy next to her, whose eyes were wide with fear, and the protestations died in her throat. What was she thinking? If she had the power to help this poor woman, she needed to do it.

But what was it she was supposed to do? Siors' book wasn't very helpful. Just a girl standing in front of a group of people, drawing in some dark mist. Was she supposed to breathe it all in? Wave her arms around? Or blast it away like some anime character?

"Lauren?" Cefin's voice echoed behind her and she began to feel stupid. She shouldn't have come here, and she shouldn't have—

"Please...do something..." Tomos was crying again.

Steeling herself for whatever horribleness was going to happen, Lauren shakily reached out her hands and placed them on the clammy arm of the woman.

She gasped and pulled her hands away. She'd never felt *anything* like that before; it was like dipping her arms into a sink filled with ice water.

"Lauren?" Cefin asked.

"I'm..." Lauren said, taking a moment to readjust. "I'm fine."

And before she could talk herself out of it, she pressed her hands on the woman again.

***

Lauren stood in the frigid darkness, as if she were at the bottom of a deep cave. She could hear the slow drip-drip-drip of water nearby. The air felt heavy and thick around her; even blinking her eyes was difficult. She shivered, trying to move in the blackness, but found herself unable to go very far.

"Hello?" Lauren called, not sure how she was a corporeal form in this weird place she had traveled to in her subconscious. She knew the tyll-whatever was there, chilling her to the bone.

"Hello?" she called again, her voice echoing in the empty space. "I have no idea what I'm supposed to be doing here...so..."

She sounded idiotic, she knew it, but she felt idiotic.

She spun around again, and noticed for the first time that everything had a red tint to it. She looked down at her chest and saw that her necklace, hidden beneath her dress, was glowing red.

She pulled the stone out and was blinded by the glare from it. It wasn't just shining—it was hot, like a lightbulb on too long. She let it drop from her hands against her chest and could feel the heat through the layers of clothes.

But with the stone shining bright, she could now see farther than her own nose, although the darkness still surrounded her.

"Hello?" she called again. "Are you here?"

Who "you" was, she had no idea, but she somehow knew she was looking for someone.

"I'm not going to hurt you," Lauren called, taking a few tentative steps forward. She remembered walking in the cave just before running into the Anghenfil—

Her stone dimmed slightly, and she heard a soft laughter. It was a familiar voice, the one that had been haunting her dreams.

Panic gripped her and the light lessoned more. Why would the Anghenfil be here, in the consciousness of this woman?

"I imagined it," Lauren whispered to herself. "It's not here, it's up in the mountains, and it's not here."

The stone glowed brighter and it gave her confidence, but Lauren knew she needed to figure out a way to clear out the tyllwyllwch before she succumbed to it.

"Okay, Dailey, if you were an empath, which you are, how would you get rid of a big dark mist?" She paused and tried to clear the nerves from her mind to think clearer. "Mist dissipates in heat, right? So maybe if I build a fire?"

As if on cue, the stone against her chest grew hotter.

"Oh, duh," Lauren said, picking it up by the gold chain. This must be how the other empath did it, too. She eyed the red stone encased in around her neck. "So...make the mist go away, stone."

It didn't do anything.

"Damn it." Lauren let the stone fall to her chest. She folded her arms over her chest and thought for a moment, trying to connect the dots between the stone growing hotter and whatever she was doing.

But as she thought about it, the stone seemed to burn brighter.

"Ah, so that's it then." Lauren nodded satisfactorily. In her mind's eye, she envisioned the stone around her neck to be like a warm morning sun, the heat evaporating the mist like on a river.

The stone burned so bright that she could see the backs of her eyelids, but she held firm, knowing that if she kept going, brighter and brighter, that...

"Lauren...Lauren..."

··*·*

The first thing Lauren registered was the burning sensation on her chest, and she weakly pulled the stone away from her sweat-covered chest. It was still hot and singed her fingers, so she could only imagine how badly her skin had been burnt.

The second thing she registered was the sound of the little boy crying and the sight of Cefin kneeling next to her, his face white and his eyes filled with something between amazement and concern.

"What happened?" Lauren gasped, her throat feeling like a desert.

"You touched her, and you began murmuring to yourself," Cefin said. "And then your amulet began glowing, and you started sweating and then you collapsed."

"And..." Lauren said, slowly pulling herself upright so she could see the woman on the bed. She was pale and weak, with the hint of a smile on her face. She was comforting Tomos as he sobbed into her shoulder.

"You did it," Cefin whispered. "You healed her."

Lauren looked around the house, realizing that the dark mist was gone. In fact, it seemed quite warm in there now; or maybe that was because she had a permanent furnace hanging around her neck. She swiveled her head farther around to look out the open door of the home and noticed the darkness still hung around the rest of the village.

"Who else?" Lauren asked.

"No," Cefin replied firmly. "You're ill; you need to rest."

"I think I just overdid it." Perhaps it was the feeling of doing something for someone else, or the fact that she could control *something*, but it made her want to go out and heal every person in that village.

"Are you sure?" Cefin asked.

"Yeah," Lauren smiled and stood up. "Who's next?"

Almost every person in Heulog, it seemed, was infected with the tyllwyllwch. Those who were still walking around still had the dark aura around them, but it was easy to clear off within a few seconds. The ones who lay in their beds like Tomos' mother were harder, and Lauren found herself waking up on the ground more than once. But she didn't want to stop, even though Cefin begged her to. The feeling of helping others was too good, too addicting, even though her head began to ache as the sun set on the village.

"That's the last of them, Lauren," Cefin said, as he and Lauren left a house where an old grandfather had just woken up.

"Is it? Don't you want to do another sweep?" Lauren asked, flexing her hands.

"If there are more, you can heal them in the morning," Cefin said. "You're pale and haven't eaten all day. You need to rest."

"I'm fine." Lauren saw the sign for a tavern in the center of the village. "But I could use a beer?"

To her surprise, Cefin's face broke from the stony concern into a wide smile.

"Well, m'lady," he said, following her into the tavern. It was filled almost over capacity with people, elbow-to-elbow around old wooden tables with sudsy beers in their hands. When the first person spotted Lauren in the entryway, he cheered, and was joined by the rest of the group. A glass was thrust into Lauren's hand, followed by a hearty slap on the back.

Elation.

Happiness.

Relief.

Emotions came to and fro as she was manhandled in the tavern, everyone wishing to shake her hand and personally thank her for saving the village. Cefin kicked away the first two people, but Lauren waved him off, now almost used to the jolting feeling of being in someone else's head after healing others all day. Besides, everyone was so happy that it left *her* feeling happy, even when the last person had shaken her hand.

She finally sat down at the table, her third beer in her hand. She didn't feel drunk, as most of her first two had ended up on the floor instead of in her stomach. She took a long swig—it was warm and tasted like urine—but it was beer and she let out a happy sigh.

"What?" Cefin asked, wiping away the suds on his upper lip.

"Just happy. Glad I'm finally useful for something."

"You've been useful," Cefin said with a mischievous smile. "You were useful entertainment when I set you to doing the laundry."

"Hah!" Lauren barked, swallowing another gulp.

"You've got a gift, you know," Cefin said, piercing her with his handsome eyes. "You saved a lot of lives today."

Lauren picked up the amulet around her neck and looked at it. It was the only thing she had on her from her old world—

Her old world.

She'd thought it so casually, like living in the old world was a dream. Her mom and dad were just figments of her imagination, Josh was just a fantasy she'd concocted. It was just as well; she wasn't going home.

She took another sip of her beer and smiled as another man came to thank her for saving his child's life, but somehow she couldn't bring herself back up where she'd been before. Something dark had settled in her chest, and she was struggling to get rid of it, even in this boisterous tavern. She felt like all of the happiness she'd experienced today had gone cold, like a cup of coffee out too long.

"We shall return to the village in the morning," Cefin said, taking a long drink. "If you are agreeable to that?"

"Mm-hmm," Lauren said, playing with the amulet around her neck.

"Are you all right?"

"Yeah, just suddenly got really tired." Lauren forced a smile on her face so Cefin wouldn't become concerned. "I think I'm going to take a walk."

"Would you like me to come with you?"

Lauren waved him off and backed away slowly. "No, no, stay here and have a good time! You work too hard. Good for you to have a break. I'll be back in a bit."

Cefin shrugged and turned to engage with the man who had just walked up to the table, presumably the leader of the village, who was thanking Cefin profusely for bringing Lauren.

Lauren took this opportunity to slip out of the tavern, leaving the warm and rowdy room for the quiet of the cool night. Wrapping her arms tight around herself, she began strolling aimlessly, hoping to find a quiet place to sit. It did not take her long to reach the edge of the town, and a thick forest that loomed in the darkness. She stepped under the canopy, sliding down the trunk of the tree.

Looking up at the moon, she allowed the loneliness that had grown in her chest to flow out. Tears rolled down her cheeks and she let them to fall without wiping them away. It was a relief to allow herself to be sad out here in the quiet forest, not having to drag anyone else down with her mood. No one else would understand anyway. She had just saved a village; what did she have to be sad about?

She heard a loud cheer from the tavern and made no move to get up.

Truth be told, she *didn't* have much to be sad about, she told herself. Sure, she was away from everything she'd ever known, in a strange land with strange powers, but she had Aerona and the twins and Cefin here. They were her new surrogate family. Cefin didn't look at her the way Josh did, but that was okay, wasn't it? He'd come all the way down to the village with her to make sure she was all right. So what if she couldn't touch him...

Her face scrunched up and she let a sob escape, simultaneously wallowing and wondering why she was wallowing. She knew this was just something she had to deal with by herself. If she could just make it until the morning, she would be fine.

"Let me take it from you..."

She sat up again, panic replacing sadness. Her eyes jumped to the sky and her ears strained for the sound of beating wings. Was it here? Why was it here? Was it drawn by the tyllwyllwch?

Was it drawn by her?

Barely remembering to breathe, she listened for a few more minutes that stretched out like hours. But all she heard was the quiet chirping of the crickets and other night creatures, and the sky, now clear of the dark fog that had surrounded it, was clear to the moon overhead.

She wondered, perhaps, if she were simply going insane and had imagined the dark voice in the back of her mind. After all, she'd heard it laughing when she'd been healing Tomos' mother, and she was sure that she'd just imagined it.

"Here you are," a different voice said behind her.

"Yeah," Lauren replied, thankful she had already wiped her cheeks. She didn't want Cefin asking about her tears, and she didn't want to worry him with thinking she heard the Anghenfil.

"You disappear a lot," he replied. "Is that just a habit from your world, or is it a trait only empaths share?"

She smiled in the darkness. "Just needed some time alone. It can get very overwhelming in there."

"I am sure," Cefin replied, coming to sit next to her.

She was comforted by his presence, but wasn't comfortable. She remembered the ease with which she and Josh used to enjoy each other's company, the trust that she could be herself and tell him everything that was on her mind without rejection. There was a wall between her and Cefin, and she wasn't sure how to pull it down.

She noticed him looking at her through the darkness.

"What?" Lauren asked.

"What does it feel like when someone touches you?"

"It's strange," Lauren said, looking up at the moon.

Cefin laughed good-naturedly. "Is that all? Just strange?"

"If I explain it, you'll think I'm nuts," Lauren smiled, before tossing him a curious glance. "What do I look like when it happens?"

"You go into some kind of fit," Cefin said. Lauren looked over at him as his eyes rolled up into his head and he began convulsing violently.

"Oh, shut up. I do not look like that."

"Maybe I overdid the twitching a bit," Cefin replied, sitting back and putting his hands behind his head.

Lauren laughed, and looked back up at the moon.

"I won't think you're...what'd you say, nuts?" Cefin asked. "I can only assume that means..."

"That you'll think I'm crazy."

"I won't," Cefin promised. "I've seen a lot of strange things today."

"Like what? Me clearing out a bunch of dark smoke from a village?"

"I don't know about smoke, but your stone was lighting up all day."

Lauren played with the amulet for a moment, hoping it would give her a little bit of courage. "When someone touches me, I guess... it feels like jumping into a pool. You're suddenly surrounded by all of these foreign thoughts and feelings. And it's like you're drowning in them."

"Feelings? How can you drown in feelings?"

Lauren recalled a quote about men having the emotional range of a teaspoon and smiled. "When they aren't your own, and when someone's struggling with a lot of different feelings...it can be overwhelming to have theirs and yours in your head."

"You still feel yours, too?"

Lauren smiled. "No, it's actually kind of nice to get out of my own head for a while."

After a few moments, Cefin asked, "Does it hurt?"

"Sometimes."

"What does the tyllwyllwch feel like?"

"It's cold." Lauren shivered. "When I go into these people's... minds, I guess...it's like being at the bottom of a dark cave."

"How did you get rid of it? The stone?"

"I figured that it was kind of like the mist on a river, that if I found some way to heat it up, it would go away. And I just closed my eyes and the stone did the rest."

"Amazing," Cefin said, reaching a hand over to pluck the amulet off of her chest. His fingers brushed her skin.

She looks beautiful tonight—

"Sorry," he winced, the stone dropping to her chest with a dull thud, echoing in the emptiness of her heart.

Lauren hissed in frustration. "I wish I didn't have these stupid powers. I can't even..."

"Can't what?"

"Nothing," she whispered. She wanted to say that she couldn't even touch him, but it would just be too painful to vocalize. And although she could touch him and know *exactly* what he was thinking and how he felt about her, it would be too awful to have that knowledge and not be able to do anything about it.

chapter eight

The next morning, Lauren was in much better spirits. It might have had something to do with waking up to find Cefin snoozing in the other bed in the room, or maybe that she had silently cried herself to sleep after he had turned out the lights. Her mother always said that crying made everything feel better.

"Morning," Cefin yawned and sat up. Lauren tried not to look at his bare chest, reminding herself that touching those chiseled abs would result in a very unwelcome intrusion into his thoughts. And when it came to Cefin, she was happier avoiding those thoughts all together.

Lauren insisted on wandering through Heulog once or twice more, just to make sure there was no darkness remaining in the village. But it appeared to be completely cleared out. To boot, it felt at least twenty degrees warmer than the day before with the brilliant sun shining on them. Still, she couldn't help but be a little disappointed that there was no one else she could help.

"You wish for more tyllwyllwch?" Cefin smiled at her as she crossed her arms across her chest.

Lauren shrugged but followed him as they hoofed it back up the mountain to Rhianu. Although she was starting to get the hang of mountain climbing after almost a week in this land, she was nowhere near as quick as Cefin, who marched upward with no regard to the steep incline.

"Hey, can we...stop for a moment?" Lauren panted, collapsing on a rock. Her calves and quads burned, and she desperately wished they'd run across a stream so she could quench her thirst.

"Of course," Cefin said, almost gliding down the mountain to meet her. "Are you all right? Still lightheaded from yesterday?"

Lauren smiled at his concern. "No, just...out of shape, it appears."

"You didn't seem to have much trouble when we trekked to see the Anghenfil." Cefin smiled, sitting on the ground next to her. She couldn't help but notice he left a wide space between them.

"I was on a mission then," Lauren chuckled. Sadness tugged at her, but she refused to give in. Not with Cefin staring at her the way he was. It gave her butterflies, and made her think about his *insistence* on accompanying her to Heulog.

"Oh, you look so pitiful," he cooed, nudging her.

She is so pretty when she smiles at me like this—

"Sorry. I keep forgetting I can't do that," Cefin said, looking forward like she had scolded him.

"No, it's fine." Lauren shrugged, now curious at the expression on his face. "It doesn't hurt or anything. It's just... shocking."

He nodded without responding, and Lauren was even more curious about what was going through his mind. She considered just getting the answer for herself, but that would have been huge invasion of privacy.

Children's laughter interrupted their tense moment and Eddy and Mairwan came barreling down the pathway, their faces alight with happiness at the sight of the two of them.

"CEFIN!" Mairwan cried, nearly flying into her cousin's arms. "I missed you!"

"We were gone for only a day!" Cefin said, but cupped her freckly face anyway. Eddy approached Lauren and grabbed her hand before she could react.

I am going to drop a frog in Siors house to see how long—

"Eddy," Lauren warned, coming back to herself. "Don't bother Siors."

His big brown eyes grew wide with realization and he scampered back behind Cefin, who was giving him a similarly stern glance. Mairwan continued gabbing about all that had occurred in the twenty-four hours since Cefin and Lauren been gone.

"And then the *chickens* just went mad!" she said, full of life and energy.

"I didn't mean it!" Eddy said, tossing a look to Lauren as though she could read his mind from ten feet away. "Honest!"

"I'm sure," Cefin said, winking at Lauren. Mairwan followed his gaze and stopped speaking, a curious look on her face as she watched Lauren.

"Your necklace..."

In a panic, Lauren's hand flew to her neck, afraid that back in Heulog she had lost her precious connection to her world. When her hand landed on the rough stone, she let out a sigh of relief. "What about it?"

Mairwan squinted from Cefin's arms. "It looks darker."

"D...darker?" Lauren looked down at her chest. To her horror, it was just a shade darker than she remembered it.

Or was it?

Were her eyes playing tricks on her?

They must have been playing tricks on her. There was no way it could be darker.

And if it was darker, which it wasn't, why did she care?

Did it have anything to do with the Anghenf—

"It doesn't look darker to me," Lauren said, forcing conviction into her voice even though she felt none.

"Perhaps you should get Siors to look at it," Cefin suggested. "You did clear out a lot of tyllwyllwch yesterday. Perhaps it left a lasting impression?"

"It's fine," Lauren waved him off, wishing that she, herself, believed her own words. "I'm not worried about it."

"I hope it turns *black*." Eddy grinned devilishly.

"Edward, why would you say that?" Cefin asked, spinning around to look at the child, who cowered.

"I dunno," he shrugged. "I just thought it would be fun to see it turn all black."

"It's not darker," Lauren said, harsher than she meant to. Cefin raised his eyebrows at her but said nothing as they continued their march up the mountain.

Lauren fell behind the group, staring at the stone in her hand. Was it darker?

"Nope," she muttered aloud to herself.

"What was that?" Cefin asked, tossing a look back to her.

"Sorry, just thinking to myself." Lauren grinned. "Oh look, it's Owena..."

Indeed, the old woman was wandering along the path. She looked even crazier than normal, wildly talking to someone that wasn't there before muttering to herself and grasping at her hair.

"She scares me, Cefin," Mairwan whimpered, burying her head into her cousin's shoulder.

"She's just...nuts," Cefin said, winking at Lauren.

But Lauren missed his flirtation, as Owena had locked eyes with her. The soulless, dead eyes suddenly filled with emotion—fear—as if the very sight of Lauren was the most horrifying thing the woman had ever seen.

She opened her mouth and an ear-splitting scream came from

her throat.

"ANGHENFIL! BLACK!"

"WHERE?!" Cefin said, dropping Mairwan to the ground and unsheathing his sword in one fluid movement. He stood in front of the children protectively, before he realized that Owena was screaming and pointing at Lauren.

"You damned fool!" Cefin growled, sheathing his sword. "You had everyone terrified. Lauren, don't—"

But Lauren was rooted to the spot.

Owena's ramblings somehow made unnerving sense. She had spoken about the Anghenfil, and she had spoken about darkness —blackness.

The Anghenfil was turning her stone darker.

"No, she's crazy." Lauren shook her head, clearing the terrifying thought from her mind. "She's confused. I told her we had seen the Anghenfil a few days ago. She's just confused, that's all."

"Damn woman," Cefin grunted before turning to comfort Mairwan, who was terrified. "Don't worry, she's just causing a ruckus for nothing. Let's get you back home. Is your mother cooking stew for dinner?"

Mairwan nodded and clung to him as they continued towards the village, Eddy following close behind. But Lauren stood in the center, watching Owena, and wondering if she were brave enough to ask more questions—like what would happen when her stone turned completely black.

Instead, Lauren turned on her heel and ran after the other three.

***

Aerona was pleased to see them return and let Lauren off the hook with helping around the house for the rest of the day. Lauren was happy to not have to engage in manual labor, but was a little wanting for distraction as she wandered around the village aimlessly, lost in her own mind. As much as she tried to convince herself Owena was making a fuss for no reason, the truth swam just below the surface, joining the rest of the things she was trying very hard to ignore completely. By mid-afternoon, she was sick with worry and finally decided to take Cefin's advice and seek guidance.

"Lauren, my child," Siors said, coming out from the back room with a pipe in his hand. "Did you find much success in Heulog?"

"I did." Lauren half-smiled. "I was able to get rid of all the tyllwyllwch. Completely eradicated."

"Excellent news!" Siors clapped before pausing. "You look troubled?"

"I just..." Sitting here with him, she found herself unable to tell him the truth. She was worried about what he would say if he knew she had heard the Anghenfil in her mind. Did she really hear it? Maybe she was imagining things. She'd just healed an entire village, so perhaps it was just exhaustion.

And was it really the Anghenfil that had turned her stone darker? She wasn't even sure that it was. Maybe she was just going crazy. It could have been the tyllwyllwch. She was probably overthinking things, as usual.

"Yes, child?" Siors prompted in the silence of the room.

"It's...my necklace," Lauren said. "The kids said the stone in my necklace has gotten darker. I guess I just wanted a second opinion."

And affirmation that it had nothing to do with the Anghenfil.

"Let me take a look," Siors said, walking around his living room for his spectacles. Finding them under an open book, he approached Lauren, his old eyes boring into the stone around her neck. She chewed on her lip in nervous anticipation.

"I mean, I'm not even sure," Lauren stammered, as his eyes conveyed no hint of what he was thinking. "Maybe I'm just being silly."

"You would second guess your own concerns?" Siors asked, sitting back and surveying her.

"Yes? I mean...maybe?" Lauren squirmed. Second guessing was second nature to her, and she'd never had anyone ask her about it before. "I mean, when I was...getting rid of the tyllwyllwch, it lit up and got very hot. Maybe I burned it?" *Please don't be the Anghenfil.*

"Rubies are known as the fire stone," Siors said. "The myths say that it shines even in the darkest places."

Lauren looked down at the amulet and remembered how it burned her skin. She still had the mark, hidden underneath her dress.

"I cannot say for sure whether it has changed color," Siors said, after examining her for a moment. "I am out of my depth when it comes to empaths. Hopefully soon I will receive a response from my scholar-brother in Traegaron."

Lauren nodded, but her anxiety did not subside.

"I would not worry, child," Siors said, making a move to touch her but stopping just before his hand clasped her shoulder. "Do you feel any different?"

Lauren wondered if she should tell him about the drowning loneliness she felt the night before, but she chalked it up to just being silly. Again, her own voice was in her head, making her feel stupid for making a fuss over nothing.

"No," she replied.

"I am sure the stone will heal in time. Perhaps it just needs a few days to finish cleansing itself."

"Yeah." Lauren nodded, forcing herself to accept what she

definitely did not believe. "Yeah, I'm sure that's what it is. Sorry to have bothered you with my stupid problems."

"Is there anything else you wish to speak to me about?"

A thousand thoughts exploded in her mind. The Anghenfil, the tyllwyllwch, the voices in her head, being an empath, her growing crush on Cefin, missing home terribly. She was to the brim with misery and worry and wanted nothing more than to release all of it into the open so that she didn't have to worry about it alone.

But instead:

"Nope! I'm good. Thanks for the chat!"

⁂

Nothing that Siors said made her feel any less concerned, but after a few hours with Baltes' animals, she was sufficiently distracted from thinking about it. When she returned for dinner after the sun had set, she was able to completely separate herself from her worries and enjoy the evening entertainment of the twins bouncing around the house. She didn't even flinch when Eddy gave her a mindful of knowledge about his upcoming plan to rearrange Baltes' living room furniture.

"Yeah, okay, Bart Simpson," Lauren laughed at him when she came back to herself.

"Who's Bart Simpson?" Eddy asked, as Aerona placed a bowl of stew in front of him. Mairwan settled at the table as well, and began carefully picking out the carrots and chomping on them first.

"Don't worry about it," Lauren said, breathing in the aroma from Eddy's bowl. "Aerona, it smells amazing. Thank you."

"You've had a long few days." She handed Lauren a bowl. Lauren hadn't realized how hungry she was until she dove in, inhaling half of it before Aerona sat down.

"Mm, healing's hungry business." Lauren grinned sheepishly,

109

as Aerona took her bowl and filled it to the brim again.

Aerona took a seat next to her. "I'm sure the families in the village are appreciative. Cefin said you collapsed many times. I can't believe you continued on like that."

Lauren speared a potato with her fork. "Oh yeah, just part of it, I guess." She wondered how often Cefin and Aerona spoke about her, and realized they were quite close in age for being aunt and nephew. Perhaps with so few people in the village, the pickings were slim for Aerona. For a brief moment, she wondered if Cefin and Aerona...but she dismissed the thought as soon as it popped into her head.

"You don't like to make a fuss, do you?" Aerona smiled at her.

"I figure people have much worse things to be worried about," Lauren shrugged, but couldn't help but add, "My problems are nothing compared to those of the rest of the world."

Aerona took Lauren's empty bowl. "But your problems are problems to you. And problems left unresolved will fester into bigger ones."

"I'd prefer to just pretend they don't exist. It's what I've been doing with my ex."

"Your ex?"

"My ex...lover," Lauren said, not sure if Aerona would get the concept of a boyfriend. "We were together a very long time."

"And why is he your ex-lover? Did he die?"

Lauren remembered that Aerona's husband died fighting the Anghenfil and felt stupid for even bringing it up. *That* was real pain, death was final. Josh *could* still come back—

"No, he didn't die," Lauren said, quickly to avoid finishing that thought. "He just...didn't want to get married. No big deal. I'm mostly over it anyways."

Aerona's eyebrows went up in suspicion.

"Seriously." Lauren waved her off. "It was amicable, we're still...kind of friends. No worries. Besides, I'm here in this world, so it's not like I can do anything about it anyways!" She finished with a toothy grin and hoped Aerona would buy it and not ask any more questions.

"And you don't think you'll ever return home?" Aerona asked, as Eddy and Mairwan left the table and jumped in their bed. "To him?"

The idea of returning home and *not* being with Josh was more painful than the idea of never going home. Being in this other world was a convenient excuse to not have to come to terms with their new, separated reality. But Aerona was close to dragging it back to the forefront.

"I...uh..." Lauren said, mask slipping a little bit. "You know what? I think I left something at Siors earlier today. I'll be back in a jiffy."

Before Aerona could stop her, Lauren hightailed it out the door.

***

The dark village was quiet, which was nice, because Lauren's head was filled with acerbic voices, each one berating her for being so stupid, for talking about Josh in front of Aerona, for opening old wounds. To add insult to injury, her mind was replaying memories over and over again—her and Josh on road trips, hanging out in the mornings drinking coffee. They were all agonizing to think about. And then she berated herself for daring to feel miserable when Aerona had suffered so much more.

In the context of all of the other things that had happened to Lauren since she'd been in Rhianu, fire-breathing dragons and such, their break-up was laughable in comparison. Why was she even still thinking about it?

"Enough," Lauren called to the darkness. She was going to *stop* being so upset over something so trivial.

Unbidden, she wondered what Josh would say to her there in the fantasy world, what he would say about her healing people. He'd probably make some crack about it, knowing him.

She hung her head, defeated. Why did she always need him when she was trying not to think of him?

She turned her attention to where she had ended up, the watcher's post. The moon was full and bright, casting a pale glow on the valley below, and onto a familiar form slumped against a rock.

"Asleep on the job?" Lauren announced, enjoying the way she startled him and he nearly fell over.

"What are you doing up here?" Cefin asked, before giving her a look. "Are you trying to sneak past to the Anghenfil?"

"If I was trying to sneak past, I wouldn't have woken you up." Lauren took a seat on a stone near to him. "What are you doing here at night?"

"Graves took the day shift since I was in the village with you," Cefin replied, yawning a bit.

"Sorry. I didn't mean to keep you—"

"It was my pleasure," Cefin grinned back at her and her stomach churned. "Did you walk all the way up here just to make sure I wasn't sleeping?"

"I needed a break," Lauren replied, playing with her necklace.

"Break from what? You've been wandering around the village all day."

"Just have too many..." Lauren trailed off. She still couldn't bring herself to be honest about what was really troubling her. She couldn't be honest with Siors, and she couldn't be honest with Aerona. And now, sitting here with Cefin, there was something keeping her from opening up.

"Has your stone gotten any darker?" he asked.

"I don't know," Lauren admitted, looking at her hands in the darkness. "I went to see Siors today, and he wasn't sure. He said he'd written someone in the city to see if they knew anything about it, or about me. I hate not knowing what's going on."

"Wouldn't it be nice if there was another empath to read you?"

She laughed and looked at him, aware of how close they were sitting.

Cefin leaned back and seemed to be sizing her up.

"What?" Lauren asked, both flattered and unnerved by the way he was eyeing her.

"I think I can read you. I don't need to be an empath to know everything about you."

"Oh really? All right then, spear-boy. What do you get off of me?"

"Lauren Dailey," he began, sounding stern. "Not from this world. Would do well as a court jester in Traegaron."

"Yes, indeed." Lauren nodded seriously. "Because I am high-larious." She ignored the pang in her heart; she and Josh used to share that phrase.

"An empath who has no idea how to use her powers," Cefin continued, and Lauren nodded approvingly. "Eager to help others, and eager not to listen to village watchers who are trying to protect her from monsters."

"And very good at listening when those monsters appeared." The monster was still with her, living inside of her head. Could she tell Cefin that? He seemed to be looking at her one way; how would he look if she told him?

"But there's one thing I don't know," Cefin said.

"What's that?" She smiled, suddenly aware of his breath on her face.

He closed the gap between them, and she barely got to register what was happening before—

She tastes so good, her lips are velvet, soft and delicate. Oh, to push her to the ground and explore all that is underneath her dress, but she is twitching, and...wait, I cannot—

Lauren gasped, her mind reeling from the reading but her body very much turned on from the kiss. Cefin's lips were an inch from hers, where he had just lifted them. She could still taste him in her mouth, but she had no memory of their kiss. All she could remember was the peculiar sensation of kissing *herself*, and it made her squeamish inside.

"I'm sorry," he whispered. "I forgot that—"

"No, don't be sorry," she whispered back, struggling against the strong urge to kiss him again, to do other things to him, knowing that he wanted to do the same to her. With great pain, she turned her head away from him to look forward.

"So we can't...really..." he trailed off.

"Appears not," Lauren said, cursing inwardly.

They sat in awkward silence for a few moments before Cefin spoke again. "What does it feel like to kiss me?"

She was suddenly very interested in the ground ahead of them.

"What? Is it bad? Does it hurt?"

"No, it's just..." Lauren said, feeling the blush rise in her face. How was she supposed to tell him that she knew the very sexual way he felt about her? She wasn't even sure if he was a virgin or not, although he seemed to have a very active imagination.

"What?" he pressed.

"I mean, it's an...well...it's an open book," Lauren confessed. "I mean, I can feel...*everything*."

Cefin didn't understand.

"Like...well...how much you...like me," Lauren finished lamely.

Cefin's face turned redder than she thought possible and she immediately regretted telling him. "So, everything?"

"Yeah."

"*Everything?*"

She knew his meaning and couldn't look at him.

"I see." He swallowed. "I am sorry."

"For what? Feeling?"

"It's inappropriate to think that way about you."

Lauren stifled a laugh.

"Is that funny?" Cefin asked. "For me to feel that way about you?"

"I mean, you're a guy. You can't help it," Lauren said.

"Oh, so your beauty is so magnetic that all the men fall madly in love with you?" Cefin asked.

It was Lauren's turn to blush.

"I didn't mean that. I just..." Lauren sighed, and the panicked jitters were back. She should have told him that she couldn't see him anymore, that she couldn't even touch him without knowing every single intimate detail about him. She should have told him that she liked him as much as he liked her.

But instead, in true Lauren fashion:

"I...uh...guess I need to get back home," she whispered, pushing herself to stand. "I'm...sorry."

chapter nine

Lauren would have been lying through her teeth if she said she didn't think about Cefin, their kiss, and some things having to do with those bedsheets, especially as she and Mairwan spent the next day at the river cleaning several baskets of bedding and clothes for Aerona. She hoped that Cefin would get the message and just stop speaking with her, saving her from having to avoid him forever.

Luckily, avoidance happened without Lauren needing to hide under a rock. Within two days of her return to Rhianu, a man arrived carting a young woman on a donkey. She was slumped over, barely breathing, and Lauren could see the trail of tyllwyllwch behind her. Lauren healed her in the street, with much applause from the villagers, who had never seen magic before. Eddy was stuck like glue to her for the rest of the day, hoping to catch a glimpse of someone being healed and the bright light from the stone.

Over the next week, sick people poured into the village, sometimes as many as five a day. Each time, Lauren walked through the darkness of tyllwyllwch and healing them with the light from her stone. She said nothing to the villagers nor to anyone else, but after every banishment of the tyllwyllwch, she spent an hour examining her stone, looking to see if it had turned darker. And after every one, no change. Although that didn't give her much comfort—if it wasn't the tyllwyllwch darkening her stone, it had to be something decidedly more beast-like.

But even though Lauren was healing the tyllwyllwch, she hadn't heard the Anghenfil's voice in her mind for a few days. Long enough that she was able to convince herself she had imagined the whole thing.

After all, it was a fire-breathing dragon; they couldn't talk.

Right?

When there was no one to heal, she quelled these unending questions during her days on Baltes' farm. She couldn't get enough of these days, which flew by quickly and left her in a much calmer emotional state than when she arrived. When she was in the mind of a goat, she wasn't worried about Cefin or the Anghenfil or the stone—her own quiet escape.

Baltes continued to talk with her as though she could hear him while she was reading animals, or maybe he just didn't care that she wasn't listening. Sometimes the twins joined her on the farm, usually supplying their own distraction.

"I SAID I WANNA RIDE!" Eddy cried as Mairwan climbed onto Bessie. She stuck her tongue out at him and kicked the horse's barrel.

"Kids." Lauren smiled to Baltes.

"Seems like the stream of villagers has ended," he noted, an eye on the children.

"Yeah, I'm hoping that it's mostly gone now. The other day, there was a villager from as far away as Traegaron."

Baltes whistled. "That's a fair journey. At least a day on horseback."

"I hope he's the only one," Lauren said. "I can't imagine if an entire city was infected. Heulog was bad enough." She began to worry again about the tyllwyllwch and the Anghenfil, and quickly replaced those thoughts with those of a nearby chicken. She let her own thoughts go and took a calming breath.

"Hey, hey!" The twins were squabbling worse than before, and Baltes had run over to calm them down. "What's this fuss today?"

"Eddy says he can ride Bessie better than I can!" Mairwan said, glaring at her twin from atop the horse. "I wanna show him!"

"All right, all right," Baltes said, walking beside the horse as she plodded along the paddock in a circle.

Lauren smiled and closed her eyes as a goat passed by her. The water trough was empty, and he was thirsty. When the presence passed, Lauren walked over to the trough and found it bone dry.

Since Baltes was busy with the kids, Lauren decided to visit the river and bring back some water for the animals. She hoisted the water bucket easily, priding herself that she'd grown stronger in the few days she'd been there in the village. She even had sort of figured out how to keep her mind under control, as long as she had some livestock nearby.

That was, until she came to the banks and saw a half-naked Cefin scrubbing himself down in the middle of the river.

"Oh, hi," Lauren said, the bucket falling out of her hand. His long hair hung around his ears, wet and sticking to his face. He swiveled around when he heard her voice, and his entire upper body grew red.

"Hello...." he said.

They stood in awkward silence for a moment, and Lauren tried not to stare at his gorgeous body.

"Do you need something?" he asked after an eternity of silence.

"Was just getting water for Baltes."

"Oh," he nodded. "Do you need help carrying it back?"

"I....um...sure," Lauren stammered.

Cefin smiled his gorgeous smile. "Let me get dressed and I'll do just that."

Lauren stared at him for a moment before realizing he *was* in fact naked and probably didn't want her gawking at his nakedness. She spun around, haranguing herself for being such an awkward twit. She tried not to think about naked Cefin, but failed miserably. His naked body was firmly in the forefront of her mind, as was their kiss, as was all of other, more sexual thoughts that were currently heating up her cheeks.

She looked around for a small mammal or bug she could read, just so she could stop the stream of consciousness. Unfortunately for her, the only living thing in the vicinity was currently the object of her erotic thoughts.

She heard him finish sloshing around and call to her that he was dressed. She spun around and swallowed a hiss—his white shirt was sticking to his chest even more attractively, defining every single ripple and definition on his upper body.

"Thanks for helping me," Lauren said, handing him the bucket. Their fingers brushed for a moment-

I can't believe I kissed her. How stupid can I be—

"Sorry," he winced.

"Don't be," Lauren said, forcing a smile on her face. She then blurted out, "And don't be sorry about the other day, either."

"Right..." Cefin blushed beet red and Lauren hated herself for speaking.

They walked in silence down the path to Baltes' farm, but there was a loud conversation in Lauren's head. These empath powers weren't only a pain in the ass for her, they were awfully invasive to Cefin's privacy. Not wanting to chance getting another glimpse into his mind, she folded her arms tightly over her chest.

Cefin noticed her distance and his face changed, but he said nothing as he carefully balanced the water bucket in his hand.

Lauren was sure that the trip to the river was much shorter than the way back, but mercifully, they reached the farm. Mairwan, still on top of Bessie, was calling out to Eddy, who was looking quite put out that she wouldn't get off and let him ride.

"Kids." Lauren shook her head, eager to break the tension between Cefin and her.

"Mm," Cefin said.

"Look, Cefin, here's the deal—" Lauren began, but a loud scream ripped through the both of them. Lauren spun around to search for the source of the scream and heard the bucket of water fall out of Cefin's hands.

Eddy was the source of the ear-piercing screaming.

Bessie was bucking, and Baltes was trying to get hold of her.

Mairwan lay motionless on the ground.

⁂

Lauren paced in front of the hut, her hands moving from covering her mouth to wringing anxiously to running through her hair. There was no sound coming from the hut, and that just made her more nervous. Siors was inside with a distraught Aerona, doing his best to calm the mother and save the daughter, who was breathing but not responsive. It seemed as though they had been in there for hours, and every passing second was agony.

Cefin was holding Eddy, who hadn't stopped shaking or crying since he first saw his sister on the ground. Baltes had said he was prodding at Bessie, trying to get the better of Mairwan. Lauren knew he must be wracked with guilt; no wonder Cefin was holding him so tightly.

Lauren spun back around to look at the door and began to feel guilty as well. She didn't even want to go near the young girl, the idea of death making her uncomfortable. She'd only seen it once before, when her grandfather died, and the sight of the once jolly man lying in the coffin had been unnerving. The idea that so much life and energy could just evaporate in an instant terrified her.

But it was more than that: Lauren was afraid of what she'd find if she touched the young girl. Would she still be there, the sweet little girl that she had come to adore? Or would it be like Owena—nothing at all.

Siors appeared in the doorway, his face grim and ashen, and Lauren's stomach fell to the floor.

"I am afraid there is nothing more I can do for her," Siors whispered to Lauren.

"Oh no," Lauren gasped, covering her mouth with her hands. She caught eyes with Cefin and his face scrunched up with unshed tears. He patted Eddy on the back, but didn't turn to keep the boy from seeing Siors.

"Aerona is making her comfortable, but I do not think she will last the night," Siors said heavily. "Perhaps you can give her some peace before she goes."

Lauren's blood ran cold, and immediately she tried to think of all the reasons why she shouldn't go in there to do the right thing. All of them died on her tongue at Siors' expression, the solemn acceptance that the village was about to lose one of its brightest lights. She bit her lip and thought of Aerona inside. The mother had been nothing but kind to Lauren, and now was about to lose her only daughter—much the way Lauren's mother probably felt right now back in California. She steeled herself as she nodded to Siors, dread spreading as she approached the small hut.

But nothing prepared Lauren for the sight of Mairwan lying in the bed she shared with her mother and brother, her face pale and lifeless, her hands folded gently across her stomach. If it weren't for the gentle rise and fall of her chest, Lauren would have thought her already dead.

"L-Lauren?" Aerona whispered, standing over the hearth. With tears running down her cheeks, she rinsed blood out of a rag that she had been using to clean the wound on the back of Mairwan's head.

"Hey," Lauren whispered, rushing over to her. She placed her hand on Aerona's back and retracted it just as quickly. Aerona was on fire and bone chillingly cold at the same time, a tumultuous sea of emotions that felt oddly similar to the tyllwyllwch.

"She's..." Aerona sobbed, rubbing the blood off of her red hands. "I don't know..."

Lauren wished she were a doctor, or knew anything about medicine. But she was just a stupid empath, and there was nothing she could do.

Except maybe stay with Mairwan until the end.

Lauren walked over to the bed, her feet made of lead. She didn't want to know what a person felt before they died, but she also knew Aerona would appreciate her staying with Mairwan when it happened. Lauren looked down at her hands, trembling with fear.

"Lauren?" Aerona asked.

"I'm gonna see if...well..." Lauren trailed off, her body not responding the way she was asking it to. She was petrified of what was going to happen, of having to face death.

"Thank you," Aerona whispered.

Lauren closed her eyes and gently touched Mairwan's small wrist, unsure of what to expect. But all that was left was... nothing. It was like touching old woman Owena.

"Did you feel her?" Aerona asked.

"Y-yes," Lauren lied. She couldn't bring herself to tell Aerona the truth. "But it's faint. Let me try again."

Lauren sat down on the bed and leaned over the small girl's frame. She sent up a silent prayer to whatever deity existed in this world and placed her whole hand on Mairwan's arm, and her other hand on the girl's warm forehead, willing her own consciousness to find something...

**

Lauren knew she was in Rhianu, or some form of the village. Everything was familiar, and yet it was different here—just as she was aware of her body, but not completely there. There was no one else there with her, and yet, she knew if she started walking towards the river, she would find the person she was looking for.

She saw the fire-red braids first, then the little body perched on the banks and looking into the white nothingness on the other side. Mairwan seemed a ghost herself—from her muted hair to her pale skin and freckles, everything was dull in color.

"Mairwan," Lauren said softly, standing next to the young girl, who didn't move to acknowledge her presence.

"Papa is calling me," Mairwan whispered.

Lauren nodded, straining her eyes to see the form of a man. But in this case, her empath powers did not give her the ability to see beyond what was in front of her.

"He's over there, on the other side of the river," Mairwan said, lifting her hand to point to the opaqueness. "He says it's time for me to go with him."

"Do you want to go with him?" Lauren asked, wondering why that thought gave her so much sadness.

"I don't know."

Lauren stood beside her for a moment, and reached out to touch the young girl's head. She didn't feel anything but air, but somehow she had connected with the girl. Mairwan turned her sad, hollow eyes to look up at Lauren.

"Would Momma miss me if I left?"

Lauren nodded. "And Eddy would too."

"I don't want to go, but I don't know the way back home."

"C'mon," Lauren said, offering her hand. "I know the way."

Mairwan slid her hand through Lauren's. It fit firmly in Lauren's hand. In fact, her whole form seemed more solid the closer they came to the village. Lauren spotted Aerona's house—or what she remembered to be Aerona's house—in the distance, and the stone at her neck began to warm. She knew if they walked through the threshold, they'd be home.

Home, but not Lauren's home.

She'd never see her home again.

The sky darkened as sadness settled in Lauren's chest, as if a cloud passed over the sun. Mairwan tugged at her arm. Her eyes were trained on something in the distance, something Lauren could not see.

"What is it?" Lauren asked.

She heard the beating of wings, and dread snaked up her spine. A shadow crossed over them, and she knew in the pit of her soul that it had come in her moment of weakness. The world, too, became darker, windier, reflecting the hurricane in her own mind.

It only grew more violent when Lauren heard the hissing laughter, as loud in this world as it was in her mind. Mairwan heard it too, and she began to cry in fear, clinging to Lauren's arm.

"It's okay," Lauren whispered, unsure if she was telling the truth or not.

With a great thud, the monster—the Anghenfil—landed in the middle of the village, smoke pluming from its flaring nostrils, and its ruby red eyes, now the same terrifying color as her necklace, stared only at Lauren.

"Get back," Lauren pushed Mairwan behind her, hoping that she'd find bravery by protecting someone else. The monster moved its head slowly as it surveyed its prey, and Lauren could hear it purring happily.

"You will not return."

The voice was at once quiet and echoed loudly, filling the dark space around them. Mairwan whimpered at Lauren's side.

"What does it want?" Mairwan asked.

"I don't know," Lauren lied.

The monster laughed, the hissing bursts of air sending chills down her spine.

Lauren tightened her grip on Mairwan; she was *damned* if she had just saved the young girl's life and this stupid monster took it again. The Anghenfil stood between them and Aerona's house, now covered in tyllwyllwch, as was the entire village. The only light, it seemed, was coming from Lauren's stone and from the belly of the beast.

"Mairwan, can you see your house?" Lauren asked.

"N-no," Mairwan whimpered. "Don't leave me—"

"I'm not," Lauren said, and she heard the monster laughing again.

"She is of no consequence. Give it to me, and she will go home."

"Give what to him?" Mairwan asked.

"Look at me," Lauren said, crouching down and grabbing Mairwan by the shoulders. "When I say run, I want you to run as fast as you can into the village."

"But—"

"I'll be right behind you."

"You can't escape."

"RUN!" Lauren screamed, nearly dragging Mairwan forward. She ran as fast as her legs could carry her, pulling Mairwan along as they narrowly missed the snapping jaws of the Anghenfil. Lauren nearly threw Mairwan in front of her, but the girl found her footing and began running on her own.

Behind her, she heard the Anghenfil roar, and then fire exploded around them, lighting the dark sky with an eerie orange glow.

Mairwan stopped in the middle of the street, the fire dancing in her eyes. "Lauren, I'm scared!"

"MAIRWAN, RUN!" Lauren screamed, turning to look at the Anghenfil as it tilted its head back and roared again, spewing fire into the sky. Ash and fire rained down on top of her, but it didn't burn or hurt the way the stone at her neck did.

"Wait, what?" she blinked, looking down at her chest. The stone was glowing as though she were cleansing the tyllwyllwch. She turned to look back at the Anghenfil, and it hissed when the light from the stone reached its eyes.

With the Anghenfil distracted, Lauren scooped Mairwan into her arms and ran forward into the village, unrecognizable in the fire. She closed her eyes and tried to remember the way it looked, how many houses down Aerona's house was from the edge of the river.

The stone glowed brighter when Lauren spied one house in the distance, and she knew it was the one. She put Mairwan on the ground and knelt down to her level.

"Lauren, I'm scared," Mairwan cried. Lauren heard the Anghenfil roar again, but she shook off her own fear, knowing that getting Mairwan to safety was more important.

"Your house is right here," Lauren said. "Walk in the front door, and you'll be home."

"But—"

"Just go," Lauren said, pushing her towards the burning house. She held her breath as the little girl pushed aside the curtain and disappeared.

Lauren breathed out; Mairwan was safe.

"You can be safe too."

"Yeah, I don't quite like your definition of safe." Lauren spun around to find the monster looming above her. It was keeping its distance, unable to look at her with the stone around her neck.

"I can defeat you with this, can't I?" Lauren said, lifting the stone by the chain.

"How can you defeat me if you still fear me?"

"I can handle this," she said, but the light dimmed and the monster cackled as panic grew in her mind.

"You have no secrets from me. I know what you fear. The things that you are even afraid to think..."

Lauren swallowed. The stone dropped against her chest, and the light vanished. Her cheeks flushed as she registered the heat of the village. The smell of the burning wood filled her nose, and the fire was suddenly very real. She coughed in the smoke, heard the monster laugh.

"I can make it all go away...just give me your pain..."

The smoke was thick now, and she choked on it. She hunched down to the ground, hoping that she could find clearer air, but found no respite. Things were starting to get hazy as fear replaced calm in her mind.

She struggled to focus, to remember that she *could* do this, she could defeat the monster.

If she could just stop own panic and *focus.*

"It is useless to fight me...just let me have it..."

Her mind turned on her, wondering why the hell she thought it was a good idea to stay and fight when she could have made her escape. She was so stupid for thinking she was strong enough to handle this.

She coughed again; the smoke and the fire and the constriction in her chest were too much. She fell to the ground as she gasped for breath. The monster towered over her, smoke pooling from its nostrils as it lowered its head.

"Let me take your pain..."

"No!" She struggled to keep herself awake, to breathe, to resist the pull of the monster.

"That's right....come to me..."

Lauren's eyes opened halfway as the burning village disappeared in a thick fog of tyllwyllwch, or perhaps that was the fog in her mind. She was very cold, the monster was very warm, and the promise of never feeling pain again was so tempting.

"You will never think of him again..."

Lauren's eyes closed.

"You will never be lonely again..."

She was teetering on the edge of an abyss, and knew if she slipped, she would never re-emerge.

"Let me take it all from you..."

It was going to be nice to never be afraid again.

"Lauren....Lauren...Lauren....LAUREN!"

⁂

"LAUREN!"

Lauren's eyes shot open and she gasped for air. She could hear voices, but the only one that mattered was the Anghenfil, hissing and sputtering in the back of her mind. She had been torn from its grip. She lay on the floor for a moment, stunned and scared that she had ventured so close to giving the monster what it wanted.

"Lauren!" Cefin cried, his face filling her hazy vision. "Lauren, what happened?"

Everything—Mairwan, the monster, the village on fire, and the Anghenfil—washed over her at once, and she found herself unable to breathe again.

"Lauren, you're safe," Aerona said, joining Cefin as a face in

128

her line of vision. "You brought Mairwan back. It's all right."

Mairwan. She had been so scared when the Anghenfil appeared, and it was *Lauren's fault* that the Anghenfil almost took her. Lauren, who stupidly decided to stay behind and fight, and cowered at the last minute.

The monster was moving in her mind, and it only served to make her more panicked. What if it was coming for her at this very second? What if it crashed down on the house and crushed everyone in it, wrapping her up in its regenerated tail and flying her to do—

"Lauren, look at me," Cefin said, grabbing her face.

Relief. I am so relieved that Mairwan is back, but guilty—I never should have let it happen, now Lauren is acting so strangely—

Lauren returned to herself, Cefin's emotions overpowering her own fearful ones. In the absence of panic, she finally took a deep breath and looked around the room.

Siors and Aerona were white, the latter's eyes rimmed with red and her hands over her mouth. Eddy sobbed in the corner, and Mairwan was...

"You're awake?" Lauren gasped, staring into those brown eyes. They blinked back at her, tired, weak, but the light there.

"Lauren, what happened to you?" Aerona asked, stepping forward. "Mairwan woke up, but...you began swaying, and we couldn't wake you up!"

The Anghenfil growled in the back of her mind and she forced herself to half-smile. "I guess I got carried away...I've never done that before."

"You looked like something was after you," Cefin said, more firmly than Aerona. "What did you see?"

Lauren caught eyes with Mairwan, and prayed the little girl wouldn't say. Or that she wouldn't remember. Mairwan seemed completely out of it, but Lauren knew that she couldn't keep the appearance of the Anghenfil a secret for long. But she *could* delay telling them until it actually became a problem.

"I'd rather not talk about it," Lauren said, pushing herself to stand. She was still wobbly, but she needed to be alone before she lost her shit in front of everyone.

The Anghenfil purred in anticipation of her impending hysteria.

On second thought, perhaps she needed to be with people.

"Lauren, I...thank you," Aerona said, stepping forward. "You saved my little girl's life. I can't ever...there's no way I can ever repay you."

"Don't worry about it." Lauren forced herself to grin and add, "Just don't ask me to do laundry ever again."

chapter ten

Mairwan continued to drift in and out of consciousness, but Lauren just knew she was going to be fine, and she told Aerona as much. Siors was in agreement, although he stayed through a cold dinner of bread and cheese. Cefin left soon after, saying he was taking the night shift again, and Eddy and Aerona, exhausted from the day, were asleep soon after the plates were cleared away.

Only Lauren remained alert and awake, offering to keep watch over Mairwan through the night. It wasn't like she was planning to sleep ever again; she was afraid what would happen if the Anghenfil was able to penetrate her mind. She could feel it back there, moving around in the space reserved for terrifying thoughts. She was still on the cliff, and it was at the bottom, waiting for her to slip off.

She rubbed her face, wishing she could just turn off her mind for once. Mairwan slept peacefully beside her, and Lauren brushed aside some of her hair to relish in the quiet calm of the sleeping mind. When Lauren lifted her fingers, she felt better for a moment, until her fears washed back of her.

One day, Mairwan would regain full consciousness. Then she would tell her mother how Lauren brought the Anghenfil to the village in her mind, how they were both nearly killed because Lauren couldn't handle it. And then what would Aerona do?

Kick her out?

Lauren's panic resurfaced, and although she did her best to quiet it, but it continued boiling. Every question grew louder and louder in her head. She was a ticking time bomb, and things were going to blow up any day now. Either the villagers would find out or the monster would tire of waiting and return for what it came for.

And what would these people do when it did? If it was a matter of saving themselves or saving her, a stranger with no connections to this land, they would give the monster what it wanted, she was sure.

She could feel herself slipping down into the darkness and struggled to keep herself afloat. It was the sadness that attracted the Anghenfil. When she fell deeper into her dark thoughts, that's when it appeared.

Needing a distraction, Lauren stood up and walked to the door, stepping outside to get some fresh air. She turned to look at Aerona's house, ghostly in the moonlight and reminding her of the vision. The desire to go home boiled to the surface again, and she wished there was some way that she could just break free of this world and go home, go to a place where monsters only existed in the movies. Where the worst thing she had to deal with was whether she made it to work on time. Where she could just show up at her mom's house and spend the night when she had a bad day, or could spend time with her childhood friends. But she was stuck in this stupid world, tangled in circumstances out of her control, and happiness remained firmly out of reach. It was at once miserable, frustrating, and disheartening.

The monster growled, reminding her of its presence. She hissed at herself, angry that she couldn't even control her own emotions. It was the exact same thing she had been struggling with since she broke up with Josh, the incessant back and forth like the world's worst game of ping-pong.

She rubbed her face again, hoping that the action would release her from her thoughts.

Which was, of course, what the monster was promising, and that's why it made it so tempting. She could just package up all of her hurt and pain and give it away before she had to endure it. But she also knew that giving into a fire-breathing monster was probably not the smartest thing in the world. It wanted to take her heart; magic or not, she couldn't live without it.

But the question now in her mind was how long she could hold out before the thoughts became too much and she gave into the temptation?

She looked at her stone, imagining the bright light and trying to will her stone to glow. But it remained dull in her hand, and she let it fall back to her chest. It was useless anyway—special power or not, she wasn't able to wield it in the face of the Anghenfil.

In the dark of the night, she let the forbidden thought cross her mind: in order to get back home, she would have to defeat the Anghenfil.

And she couldn't.

Stuffing that thought back into the back of her mind, she considered other options. If she could keep it at bay, if she could fill her mind with goodness and happiness, perhaps it would lose interest in her and move on.

She closed her eyes and thought about all the things that made her happy. But she struggled to remember anything that wasn't tainted with a longing to return home, or clouded by the memory of Josh. Even the new memories she'd made here—Aerona, Siors, the twins—while they were loving and kind to her, but there was a wall between them. And Cefin, sweet handsome Cefin. He could be a suitable replacement for Josh, except that she couldn't touch him.

So she was alone, as she had been back in her own land. It began to settle in her chest, the separation, the loneliness, and tears pricked at the corners of her eyes.

"Give it to me, and you'll never feel this lonely again."

"GO AWAY!"

✴✴✴

The next morning, Aerona was already awake and tending to Mairwan. Aerona looked as if she'd gotten very little sleep as well but seemed to be pleased with how Mairwan was progressing.

"Good morning," Aerona whispered, gently stroking Mairwan's cheek.

"How's she doing?" Lauren asked quietly.

"She's going to be all right. I can't thank you enough."

"It was my pleasure," Lauren replied, crossing the room to sit down on the bed next to Mairwan. She placed a hand on the girl's small leg. Mairwan was still dreaming peacefully, and the feeling was stronger than the night before.

When Lauren returned to herself, Aerona was giving her a curious look.

"What did she say to you just now?" Aerona asked.

"She didn't say anything...it's more like a feeling. Just wanted to make sure she was still there."

"And?"

Lauren smiled and nodded, "She's dreaming happily. Nothing to worry about."

Aerona looked down at Mairwan and ran her fingers lovingly over the little girl's forehead. Lauren was strongly reminded of her own mother, and wondered what she might be doing back home. Had she given up hope that—

Those kinds of thoughts, she reminded herself, were what

drew the Anghenfil.

"Thank you for bringing her back," Aerona whispered. "I don't know...after Ieuan died... And Cefin is always putting himself in danger..."

"Cefin told me what happened," Lauren said, happy to talk about anything but what was worrying her.

"I know he regrets it," Aerona nodded, brushing Mairwan's cheek. "He was just trying to protect the village. He was trying to make sure the twins had a father and..." She sighed. "He hasn't forgiven himself, and I know that's why he doesn't come around as much. He can barely look me in the eye."

Lauren cocked her head to the side. "You aren't that much older than him, are you?"

Aerona smiled and shook her head. "We played together as children, and I always considered him to be a brother. Our families were close even before I married Ieuan." She noticed Lauren's curious expression and added, "Ieuan was ten years my senior when we married. He and his brother—Cefin's father—were inseparable. So it's no wonder that he followed his brother into danger."

Lauren watched the way Aerona spoke and wasn't sure if the adoration was directed towards her late husband or towards Cefin. She could tell Aerona cared about Cefin; nephew or not, they had a bond that seemed to extend past her previous marriage.

"I wish Cefin would allow himself to move on." Aerona sighed, looking at the door before turning to smile at Lauren. "I think he's sweet on you, though."

"Yeah, well..." The wall was still there, keeping her apart from everyone. The Anghenfil purred in anticipation and she turned to smile at Aerona, forcing the monster back down.

"Do you think there will be new villagers with tyllwyllwch

today?" Aerona asked. "Mairwan will be fine, it seems. I don't think you need to stay here if you don't want to."

Lauren nodded and played with her necklace, lost in thought.

"What's the matter?" Aerona asked. "You know that you can talk about anything with me, dear."

"Just a little tired from yesterday," Lauren waved her off. "But you're probably right. I should—"

"Lauren," Aerona said, looking at Lauren's necklace, "is your stone darker?"

A chill ran down her spine but she forced a smile on her face. "A little bit, but Siors said that it was fine."

It was a complete lie, but Lauren hoped that it would cease any of the other questions.

Aerona looked down at her hands. "You know, I wish I was as strong as you."

"What?" Lauren blinked.

"You just seem to take everything in stride. You didn't even flinch when Mairwan was....you just did what needed to be done."

Lauren swallowed.

"And..." Tears gathered in Aerona's eyes. "I don't think that I will ever be able to thank you for everything you've done for us—for me. You are a blessing, Lauren."

Lauren nodded and imagined the look on Aerona's face when she found out how close Mairwan had come to being devoured by the Anghenfil. They were all in danger, every person that was around her, because if she slipped up just once, the monster would come for her—and destroy everyone in its path.

Lauren smiled and nodded at Aerona, promising herself that she would do better from now on. No more sad thoughts from here on out.

The Anghenfil chuckled in the back of her mind.

There was no one in the village with tyllwyllwch, and Lauren didn't feel like walking up to Baltes' farm. She was focused on the idea that she needed to be happy to keep the monster at bay, to protect everyone from her own temptations, and she was on a mission to find the things that made her happy. She felt in control of her mind for once, bolstered by the idea that she could bury the Anghenfil under a pile of positive thoughts.

It was certainly a pretty day out, so that was enough to put her in a good mood. She smiled at a couple of villagers, who were too busy with their own work to stop and talk to her. None of them looked like they needed any help, and they told her as such when she asked.

In the absence of anything else to do, she wandered up the path to the watcher's post. Cefin was a nice distraction—at least, he was lovely to look at. And if she pretended, she could almost forget that they couldn't be together.

When she arrived, her heart warmed at the sight of him on the watcher's post, staring off into the sky. As she got closer, she saw the worry and concern etched on his face.

"Cefin? Are you okay?"

He nodded in welcome, but didn't look at her.

"What is it?" Lauren asked, coming to sit cross-legged next to him.

"I just can't stop thinking about Mairwan."

"She's going to be fine. Siors said—"

"I promised Aerona I would take care of her and the twins."

"Cefin," Lauren said. "You can't protect them from every little thing that happens. Your job is to protect the village from the Anghenfil."

The Anghenfil which was currently taking up residence in

the back of her mind and had become much more vocal in the past day. But she was trying to ignore it and bury it under a mountain of happy feelings, she reminded herself. Perhaps if she helped Cefin, it would be just the thing to push it out completely. After all, she had felt better in Heulog after saving the lives of the villagers.

"And yet...that happiness was fleeting...gone in the blink of an eye..."

"Shut up," she hissed under her breath. She cast a nervous look to Cefin, hoping he hadn't just heard her talking to herself (or worse, talking to the Anghenfil), but he seemed too absorbed in his own pain to notice her.

"It's my fault."

She almost didn't hear it, as quiet as he spoke. In fact, she wondered if she *felt* it instead. She could almost see the guilt radiating off of him like tyllwyllwch.

Tyllwyllwch, she thought to herself as she clutched at her stone. It warmed comfortingly in her hand. She knew what she needed to do. "Cefin...can I help you?"

He turned his head slowly to look at her, but didn't respond.

"I think..." She smiled and the stone warmed more. "I think I can help you."

"I don't want you to hate me."

Lauren laughed. "I'm not in any danger of that, I promise you. Let me help you. No judgments here."

In the back of her mind, she could hear the Anghenfil chuckling at the hypocrisy of what she had just said.

"Stay out of this," she hissed under her breath. When the Anghenfil did not return fire, she nodded and turned to Cefin again. Still blissfully unaware of her internal arguments, he seemed to be considering her words about helping him, before shaking his head in defeat.

"There's nothing that can help me," he said sadly. "Nothing that can bring them back."

"Bring them..." She gasped as she made the connection. "Your father and uncle?"

Cefin grimaced and turned farther from her.

"Cefin, that was years ago," Lauren said, not sure if the memory in her mind was hers or Aerona's. "And you made a mistake"—she snorted ruefully—"one that I made as well. You can't beat yourself up forever over something you did as a kid." She paused, beginning to understand him as she hadn't before. Almost everything about him, from his obsession with protecting the village to his attentiveness to the children, was from the guilt of leading his father and uncle to their deaths. She sat back, absorbing this new information, and again, the stone reacted at her neck.

Cefin remained silent and Lauren wondered if he was going to be silent for the rest of his life. She had the strongest urge to grab his hand and peer into that brain of his, but didn't move. She had already invaded his privacy once; she didn't want to do it again without his permission.

"I want to help you, Cefin," Lauren repeated.

"Why?"

"Because..." Lauren trailed off. Because she couldn't help herself so she wanted to help others? Because doing for others was a surefire way of getting the Anghenfil out of her own mind? Because after all they had been through, she still thought he was handsome and she wanted to be close to him? "Because you're hurting."

"What are you going to do?" he asked, turning to look at her.

The stone was hot now. Very gently, she reached to take his hand.

***

"You are not old enough to go up the mountain." The older man stood in front of Lauren, eliciting a spectrum of emotions, from respect to anger to love. He carried a familiar spear on his back, and a sword at his side. For a moment, she was confused, but then realized that she was seeing this scene the way Cefin had experienced it in his youth.

As if to prove her point, her own voice came out as his, younger and filled with impudence. "But Father—"

"There is no discussion," the other man said. "Ieuan will continue the night shift."

"But Aerona!" Lauren-as-Cefin said. "It's not right to ask him to stand guard."

"I stood guard when you were a babe," he said. "It is a privilege to protect this village." He paused, smiling grimly. "One you will inherit when the time is right."

Lauren could feel the anger bubbling as she left the small hut. Ieuan would be a father any day now, and it would not be right to ask him to give his life. Cefin knew what it was to have a father wedded to protecting the village, and did not wish it for his new cousins. For Aerona, whom he cared for very much.

Lauren was now climbing the rocky paths, a makeshift spear on her back. Cefin wanted to prove to his father that he could protect the village—he wanted to defeat the monster that lived in the caves, once and for all.

Stupid, foolish, moronic.

He stood in the mouth of the cave, banging his spear against the rock and calling into the darkness for the beast to show itself. His confidence shook as the beast showed its true self, growing larger than anything Cefin had ever seen in his life. He fell backwards as the monster loomed over him.

Why did I have to go up to the mountain?

"GET AWAY FROM MY SON!"

Cefin's father appeared, like a vision from a dream, followed by his uncle. They were fearless, approaching the monster with their spears and swords.

"Cefin, get out of here!"

Cefin scrambled away, watching the two men battle the beast. His uncle tossed his spear, which the beast knocked away with a simple flick of his mouth.

Stupid, foolish boy.

The Anghenfil opened its great, wide jaw, and fire filled the forest, engulfing the two men in a hellish blaze.

Stupid, foolish boy.

Lauren heard their screams of pain as they burned, and guilt burned at her just as badly.

Stupid, murderous, foolish boy.

Murderer.

Lauren was sucked in deeper into the misery, bombarded with regret, shame, misery, and the longing desire to make right what could never be made right. He was carrying this weight on his soul, driving him to flagellate himself with long watches over the pass to deprive himself of being simply a young man.

"Cefin, why are you blaming yourself?" Lauren found herself asking. Her voice was ethereal, her body non-existent, but she was there with him in the darkness.

His response was a jumble of emotions so loud that she couldn't make sense of it.

"Cefin, you need to stop—" she tried again, hoping that one voice would echo out of the darkness. The response was jumbled again, but one voice stood out.

"It's my fault they're gone," it said.

"Cefin, you made a mistake, and you don't have to beat yourself up forever," Lauren cried, trying to speak over the voices. "You have to forgive yourself—"

The response was so deafening that it hurt her nonexistent

ears.

"Cefin, you are allowed to make mistakes," Lauren said, hoping that would resonate.

"THIS WAS NOT A MISTAKE!" the chorus of voices spoke in disorganized unison, but Lauren got the message. She began to feel hot, as if he were trying to push her out of his mind.

"You were young!" Lauren replied, pushing back against him. "Cefin, don't push me out."

The chorus of different voices began talking again, a low roar growing into an echoing cacophony of angrier and angrier words towards himself and towards Lauren. She struggled against the emotion, feeling him falling deeper and deeper into his misery, and she worried that she was going to lose him forever.

She ran through the voices, each word lashing her like a whip, as she searched for the center, for the true center of what Cefin was really feeling, why he was hurting, and where she could plug the hole in the dam before it broke.

"Show me," she called to the darkness as it closed in around her.

She heard crying, very faint in the corner. She turned to follow the source of the crying, knowing that it was the one memory, the one thing that kept him in this place of darkness.

He was fifteen, crying over his father's mutilated body, begging for forgiveness. He wasn't speaking, but Lauren could hear a single thought echoing off of him in waves.

"I cannot live when others died because of me."

"Cefin," Lauren said, kneeling beside him. "Your father, he chose to come after you. He chose to sacrifice himself so that you would live."

"It's my—"

"He made his choice. He chose you instead of himself. Even though you made a mistake, he and your uncle loved you so much that they chose for you to live instead of them."

The darkness that flowed above them began to slow, and Lauren knew she was making progress.

"You need to let this go, Cefin," Lauren said. "Let this go and live your life, because that is what they gave theirs for."

She began to see a light above them, as the body of his father began to fade in front of them.

"Let him go," Lauren said, brushing his now adult hair out of his face.

"Thank you," he whispered.

***

Lauren blinked in the sunlight. Her head was dizzy, and her whole body felt like she had hand-washed fifteen buckets of laundry. But she felt satisfied, like she had just done something truly powerful in someone else's life.

She sat up and saw Cefin standing on the riverbank. She pulled herself to standing, as the blood rushed to her head, and shuffled over to him.

"Hey," she whispered. His cheeks were wet, and when he didn't turn to look at her, Lauren worried that he was angry with her for dredging up such terrible memories.

"I've been carrying around the memory of my father's death for years," he said, his voice thick. "Every day when I walk to the watcher's post, I think about him, and tell myself it's my fault that I am making this journey and not him. Every time I look at the twins, I remind myself it's my fault they don't have a father and Aerona doesn't have a husband."

"Cefin—"

"But now, for some reason. I feel at peace." He smiled finally.

Lauren half-smiled back, and the stone warmed at her throat.

"I wish I could hug you," Cefin said, looking out in the distance. "But I'm afraid of what other demons you would unearth."

To that, Lauren let out a barking laugh. "I only use my powers for good."

"If there's ever anything that you need to speak of," he said, rubbing his hands over his face, "anything at all...I can never repay you for relieving me of this burden."

Lauren opened her mouth, but nothing came out. All she could see was Cefin's face melting into horror as she told him the monster that had killed his father was living in her head. The wall was still firmly between them—because of her powers and because of her secrets. He was brave enough to let her see his demons, but hers were much more terrifying. Cefin's guilt was misplaced, but Lauren's was real.

She struggled to reach for the feeling of accomplishment and satisfaction from helping Cefin through his inner demons, but it was gone. And even worse, the darkness settled on top of her chest—the very same that had come over her in Heulog.

She glanced down at her stone as, before her eyes, it horrifyingly turned another shade darker.

And even more terrifying, she could hear the Anghenfil taunting her.

"Lauren?" Cefin said. "What is it? Is it your stone?"

Lauren dropped the stone and forced a smile on her face. "But you're better?"

"Lauren, you looked concerned."

"Nope, I'm good," Lauren said, not looking at him as she scrambled to her feet. "But I think I need to get back to Aerona. See you later!"

And before Cefin could say another word, Lauren was halfway back to the village.

chapter eleven

Lauren didn't go back to Aerona's house after talking with with Cefin. Instead, she wandered around the village, chewing on her lip and wracking her brain for ways to pull herself out of the low spot she found herself in. But she could no longer hide from the truth: she needed to talk to someone about what she was going through, if only to get it off of her chest.

So for the past hour, she paced in front of Siors' house, practicing her speech.

"Hi, Siors, I can hear the Anghenfil in my mind. Have any ideas on how to fix this?" Lauren said and immediately rolled her eyes. It sounded stupid in her head, and it definitely sounded stupid out loud. Siors may have been more knowledgable on the subject than most, but she wasn't sure she should start with telling him that.

Taking a deep breath, she walked up to the door and knocked. When he didn't answer, she pushed the door open and poked her head in. As before, the room was thick with heat from the fire and the smell of perfumes and spices, filled to the brim with books and scrolls. There was barely any room for the old man to sleep. She called for him again, but didn't hear him in the house. She supposed he might have been tending to Mairwan, and she also supposed she should wait for him to return before poking around.

empath

But a book caught her eye. Or rather, the image of a ruby on the page. Pulling the book closer to her, she began to read.

The fire-stone ruby is one of the rarest healing stones known in this realm. It has been used as a talisman against sadness and foolish thoughts. A symbol of the sun, it glows with an inextinguishable fire that shines even in the darkest of places.

In the hands of an empath, it can amplify the already sensitive powers. For one with empath tendencies, it can allow the penetration of the mind of another, and cleanse of dark thoughts or sickness.

She saw a scribbled note in the corner, and she presumed it to be Siors writing.

Bring back from the dead?

Lauren hadn't told Siors about what *really* happened when she'd saved Mairwan, afraid that if she strayed too close to the truth, she'd come clean about it all. So, of course Siors would think that she could revive the dead.

She flipped to the front of the book titled *The Compendium of Stones*, then leafed through the pages, each showing a different stone. She saw no more mention of empaths or empathy, but rather a glittering array of different gems and their alchemical uses. She stopped again on the ruby page and lifted a hand to her necklace.

...a talisman against sadness and foolish thoughts...

Maybe her ruby was defective, because she was often filled with sadness and foolish thoughts. Or maybe, because she was an empath, it didn't work on herself.

Or maybe, she thought with a nervous bite to her lip, it didn't work because the stone was growing darker.

She began rummaging through the other books on the table, ranging in topic from gardening to philosophy to mathematics. Siors was truly a varied individual, but it didn't help her figure out more about the Anghenfil.

She was about to turn around and leave when she saw an

open letter on the ground. It must have fallen off the table when she was mucking around. Figuring she'd already invaded his space enough and a little more wouldn't hurt, she picked it up to read:

Brother Meirion,

Intriguing news about the arrival of the empath. Please send her to Traegaron as soon as able.

Brother Probert

"Traegaron?" Lauren murmured to herself.

She looked around the small hut, and at all the books that lay before her. When she first arrived in this world, Siors said at the king's castle, that there was a great library, one that might contain information about her powers. So she'd wager to guess that it would probably have some information about the Anghenfil as well. And maybe, even a way to get home.

Folding the letter, she walked out of Siors' house and scanned the village before her. Traegaron was at least a day's journey, so Cefin had told her. She'd probably have to walk it as well, as she hadn't yet seen a car here in Rhianu.

She could always take the Anghenfil for a ride.

The image was so amusing to her, she snorted. Well, that was the first step, she thought. Laugh at the beast and perhaps she would stop fearing it.

She spotted movement at Aerona's house, and Cefin emerged, his spear on his back. Aerona was grasping his shoulder and had a smile on her face. It warmed Lauren's heart a little bit, knowing that she had been able to help Cefin make amends with Aerona.

And it also made her hurt a little.

After all of this, could she ask any of them to accompany her? Mairwan was still recovering, so Aerona wouldn't even dream of leaving her side. Cefin, he had his position as the village watcher. And Siors might have accompanied her, but the trip could be too much for him.

"You don't want them to know."

"Shut up, stupid monster," Lauren growled. It was bad enough she had her own running commentary in her mind, but she didn't need more from a fire-breathing peanut gallery.

She looked through the village, faces and names of villagers she had seen but didn't know very well. Could she ask any of them to put their lives on hold to take her to the great castle?

Would they go with her knowing she could lose her grip and call on the Anghenfil at any moment?

She imagined the great beast in the village, the same way it had landed in her vision with Mairwan. Only this time, it would endanger everyone in Rhianu. Aerona, Mairwan, Eddy, Siors. Cefin would step forward to give his life without hesitation. He had escaped the Anghenfil twice now. Would he escape a third time?

She stuffed that vision in the back of her mind, and rushed down the mountain path before anyone noticed she was gone.

❖❖❖

Lauren reached Heulog just as the sun was setting on the mountain range, and just as she convinced herself she was doing the right thing. Even at the end of the day, the village buzzed with activity. With the tyllwyllwch gone, people milled about, talking and chasing their livestock. Children ran up and down the street, laughing and calling to each other. For the first time, Lauren realized how barren and empty Rhianu was. The Anghenfil—

No, she told herself firmly. She was not going to think about that stupid thing. Not until she reached Traegaron anyway.

She wandered through the streets, holding her arms closer around herself as the sun and temperature dropped. Right above the tavern, she spotted the inn where she and Cefin had stayed and hoped she could sweet talk her way into staying another night for free. After all, she *was* the empath who had saved the village from the tyllwyllwch, that had to count for something.

The tavern smelled like old beer and body odor, something she hadn't noticed the first time she was there. Then, it had been filled with people and happiness, now it was quiet, with a scullery maid cleaning tables with an old rag.

"H-Hi," Lauren said. The maid stopped in her scrubbing and looked up at her, giving her the once over. Lauren immediately knew the maid didn't recognize her.

"What'ya want?" the woman barked.

"I was wondering if you could tell me where the owner is?"

"He ain't here. Out buying bread for dinner tonight. You looking for a job?"

"No, I was hoping that..." Lauren trailed off. She was sure the woman would laugh at her for even thinking about asking for another free room. "Well, I just need to talk to him, all right?"

The scullery maid sniffed and continued scrubbing, muttering something unpleasant. Lauren turned on her heel and walked out the door into the frigid air outside. She shivered for a moment, looking around the city, and for the first time, began to second guess her decision to leave Rhianu without anyone to accompany her.

She didn't know the land. She was still relatively new in this world and didn't even know what kind of money there was. Dollars? Gold coins? Of these she had none, and it was starting to get very dark.

She turned to look back towards Rhianu and the dark mountains. Even if she wanted to go back, it was too dangerous in the dark. She was *stuck* here.

Just like she was *stuck* in this world. And—

"It's you!"

She twirled around at the sound of a young voice behind her and was relieved to see Tomos. He was carrying a basket in his hand that was nearly bigger than he was.

"It's me!" Lauren smiled, bending down to his level. "How's your mom, Tomos?"

"She's well, thank you," Tomos said nervously. "Is it back?"

"Is what back?" Lauren asked, before her brain connected the dots. "Oh, no. The tyllwyllwch isn't back, don't worry."

Tomos' face relaxed into a smile.

"I'm actually on a little bit of a road trip," Lauren said.

"A road trip?" Tomos said, confusion crossing his face.

"A...quest, I suppose. I'm headed to Traegaron."

"Ooh!" Tomos' grin grew wider. "I've never been, but the travelers tell stories of a great castle! Are you going to see the king?"

"Maybe?" Lauren hadn't considered that she'd be a guest of the king. "But I obviously can't go any farther tonight. I was hoping maybe I could find a place to stay."

"You shall stay with us!" Tomos announced, quelling Lauren's anxiety immediately. "It is the least we can do, after you saved my mother's life."

Chalk one up for being an empath, Lauren thought to herself, happily following him.

Lauren hadn't gotten a chance to take in Tomos' house the last time she was there, but she was glad to see it completely free of darkness. Tomos' mother Cadi was kind and gentle, hugging Lauren before the empath could stop her and giving Lauren a glimpse into the goodness inside. She made sure to give Lauren three helpings of stew, filled with more vegetables and meat than any Aerona had made.

"Heulog seems to be busier than Rhianu," Lauren said, swallowing her mouthful of food. "And richer."

Cadi smiled and ladled more stew into Lauren's bowl. "Travelers do not venture up to Rhianu often to trade. The climb is very hard and then there's the..." She trailed off and looked at Tomos who was reading a book in the corner.

"The monster," Lauren finished quietly.

"I've never seen it, myself, but I've heard tales."

"The tales aren't as impressive as the real thing, I can assure you." Lauren said it under her breath, but Cadi heard and gasped.

"So you've seen it?"

"Y-yeah," Lauren nodded, looking down at her stew. "Cefin...the guy who came with me the last time...when I first arrived here, I made him take me up to the caves."

Cadi's eyes widened in fear. "Why would you do a thing like that?"

"Because I didn't think it was real." Lauren shrugged. "I mean, who believes in fire-breathing dragons, right? They only existed in movies where I came from."

"Movies?"

"Moving...pictures?" Lauren tried, wondering how to explain it.

"Tell me of your world," Cadi said, a wistful tone in her voice.

"My world is...." Lauren trailed off, the memories too painful to talk about. "Somewhere that I'd like to get back to very soon. Which is why I'm going to Traegaron. Siors, our village....elder, I guess, he said that there is a great library there that might have something to help me get home." *Without having to go through the Anghenfil*, she added silently.

"Traegaron is a day's journey from here," Cadi said, standing and walking to the wall. She pulled a long rolled up piece of paper from a stack of them and spread it across the table. Lauren ran her fingers along the map, fully taking in the world that she had only seen the tip of.

Rhianu was drawn into the mountain range on the extreme right side of the map, Heulog right at the edge of the range. A vast plain devoid of cities and towns fanned around the mountain range, with a forest lining the northern edge of Heulog, and a sea to the south. On the extreme western edge of the map sat a large dot called *Traegaron*.

"Why aren't there any cities along the path?" Lauren asked, looking up from the map.

"The land is not fertile, and there are no rivers nearby." Cadi pointed. to the forest on the map. "I advise you to steer clear of the forests of Myf. Bands of thieves are known to attack travelers who venture too close."

Lauren nodded, dragging her fingers to the drawings of the trees north of the plains. "Roger that, no trees."

"Who is Roger?" Cadi asked.

Lauren sighed; she was getting tired of no one understanding her references.

"So steer clear of the trees," Lauren said, looking at the distance between where she was and where she was going. Even on the map, it looked quite a distance. "I don't suppose that I'd be able to find a horse to take with me, huh?"

"I'm afraid that horses are hard to come by, even for the great empath who saved the village."

"This is going to suck," Lauren whispered to herself. She remembered a trip to Washington, D.C. a few years back with her parents. The three of them had walked all day along the mall and through monuments and museums, and Lauren had felt like her feet were going to fall off. The shoes Aerona had given her were all right for wandering around the village, but for traveling this distance? She already dreaded the blisters.

"You have a long journey ahead," Cadi said. "You should get some rest."

Lauren nodded and rose from the table. Before leaving, she paused to smile at Cadi. "Thank you for everything. I was a little worried that I was in over my head."

"If it weren't for you, I would not be here," Cadi smiled, before adding, "You are welcome at my hearth anytime."

***

If Lauren had thought that walking to Traegaron was a good idea at some point the day before, she definitely did not think so by mid-morning the next day.

Her feet ached, her back ached, and the sheep's bladder that Cadi had given her filled with water was completely dry by mid-morning. The sun beat down on her unrelentingly, and she had a headache in a particular spot above her left eye which felt like someone had jabbed a knife in there.

Yet she continued on, with no sign of shade, and no idea how far she had gone or how much farther she had to go. The only thing she knew was that she was headed in the right direction—due west, based on the position of the sun above her.

Stupid, stupid, stupid was the chanting in her head. She should have brought someone with her. She should have gotten over her fear and asked Cefin to come with her, or Siors or someone who knew where they were going. Or perhaps, she should have tried a little harder to get a horse.

Or perhaps she should have just stayed in Rhianu.

She stopped in the center of a field, rubbing her face to clear her mind. Her eyes drifted to her right, to the blessed trees of the forest that lined the plains. Every time she looked at them, she remembered Cadi's warning. Thieves, she'd said. Mean and evil thieves who would probably do terrible things to her.

She turned her head forward and marched on. It was no

wonder there weren't any farms out here; the low lying grass seemed barely alive as it crunched under her feet.

She reached for the bladder again, her throat parched, and whined when nothing came out. She stopped and unfurled the map under her arm, a parting gift from Cadi. She spotted Rhianu and the river that began at the mountain and passed through the village of Heulog before continuing down to the sea to the south. She was too far along to turn around and get more water, but she desperately needed some.

There was another blue line that ran through the forest, but —again, there were thieves in the forest.

Thieves, she reminded herself, that would do terrible things to her.

She rolled up the map again before she made a stupid decision.

Five steps later, she stopped, unable to keep to the course.

Thieves weren't that bad. Maybe she could lie and tell them they had tyllwyllwch and heal them and they'd leave her alone.

Myf was a big forest on this map. Maybe they wouldn't even find her.

In any case, she knew if she didn't get to shade soon, she'd have much worse things to worry about than thieves.

**

Relief was immediate when Lauren stepped underneath the shadow of the forest. She allowed herself a moment to relish the coolness and the lack of the sun on her face. It was only a moment, though, because she needed to keep moving. She hiked up her skirt, keeping her ears open for the sound of men doing thieving things. She heard birds and crickets but no men, and she relaxed a little bit, looking up at the trees and the forest around her. The trees were unfamiliar, a mixture of tall trees falling over and shorter, newer trees, struggling to reach the sunlight above.

Once or twice, she saw a small rabbit appear and disappear under a log, and it made her smile.

After a while, her ears picked up the faint sound of running water. A smile broke out across her face, and she headed farther into the forest towards the sound, focused on quenching her thirst. She stumbled through, her dress ripping on the branches and thorns growing out of the unclear path, but she carried on, seeing the split in the ground up ahead. Approaching the river, she sent a thankful prayer to the universe that it was flowing and looked relatively clean. She bent down and unscrewed the top of her sheep's bladder then dipped it into the cold water.

When it was full, she gulped it down, then repeated the action until she felt full of water. She sighed in happiness and relief, grateful that she had found shade and water and—

"Hey...."

She looked up, realizing she had stopped listening for the sounds of other people in her euphoria of finding running water. She was now aware of voices, men's voices, cackling and catcalling nearby, growing more numerous as the seconds ticked by.

Those thieves Cadi had warned her about.

And she, a young woman alone with no weapons and no real fighting skills.

Fantastic. If it wasn't one thing in this stupid world, it was another.

"Back off, jag weeds," Lauren snapped in her meanest, most metropolitan voice. She'd been leered at back in California too many times; it was rare that she could walk down the street without getting honked at. Maybe if these men thought she *could* take care of herself, they'd leave her alone.

But they had surrounded her, at least eight of them with unshaven, dirty faces and missing teeth. They were thieves all right, and looked like they hadn't seen the inside of a shower in years (not that there *were* showers here in the first place).

"What do you want?" she said, the words sounding stupid in her head as she said them.

The grotesque men simply chuckled, one pulling out his knife menacingly.

"That's a pretty necklace," another said, "pretty necklace for a pretty girl."

Lauren's hand flew to the rock around her neck—the rock that had brought her there and was quite possibly her only way home. She had nothing else of value on her, but she was damned sure not going to give them her necklace.

"You can't have this," she insisted.

"Darling, you aren't in any position to make demands," one cackled, moving towards her. Lauren backed up a step, but her foot fell into the water.

For the first time, she realized that she was trapped and in real trouble. There was no one else for miles around, no one to hear her screaming. No one to come save her.

Why didn't she want Cefin to come again?

"You're very pretty." The thief was missing at least three teeth and his breath was putrid. "You come here all alone?"

"Get away from me," Lauren stammered, her confidence slipping away as fear took over. She'd never been in a situation like this before, with men who were definitely interested in hurting her—or worse—and she wasn't sure how she was going to get out of it.

And then she remembered that whole bit about being an empath, and her eyes widened even farther. If they touched her, she'd collapse and be completely defenseless.

"D-don't touch me," she stammered. "I have tyllwyllwch."

They laughed at her, and the one closest to her moved even

closer.

"I seen people with the darkness, and you ain't got it," he said. "Eyes too clear."

"Yeah well, it's early stage," Lauren said. "Please, you don't want it. It's really quite terrible."

He grabbed her arm.

Pretty girl, pretty necklace—would catch a fair price. Pickings are slim and morale is low. I need this boost for the men. Why is she twitching like she's having a fit? What's wrong with her—

Lauren gasped loudly and found herself on her hands and knees. Her feet were soaked from the river, and she was breathing heavily.

"What kind of witch are you?" The man—Cael was his name—backed away from her in fear.

"Empath, actually."

"An empath you say?" Cael said, scratching the stubble on his chin. "That'd fetch a fair price in Traegaron, you know."

"Oh good, because I'm headed that way," Lauren said, but knew she wouldn't be traveling with them as an honored guest. The men laughed in that way that told her still in deep trouble.

"You'll be going to Traegaron," Cael said. "But after we get our fill of you."

Lauren paled. "But I'm a witch, remember?"

More laughter. "You're nothing but an empath, and empaths don't bother us much. Make you more pliable."

Lauren grimaced. "You're disgusting," she spat, coming to her feet. Cael unsheathed his sword and stuck it in her face.

"You'll walk," he ordered.

"And if I don't?"

The sword tip moved closer.

"Fine," Lauren said, wondering how she was going to get herself out of *this* mess.

chapter twelve

Lauren stumbled deeper into the forest at sword-point, the sharp edge digging into her back when she slowed. Cael pushed her along mercilessly and his motley crew whistled and whooped behind them. They arrived in the thieves' village and Lauren saw more of the grotesque, disgusting men around campfires and in front of small thatched huts. She knew they were very far into the forest now, removing all hope that she would be found by a passer-by. She found no friends in the camp either; most of the men watched her like she was tonight's dinner.

Cael tossed her into one of the small cabins and disappeared, leaving her to contemplate the horrifying events about to occur.

And then she realized that she *was* terrified—so maybe the Anghenfil would finally come to eat her.

"Okay, Anghenfil, whenever you want, come get me," Lauren whispered, her voice shaking. When the monster didn't respond, she scoffed at the irony. The monster wasn't interested in her real problems; just the ones she made up in her head.

The flap to the one-room cabin opened and her heart stopped. Cael walked in, a satisfied look on his face as he surveyed her.

"You'll be a fine lay," he commented, setting to unbuckling his belt.

"So morale is bad, huh?" Lauren stammered, pressing herself

against the wall. She had to stall him—for what, she had no idea. Delaying the inevitable?

The tactic seemed to be working as Cael paused and glared at her.

"Whatdya mean by that?"

"I read your thoughts, remember? Morale is low, and you want everyone to sleep with me to raise it?"

He grunted and smiled, continuing to unbuckle his belt. She scraped at the bottom of her mind for something to distract him.

"What's the problem? Too few stupid wenches coming into the forest?" Lauren said, nervously laughing. "Too few travelers? Or are you just an ineffective leader?"

That last one seemed to strike a nerve.

"If you don't close your stupid mouth, I'll knock you out," he growled.

"I mean, if you're gonna have your way with me before any of the other men, that definitely smacks of bad leadership." Lauren shrugged, trying to sound nonchalant. Somewhere in the back of her mind, she remembered a leadership course she took in college and could not believe she was applying the lessons learned to a man about to rape her.

Cael narrowed his eyes. "I don't need to be told how to lead my men."

"Look, I was only in your head for a second, but from what I can tell, you're pretty insecure about the whole thing," Lauren said, grateful that she was buying herself some more time, but unsure if the tactic of pissing him off was going to work in her favor. "I mean, you *just* got the position about two months ago, and you guys haven't so much as pilfered anything in weeks—"

"SHUT YOUR WHORE MOUTH!"

"Just saying," Lauren winced as his voice echoed in the small room. "You might want to consider giving me to one of your men *first*, as a show of good faith?"

Cael considered her words, and to her relief, he buckled his belt again. Saying nothing, he stormed out of the room.

Lauren breathed a sigh of relief and sank down against the wall with her hand over her racing heart. She really wasn't sure how she picked up all of that from just a second of touching him, but it worked. She crawled along the floor and opened the flap of the house, looking out into the village square. Cael was in the center, talking with the group of men. Talking wasn't a good word; arguing was more like it.

In fact, they seemed to be arguing about who was going to take her first.

"I says, I'm the one who saw her walking to the river, I should get her first!"

"Yeah, but you also let a wagon go last week. I'm the one who finds the most gold!"

Too engrossed in their arguing, none of them were watching the hut. Lauren took a deep breath and slid out the door, creeping around to the side of the house and out of sight. She pressed herself flat against the outer wall and waited for the yelling of someone seeing her escape.

"You'll do it all wrong!"

"That's not what yer mother said!"

Lauren pulled herself behind the house and closed her eyes, saying a prayer. Then, without another word, she ran like hell.

***

Lauren ran and ran and ran. She wasn't actually sure if she was running into the forest or out of the forest, but she knew she just needed to *run*. The trees weren't getting any thinner and she hadn't seen the plains yet, but she knew once the thieves realized she was gone, they'd be after her.

But she was tired—adrenaline and fear now washing away

and leaving nothing but exhaustion. She'd been walking all morning, was nearly gang-raped, and now she wasn't even sure where she was going.

She slowed her running to a walk and listened for the sound of anyone following her. When she didn't hear anything, she slumped against the nearest tree and held her head in her hands.

She was such an idiot, leaving Rhianu without anyone to go with her. Now she was lost in a forest crawling with men who thought she was a piece of meat. She was hungry, she was cold, and she really needed to pee. She let the weight of the situation fall on top of her and leaned her head back against the tree.

She wasn't sure how long she'd been asleep, but her body jerked awake when she heard someone moving in the forest. It was pitch-black dark, but she definitely heard someone step on a tree branch nearby.

Trembling, she searched the dark forest floor for anything to defend herself with, and her hands fell on a rock. It was heavy, but she could use it to knock out whoever was approaching and make her escape.

With the rock gripped in both of her hands, she pulled herself to her feet, pressed herself against the tree, and waited for whoever it was to walk by.

A shadow crossed next to her and she cried out, throwing the rock.

"OW!" A familiar voice replied.

"C...Cefin?" Lauren squeaked. Was she dreaming?

"Lauren?" The voice sounded relieved to hear her voice and definitely real.

"Cefin!" Lauren threw herself towards the shadow. It was too good to be true—too perfect for him to have found her.

"Wait, wait," he backed up before she could touch him. "Empath, remember?"

"Oh right," Lauren sniffed, unable to hold back her tears of joy. She was so relieved, she was *saved*.

Cefin sounded similarly relieved in the darkness. "Are you all right?"

"What are you doing here?" She desperately wished she could curl into his arms for comfort. "How-what? I don't even...how did you find me?"

"Siors said you'd taken his letter," Cefin said. She felt the tip of his spear touch her leg. "Hold onto this and I'll guide us out of here."

She obliged happily, letting him take control.

"I stopped in Heulog first," Cefin said, "and ran into our little friend Tomos. He said that you had stayed with them last night, and were on your way to the castle."

"But how did you find me in the forest? This place is huge and—"

"I almost didn't check the forest," Cefin said, sounding annoyed. "But a young woman traveling alone, I wanted to be sure. I heard them arguing near their camp and figured you had escaped. I was able to track you to your hiding spot before they did."

Lauren chuckled and gripped the spear harder. "Wow, climb mountains *and* track in the woods? You certainly are a man of many talents."

"Is this funny to you?" Cefin boomed, turning on her. She could feel his anger radiating off of her and it took her breath away. "You could have been *hurt*. You could have been *killed*—they were going to...to..." He swallowed, trailing off. "And all because you were too stubborn to let any of us help you!"

"Look, I know I made a mistake, but I just—"

"Do you hate my company so much that you won't stand me to take you to Traegaron? So much so that you didn't bother to ask me at all, or say goodbye?" Cefin's eyes pierced her in the dark.

"It's not that," she whispered, unable to elaborate.

Cefin angrily tossed up his hands. "I wish I was an empath, so I could know what you're thinking!"

"You don't want this!" Lauren cried. Unable to touch anyone, unable to be in a crowd, and a fire-breathing monster lurking in her mind? She wouldn't wish this on her worst enemy.

"Since I can't have your powers, at least talk to me," he pleaded. In the darkness, she locked into his eyes, and was reminded of how pretty he really was.

And of their kiss.

God, she wanted nothing more than to climb into those strong arms of his and let him hold her close while she told him everything that was on her mind, everything that was bothering her, everything that she was afraid of.

"I..." The truth was on the tip of her tongue, but she couldn't push it out. "I wanted to know more about my powers. And I thought, with Mairwan in the state she was in...and you had to protect the village."

Cefin softened a little. "*You* are a villager now, and it's my job to protect you."

"But you can't leave—"

"Lauren, I left for you, because I was worried about you."

A wave of guilt crashed down on top of her and she sighed. "I'm sorry."

"Now promise me, no more lies," Cefin said, stepping closer to her. "You can tell me anything that's on your mind."

What was she supposed to say to him? Could she tell him about the Anghenfil? Could she tell him about how it lived within her, how it fed on her sadness? Could she tell him about how lonely she was?

The answer was a resounding no as she nodded to him. "No more lies, I promise."

"Good. Now, we have to find the carriage," Cefin said, turning to continue on.

"Carriage?"

"You didn't think I walked here, did you?" he asked, with a knowing smile. "I would have to be a complete fool to want to walk to Traegaron on foot."

Lauren wished she could smack him, but her attention drew to the familiar-looking horse in the moonlight ahead.

"Bessie!" Lauren said, spying Baltes' old horse attached to a carriage. She had never been so glad to see something so familiar. Or something with wheels. Her feet were killing her.

"Baltes let me take her down to Heulog, and I bartered with a local merchant to sell his wares in Traegaron in exchange for his wagon," Cefin said, hopping up on the driver's seat.

"You did all this for me?" Lauren whispered.

"I told you, you're a villager now, and it's my job to protect you."

Lauren caught the affection in his eyes and allowed herself a smile. She'd never had anyone do so much for her before, and it was kind of nice to be thought of so highly.

"Hop on already," he ordered. "We've still got a ways to go before we reach Traegaron."

He reached his hand to help her onto the carriage and retracted it just as quickly with a pained expression. For the millionth time, Lauren wished she didn't have her empath powers as she climbed into the bed of the carriage, leaving space between the two of them. Cefin snapped the reins and Bessie lurched forward, moving them out of the forest and into the open night air.

My heart is beating so fast, she's so close to me. Gods above, she is beautiful, and I'm just a simple farm boy. I wish I could lay her in the back of the carriage and—

The carriage went over a bump and Lauren rudely woke up, not even realizing she'd fallen asleep but knowing immediately that she'd been leaning against Cefin.

"I wondered if I should wake you," he said, sounding guilty, "but you seemed so peaceful..."

She mumbled and rubbed her eyes, trying to clear her head of Cefin's feelings. She replayed his fantasies about her in the back of the wagon, and rather wished that he would act on them.

"What is it?" he said, the reins lazily resting in his lap as the mare pressed forward.

"How much farther to the castle?"

"You can see it in the distance." Cefin pointed to a small spot on the horizon. "I'd say a few more hours and we'll be there."

Lauren yawned and rubbed her stomach. She hadn't had a proper meal in a day.

"Do you have any munchies?" she asked, still half-asleep.

"I...what?" Cefin blinked at her.

"Food."

"Oh yes, some bread in the bag under the seat," he said. Lauren slid back into the wagon and pulled out the bag stuffed under the seat. She let out a happy sigh as a few loaves of bread spilled into her hands. "God bless Aerona."

"She sends it with love and a little bit of anger. Hand me one?"

Lauren placed the loaf next to him and sat in the wagon bed, nearly inhaling hers.

"You're funny when you eat," he said, tearing off a piece and smiling at her. Lauren noticed him watching her and shifted uncomfortably.

"I'm hungry," she said, leaning against the seat, far enough away that they weren't touching. She wished they were. "What's Traegaron like?"

"Busy," Cefin said, looking out in the distance. "More people than in Rhianu or even Heulog. Giant walls surround the castle and the city, and the castle itself is a sight to behold."

"Do you think the king is going to want to see me?" Lauren asked, pulling out the letter and reading it for the millionth time. She wasn't sure how she was going to get into the castle—perhaps just show them the letter and hope that they didn't think it was a fake. Somehow, she had a bad feeling about the king. She'd seen enough many movies to know that it could end with them running out of the castle with an army behind them.

"King Idris is a good and fair king," Cefin said, looking down at her. "I'm sure he would be pleased to meet the famous empath."

"And by meet, you don't think that means burn me at the stake? Or chop off my head?"

To her surprise, Cefin laughed, and it dissolved some of the tension in her shoulders. "I doubt the king would order such a thing. It'd be a waste of your brilliance."

"Oh well," Lauren blushed at his compliment. "As long as he's not married to the Queen of Hearts, maybe I'll be okay."

The joke fell flat on Cefin as he blinked at her.

"Never mind." Josh would have gotten that joke, and probably followed up with a quip of his own. Cefin was gorgeous, but he didn't have Josh's sense of humor.

She caught herself thinking of Josh and scathingly and silently rebuked herself. But then again, she couldn't be with Cefin, so what did it matter anyway?

"You worry too much," Cefin said, adjusting the reins in his hands. "Can't you use your empath powers on yourself? Calm yourself the way you...calmed me?"

Lauren's cheeks warmed when he looked down at her. He did seem more relaxed than before she had helped him through his guilt. And he had allowed himself to leave the village to find her.

God, he *left the village to come for her.*

Josh wouldn't even come take care of her when she had the flu. And this guy was...

But she couldn't be with him. She was an empath.

"Lauren?"

"Sorry." Lauren shook her head. "I think the empath thing only works on other people. And animals."

"But I would think you'd be pretty good at fixing yourself, right? You seemed to know exactly what to say to me."

"I wish it was that simple," Lauren replied quietly. Other people's problems seemed fixable. She could control *that.* But the storm in her own mind blew ferociously and uncontrollably. Even now, she bounced from thought to thought to thought without any hope of landing.

And the Anghenfil was always in the back of her mind, although she realized she hadn't heard from it since before she was caught by the thieves.

"You're thinking again," Cefin said gently. "You have a look on your face."

"Well, I have a lot of things to think about." Lauren laughed, turning her head upwards. He was really breathtakingly, adorably handsome.

And he had come all that way for *her*, which sent her mind careening in a whole different direction.

"And what are you thinking about?" Cefin asked.

Josh, missing home, being in a strange land, being an empath, being unable to touch anyone and having a major crush on the guy sitting next to her, the Anghenfil that haunted her dreams.

"I'm thinking I wish I wasn't an empath."

Their conversation ceased when the castle rose before them. It looked like something out of a fairy tale or a history book, Lauren wasn't sure which. It was massive. Stone turrets rose towards the sky with flags waving from the tips of the roofs.

"Wow," Lauren whispered, climbing to sit next to Cefin. She wished for him to put his arm around her, but his hands remained firmly on the reins as the old horse pulled them over the drawbridge over the moat surrounding the castle. Lauren looked up at the castle walls as they passed through the entrance, taking in every sight, sound, and smell.

"I told you it was impressive." Cefin smiled at her as he pulled Bessie to a stop. He slipped out of the carriage so he could walk them through the crowded streets of the city. The castle was huge, but the city inside the walls was even more interesting. People milled about as Lauren and Cefin passed, surrounded by chickens and foul-smelling bales of hay. Since they were used to visitors, they gave Lauren and Cefin no notice. Houses lined the streets, looking much more impressive and sturdier than those she'd seen in this world so far. She looked upwards, taking in the sight of the castle. She felt small and insignificant and wondered how long and how many men it took to build it stone-by-stone.

She was pulled from her thoughts by the three soldiers who had marched up to their carriage.

"Announce yourselves, travelers," one soldier said to Cefin.

"This is the empath," Cefin said, looking back at Lauren. "Brother Probert has summoned her."

"An empath, huh?" the soldier replied, reaching up to yank Lauren down.

Who is this girl? Another fake empath here to swindle unsuspecting villagers? The man has a spear. What if I don't return home to my children—

168

When she came to, she was face-down in the muddy street, Cefin's angry voice mingling in with the voices of the soldiers.

"I said don't touch her!" Cefin growled, standing above Lauren. "She's an empath. Don't you understand?"

"We get empaths all the time," the soldier said. "Just some charlatans looking to make some coin in this city."

"I wish I was a charlatan," Lauren grumbled, coming to her feet. "Do you think I would fake this?"

"We see lots of young women who faint. Don't mean they're the real thing."

"How about this, then," Lauren said, shoving Siors' letter into the soldier's hand. "I've been summoned."

The soldier looked over her letter, and Lauren hoped that he would recognize the signature.

"You stay here," the soldier ordered. "I shall confer with the palace soldiers."

"Are you all right?" Cefin asked, his hands itching to help her back up onto the wagon.

"Be easy on him," Lauren mumbled, climbing up on her own. She sat on the driver's seat and looked out on the whispering and pointing crowd that had assembled. "He's just worried he'll be killed on the job."

Cefin glared the way the soldier left. "He shouldn't be so short."

"He can't help it," Lauren said, hating how she understood this man and couldn't share in Cefin's consternation for the rough way the soldiers had treated them. She tried to dredge up the hatred towards the soldier, but couldn't get the soldier's fear out of her head.

"There she is!" a voice cried out.

Cefin jumped in front of the wagon, his hand on his sword as the soldiers rushed over.

169

"Stay back," Cefin growled.

"Calm down, my boy!" An old man was pushing his way through the soldiers. He looked as old as Siors, with a long white beard and kind eyes. He was wearing a long, beautiful dark blue robe, and his face looked cleaner than any peasant Lauren had seen so far.

"Brother Probert?" Cefin asked, relaxing only a little bit.

"Yes, my boy!" The man's eyes landed on Lauren and lit up. "Twim Probert, at your service."

"Scholar, you believe this girl?" the soldier asked him, giving Lauren a curious look.

"My scholar-brother in the village of Rhianu told many tales of her powers," Probert said, which Lauren thought odd. Siors had only sent one letter, and that was before tyllwyllwch or Mairwan or any of that.

"Yeah." Something about him set her on edge, but she couldn't place her finger on it.

"Now, now, all of this fuss," Probert tutted, looking at the soldiers. "Why don't we get our esteemed guests settled into the castle?"

He reached out a hand to Lauren and she didn't take it, but offered an apologetic smile.

"I'm sorry, but I can't—"

"Ah-hah, my dear, but of course," he said, something in his eyes. "Please forgive an old man for his habits."

She began climbing off of the carriage when Bessie whinnied and charged forward. Lauren stumbled and flew off the wagon, right into Cefin's arms—

I'm so unsure about all of this. Something feels wrong, something about this castle makes me feel boxed in. But she's in my arms, what I wouldn't give to never let her go.

She heard herself gasp as Cefin's arms left her upright.

"Sorry," he murmured, throwing a look to Probert who

gaped at her in awe.

"So it's true then," Probert said, awed. "You are an empath... what did you feel when he touched you?"

Lauren exchanged glances with Cefin again and he understood that she knew what he'd been thinking.

"Nothing important," she said, wrenching her eyes away from his. "You said something about the castle?"

chapter thirteen

Inside the castle was as opulent and beautiful as the outside. Red carpets lined the stone floors, and almost every hall was adorned with oil paintings and beautiful tapestries. Probert was more than happy to give them a tour, pointing out the history of every portrait and suit of armor that lined the hallway.

Cefin walked behind them, his watcher eyes scanning the room for any sign of trouble. His uneasiness was catching; Lauren couldn't help but jump slightly at every person that walked down the extravagant hallway.

Yet, there didn't seem much of anything to be concerned about there, unless she counted dying of boredom. After an hour of walking through the castle, Lauren caught Cefin yawning behind them, and smiled at him. He was a simple man from the mountains; this was probably boring to him.

And also, he hadn't slept a wink the night before because he was scouring the countryside for her. She couldn't believe that he would put *her*—a veritable stranger—above Aerona and the kids and his duty to the village. She knew that he thought she was cute, but those were the actions of someone who thought she was more than just a cute girl. She stifled a grin as he yawned behind them.

"You know," Lauren said, interrupting Probert's long monologue about the history of the castle, "it's been a very long journey, and I'm afraid I'm getting a little tired."

"Of course, of course!" Probert smiled. "The king has graciously allowed you to stay here in the castle, in the east wing. I shall take you there at once!"

Cefin tossed Lauren a grateful look as Probert walked a little faster down the hall, only stopping for a moment to point out a painting or sculpture that was interesting. But it was Lauren who stopped suddenly, staring into the face of a girl.

Or rather, the very familiar-looking ruby hanging from her neck.

"The last empath," Probert noted solemnly. "This painting was completed just a few days before her untimely death."

"That's my necklace!" Lauren whispered, walking up to the painting. "She's got my necklace!"

"Eh?" Probert said. "But of course, the ruby is said to be the empath's stone."

Lauren was transfixed on the stone around the girl's neck, her mind spinning. In the hectic absorbing of her new reality as an empath in Rhianu, she'd never paused to replay the exact sequence of events preceding her arrival. She had purchased this necklace, the very one hanging from her neck right now, the one that seemed alive and attuned to her thoughts, before the earthquake—

—when she'd first heard the Anghenfil.

She shook her head, ignoring that knowing voice and focusing on the necklace. Maybe she didn't have to deal with the Anghenfil to get back home. Maybe she was just using her necklace the wrong way. After all, it was capable of getting rid of tyllwyllwch, and—

—And defeating the monster. If she could just be brave enough.

She pushed that thought out of her mind and angrily pulled

her thoughts in line. The desire to go home, the one she'd put aside because she felt it impossible, returned with a loud roar.

"Brother Probert—"

"Twim, my dear. Twim is fine."

"I actually wanted to know if tomorrow you could let me look in the castle library," Lauren said. "I wanted to know more about my powers and...well, now I want to know more about my necklace."

"Why is that, my dear?"

Lauren thought of the girl again, and of perhaps going home. "I'm not from around here, and I'd like to go home soon. Maybe there's something in the library that can help me get there."

She didn't miss the way Cefin stiffened and kept walking.

"Of course!" Probert said. "First thing in the morning!"

"Thank you," Lauren said as they came to an open staircase.

"Your rooms are right up the stairs. I shall have the servants bring a light dinner in a few hours, yes?"

"That would be great," Lauren smiled, watching Cefin start to ascend the stairs. Something about his demeanor had changed, and she needed to talk to him. "Excuse me." She nodded to Probert.

She hurried after Cefin, which was quite difficult based on the rate at which he was climbing the stairs. He didn't pause when she called out to him.

"Cefin, wait!" Lauren said, doubling her efforts. "What's wrong?"

"Nothing."

"Dude, I'm an empath; it's no use lying to me." Lauren rolled her eyes and followed him up the spiral staircase. He ignored her and kept walking, the lines of anger on his face.

"Cefin!" Lauren tried again, running up the stairs and standing in front of him. "What the hell is your problem?"

"I'm very tired, and I would like to sleep," he said, trying to get around her.

"Please don't make me use my powers on you."

Cefin placed his hands on her shoulders.

Why does she want to go home? She should stay here with me forever. I want to be with her so badly. Why did she say she felt nothing when I touched her—

Lauren came back to her senses and slumped against the stairs. In the distance, she heard Cefin's door slam shut.

***

Lauren did not sleep much that night, her head filled with questions about staying and going and Cefin and necklaces. Her room was extravagant and like something out of a dream, and it was nice to sleep in a bed that wasn't made of straw. But she couldn't appreciate it.

The girl in the painting, something about her was so familiar. Perhaps because she was also an empath or perhaps it was just that necklace.

Lauren lifted her own stone to examine it in the low light, grimacing at the darkened shade. She wondered if the Anghenfil had been in the other empath's head the way it had made a nest in hers. The girl's eyes seemed so sad in the painting; perhaps that was why Lauren identified with her so much. Did the Anghenfil promise to take away her pain, too? Did the girl finally give in?

Is that why the Anghenfil took her?

"It doesn't matter, I'm going home," Lauren announced to the quiet, dark room. The library and the untold knowledge therein was a beacon in the darkness, and she was sure she could find a way back to her world without having to slay a dragon.

But a new thought emerged; if she found a way home, would she even go?

She sat up in the bed, the question arising unexpectedly from some corner of her soul. She looked at the wall and beyond, where Cefin was presumably asleep on the other side. He felt betrayed by her desire to go home. He wanted her to stay with him. The thought was distracting, to say the least, and drove comparisons of his attention to her vice Josh's. Cefin was handsome as sin, of course, and he was very interested in *her*—

But she couldn't even carry a conversation with him.

But he was handsome. And interested in her, which was more than Josh ever was. Why was she really fighting to get back home anyway? To return to a life of crying by herself at night and boring data entry? Going out to bars with girls who were moving on with their lives and had boyfriends who gave them shiny diamond rings? Having to be reminded of Josh every second of the day?

Cefin, at least, offered escape and would probably marry her. After all, there was no one else for him in the village but Aerona —

—who seemed like a much better match than Lauren—

"Can you stop, please?" Lauren said, preferring the voice of the Anghenfil over the one that sounded like a much meaner version of herself. But the Anghenfil hadn't made its presence known since she'd left Rhianu.

She sighed, rolling to the other side. Even if she did stay here with Cefin, there was still the problem of her being an empath. Kissing him was just strange, having sex with him was probably a mindfuck (she snorted—pun intended).

But it wasn't just the empathy; that was the least of her problems with him. There was a barrier between them, a fear that sat underneath her skin and prevented her from being honest with him. For as much as he had demonstrated his interest in her, finding her in the forest, taking her here to Traegaron, protecting her from danger...she couldn't shake the image of what his face would look like when she told him about the Anghenfil's voice in her head.

Or about the way she'd nearly given in twice to its seduction.

That, more than anything, was why she knew she could never be honest with Cefin.

She rolled over again, looking up into the dark room, and prayed for sleep to quiet her mind.

**

When the first rays of sunlight hit the room, Lauren was up and about. She was still teetering between staying or going, but sometime in the middle of the night, she had decided that she would make a decision when she had all the answers. Pausing by Cefin's door, she briefly wondered if she should wake him so he could accompany her to the library, but her fingers stopped inches from the dark wood. Instead, she spun on her heel and scampered down the stairs.

She caught a passing servant who was kind enough to lead her to Probert's offices, where she was assured he was most certainly already awake. Indeed, he was behind his expansive desk, smoking a similar pipe as Siors, and his face lit up when Lauren walked into the room.

"Good morning to you, empath! To what do I owe the pleasure?"

Lauren still couldn't shake the slimy feeling from him, but she dismissed it. "Hoping I could get a full day in the library."

"Then please, let me accompany you," he said, leaving his desk and offering his arm.

She held up her hands and stepped back, needing to put space between them. "No thanks. I can't...with the empath thing..."

"But of course, but of course. Shall we?"

The library was down a hall, then another hall, then another hall—so much that Lauren wasn't sure she could find her way back to the tower if she tried. Instead, she decided to focus on listening to Probert, who was a wealth of information about the city.

"Why yes, my dear," Probert nodded. "I have been the scholar here since I was but a little boy. Brother Siors and I spent years studying together in this very library."

"Siors didn't know much about empaths."

"Ah, well, empaths have always been a bit of my own personal obsession," Probert replied with a small smile. "They fascinate me, you know."

Something inside Lauren didn't like the way he was looking at her, but she dismissed it. "So the king—is he pretty cool?"

Probert gave her a confused look.

"I mean, is he...well, does he think empaths are a good thing or a bad thing?" Lauren asked nervously. She had a vision of being burned at the stake and suddenly wished she'd brought Cefin along.

"A real empath is always welcome." Probert smiled as they walked into the library. Lauren's eyes widened, and she craned her head backwards to take it all in. Rows and rows of shelves fanned out before her, crammed with thick old books. Even if she started reading now, she'd never be able to finish all of them in her lifetime.

"So, my dear," Probert said kindly. "What in particular are you looking to learn?"

"To be honest, I don't know anything about being an empath," Lauren said, running her fingers along the old spines in the shelf nearest her. "And now I find out this necklace is somehow connected. I just want some answers."

"Empaths are rare, interesting creatures indeed. Cassidy was also a strange creature."

"Cassidy?" Lauren blinked, the name so familiar and normal.

"Her name was Cassidy?"

Probert nodded. "It's been many years, but I do believe her given name was Cassidy. Does that ring a bell?"

"It just sounds like a name from my world," Lauren replied. The parallels between her and this other empath were becoming more and more pronounced.

"The poor girl was very troubled." Probert shook his head sadly. "Even the slightest touch would result in her empath fits, as I like to call them. She barely let anyone in the same room with her."

Lauren felt a surge of camaraderie with this girl she'd never met.

"She had my same necklace, too, didn't she?" Lauren said, fingering the stone at her neck. "Did she say anything about it turning darker? Did she ever heal anyone with tyllwyllwch?"

"I cannot say we had much interaction. I was a very young man. Fifty years have passed since she was...taken."

More than likely, she gave into the Anghenfil's tempting promises. Lauren remembered the young girl in the painting, and imagined what it must have been like for her when the Anghenfil arrived to pull her from her misery.

Lauren wondered what it would look like when the Anghenfil finally takes *her*.

"Do you know why the Anghenfil took her?" Lauren asked, loud enough to stuff the image back into the box it had escaped from. Maybe there was some other reason for it, and not the one that was obviously staring her in the face.

"A terrifying day." Probert shook his head. "She had been the King's guest but a month when the terrifying creature arrived out in the gardens, great big wings beating like a drum. It wrapped its great serpentine tail around her and carried her to the mountains near Rhianu."

"I'm familiar with the creature," Lauren said. When the Anghenfil wrapped its tail around *her*, she'd been forced to relive her (laughably benign) worst memory. She wondered what Cassidy saw when the monster wrapped its tail around her. What was her worst memory?

"I have never known why the Anghenfil was drawn to her," Probert said. "Empaths are pure of spirit, so the texts read, which is why they can cure those afflicted with tyllwyllwch."

"The tyllwyllwch," Lauren said, playing with her necklace. "I still don't understand how I did that, either."

"An entire village, I hear. There are some that say the tyllwyllwch is borne from the spirit of the Anghenfil."

"Really?" Lauren said, looking up at him. The tyllwyllwch was nothing but misery and desolation, definitely the same sort of thing the Anghenfil made her feel. But she had been able to defeat the tyllwyllwch with her stone; did that mean she could defeat the Anghenfil with it too?

The creature certainly hadn't liked the stone in Mairwan's dream. Lauren imagined herself with a sword in hand, facing the Anghenfil the way Cefin had bravely faced it.

The idea was laughable. She'd already tried to face the monster and failed miserably.

"Lady Lauren?" Probert's voice brought her back into the room.

"Sorry," Lauren said. "This is just a lot to think about. The tyllwyllwch, the Anghenfil...none of it makes sense to me."

"I would not worry yourself. We are far removed from the mountain where the beast has made its nest. It hasn't been seen in Traegaron since the day it came for the empath."

Perhaps that was why she hadn't heard it in her mind these past few days—not since she'd left Rhianu. That knowledge comforted her only a little.

"Lady Lauren." Probert had moved very close to her while she was wrapped in her own thoughts. "Would it be too much trouble to use your powers on me?"

"I...what?" Lauren said, turning around so she could face him head-on. Something about his closeness unnerved her.

"Word has reached us about your talents," he said, his fingers flexing gingerly. "Cleansing an entire village of tyllwyllwch and bringing a girl back from the dead."

"The village, yes, but I didn't bring anyone back from the dead. She was just knocked out," Lauren said, backing up further as he approached her. "But with normal people, I just feel what they're feeling."

"Then you have only touched the surface of your powers," Probert said, continuing to walk closer as she walked backwards. "You have the ability to cleanse others of all of their negative energy, to fill them with joy."

"I've never..." Lauren shook her head, but remembered Cefin. She *had* healed him, hadn't she? But that was only her walking him through his own misery. That wasn't like the tyllwyllwch, where she used her powers to bring light to others. "I don't understand..."

"It's very simple. Those who study the art of emotional transference know how to move a bad feeling from one person to another. You, the empath, simply take those feelings as your own, leaving the transferor to be purified of his evil thoughts."

"I have enough evil thoughts, thanks," Lauren said, as her back hit the library wall. Probert moved even closer to her, and she felt trapped. She'd nearly drowned in her tears after a day of tyllwyllwch and healing Cefin, she wasn't sure if she could handle someone intentionally giving her bad thoughts.

"Pity," Probert said, reaching out and grabbing her arm anyway.

empath

Lauren gasped, not out of shock, but out of *pain*. She wasn't reading him, but he was pushing something into her, little ants crawling up her arm and overtaking her senses. The electric shocks traveled down to settle in her heart and surrounded her lungs until she couldn't breathe. The box of forbidden thoughts in the back of her mind burst open, stampeding through her mind like a herd cooped up too long.

"—You can tell me anything that's on your mind—"

"—Cefin will hate you if he finds out—"

"—I was soooo excited when he proposed—"

"—Nobody will ever want you like that—"

"—You're the best person I've ever known—"

"—but not good enough to be with forever—"

"—The Anghenfil knows what you are afraid of—"

"STOP!" Cefin roared somewhere in the distance.

The connection severed as Probert's hand lifted off of hers and she collapsed onto the ground. Cefin was standing over her body, looking murderously at Probert. Lauren wasn't even sure when he arrived there or why he was there, but she was thankful that the pain had stopped. She just wished the echo chamber of thoughts would stop, too.

"What did you do to her?" Cefin growled.

"My dear boy, she's an *empath*," Probert replied, grinning like Cefin had just handed him a pile of money. "She can remove all bad feelings, leaving nothing but elation. It's perfectly normal."

Lauren shuddered and wrapped her arms around herself, struggling to keep the tears from spilling down her cheeks. The Anghenfil simply made her relive her worst memories; Probert added a scathing commentary that made them a thousand times worse. If given the choice between this torture and the Anghenfil, Lauren could see why Cassidy made the decision she did.

"She never looked like that after she touched anyone else!" Cefin snarled.

"Of course not, they were not using her correctly. Most people just give all of their feelings, but if used properly—"

"I think we've heard enough." Cefin grabbed Lauren by the arm before she could stop him.

Fear, fear for her. She was so pale, she was possessed when he touched her. He did something bad to her and I will kill him for it.

"C-C-Cefin," Lauren sputtered, pushing him away from her. She latched onto a nearby window, as her knees gave out underneath her and she fainted.

***

Lauren awoke in her own room, the late afternoon sun streaming into the castle windows. She felt like she had spent the entire day drinking. Her head thudded dully and her body sore and sluggish. She turned her head to the corner, where Cefin was staring out the window, his lips pressed into a thin line.

"Hey," she whispered.

"Lauren," Cefin said, rushing over to her. He knelt next to the bed, worry etched on his face. She wanted him to touch her but settled for the closeness instead.

"I'm fine," Lauren murmured, but they both knew it was a lie. "What happened?"

"I got you out of that library with that stupid..." he trailed off angrily. "And you fainted. You've been asleep all day." He leaned in closer, and she breathed him in. "What did he do to you?"

Lauren furrowed her brow. "He said it was some kind of emotional transference, that most people didn't know how to do it, but that he could just push all of his bad feelings over to me and I'd deal with them."

"Like when you...? Did I make you feel like this?" Cefin's

183

face twisted in guilt and worry.

"No, no," Lauren said, wishing she could brush the stray hair out of his face. "That was...different. This was terrible."

"How so?"

Dread filled her chest, and all she could do was shake her head. Telling Cefin about what she saw was too terrifying. But the act of keeping the thoughts away unleashed them in a torrent, and tears burst forth from her eyes as it echoed in the space between her ears.

"Lauren, ssh—"

Please stop crying, my darling

Lauren's skin tingled like he had just brushed a tear from it, and his thumb was an inch from her skin. But his intrusion into her mind stopped the raging storm and she was able to take a deep calming breath.

"Sorry," she whispered, wiping away her tears. "I shouldn't fall apart like that."

"I think we should return to the village."

"But..." She didn't even get to look in the library for any answers to her questions. She was as ignorant today as she was before she embarked on this journey. Except for the knowledge that the empath before her bore the same necklace.

She looked into Cefin's eyes and remembered his strong desire for her to stay. Maybe she should have let sleeping dogs lie. She knew that the only way to get home was to face the Anghenfil and defeat it, but there was no way that was ever going to happen.

"You keep coming to rescue me," Lauren whispered, instead of voicing her thoughts.

"I told you, you're—"

"Cefin, don't try to tell me it's because I'm a villager. I read your emotions, remember?"

"You said you didn't feel anything," Cefin whispered.

"Did you want me to tell Probert and everyone in the kingdom that you're madly in love with me?" Lauren said, the words tumbling out before she could stop them.

"Yes," Cefin replied without any hesitation. "Because it's the truth."

Lauren swallowed nervously. She had never pictured herself falling in love with someone other than Josh, or pictured anyone else falling in love with *her*, but here she was. And she remembered everyone telling her that she would find the love of her life, she would find *The One*, and she'd forget all about Josh.

And it appeared to be staring her right in the face.

Cefin had been trying to protect her from the very first day, and he had been the one to save her life. If not for him, she would be buried in the cave still—or worse. And then he took her to the Anghenfil, a bone-headed idea, sure, but he had been the one to save her.

Even now, he had left Aerona and the village to be with *her*. He was her knight in shining armor, the one she had been waiting for. He was her savior.

Except that she couldn't be with him. Not as an empath.

She bit her bottom lip and tried not to cry again. Nothing was fair, and no one would ever lo—

She stopped that thought before it could finish.

"Lauren, I didn't..." Cefin said, turning away from her. "I'm sorry if I upset you. I shouldn't have, if you don't feel the same."

"It's not...I can't touch you," Lauren whispered.

"So you...feel the same way?"

"What does it matter?" Lauren sniffed, looking out the window. "I'm stuck being a stupid empath, and I'm just...alone." Again, the forbidden thoughts threatened to break free.

"You're not alone, Lauren," Cefin said, moving his hand

closer to hers. Just another inch and his hand would be on top of hers. If he moved just a bit more, she would be in his arms. It just made her ache for him.

A knock at the door interrupted their moment, and a stuffy servant walked inside, taking no notice of the intimate scene playing out on the bed.

"The king has returned and requests your company immediately," he said, bowing low.

chapter fourteen

"You don't have to go," Cefin said, following Lauren down the stairs. "We can turn around and go back to the village. We can protect you from him there."

"I'm sure he'd come after me and I don't want to put Rhianu in that kind of danger," Lauren whispered back. "Look, let's just do the meet and greet, and I'll read him and we can get out of here."

Cefin clenched his fist. "I don't trust Probert, and I don't trust anyone in this castle. What if the king tries to do what Probert did?"

Lauren swallowed, sharing his fear, but shrugged noncommittally. "I'll refuse, and you and I run like hell to the stables to get Bessie."

Cefin smiled, the first she'd seen in a while, and it was like a salve to her anxiety. His love for her was out in the open now, and she was acutely aware of his gestures of affection. She couldn't be with him, sure, but at least she knew someone cared for her at all.

Again, the urge to hold his hand, crawl into his arms, touch him *at all* roared strong.

Her nerves went into overdrive when they walked into the great hall. The room rivaled the library in size and splendor, but this place was filled with people instead of books. Beautiful women in dresses, men in frocks and tights with white wigs, and Lauren the object of their attentions. She felt a little jealousy of the women who eyed Cefin, but pushed it down. Jealousy, at this point was a waste of energy when there was so much more to be focused on.

"Stand here," the servant ordered before disappearing into the mob of people.

"Are you all right?" Cefin whispered.

"Yeah, you know," Lauren said with a shrug. "I see lots of kings and queens."

"Really?" Cefin asked, surprised.

"No, Cefin."

"You make too many jokes in serious situations." Cefin sniffed, adjusting his shirt sleeve as a man walked by and scoffed at him. "I don't like it here."

"You and me both, bud."

Roaring trumpets blasted in the room, and the inhabitants turned to the front of the room, their faces alight with expectation and suspense. A very well dressed man came to the front of the room with one of the aforementioned trumpets clamped to his side. He took a deep breath and his voice boomed.

"KING IDRIS APPROACHES!"

Lauren's hands shook as the king walked into the room. He was already a formidable person, but the addition of a bright red velvet tunic and long red robe behind him, complete with a gold crown atop his head, gave him the aura of an even more fearsome man. He surveyed the room as if he owned it (which, Lauren supposed, he probably did).

"I wish to see the empath," Idris bellowed. Lauren felt even smaller when they landed on her. Of course she would stick out like a sore thumb; she and Cefin were the most underdressed people here.

"It'll be all right," Cefin whispered, motioning for her to go forward.

Lauren took a few tentative steps. She stopped when she saw Probert appear at the king's side, a satisfied look on his face. Narrowing her eyes at him, she continued the seemingly endless journey to the front of the room. Men watched her curiously as they moved out of her way, while the women judged her with scathing looks of reproach.

Finally, she stood in front of the king, and swallowed hard, her mind drawing a blank.

Was she supposed to bow?

She curtsied, and immediately felt stupid doing it.

"Hi," she said, continuing her demonstration of her complete lack of decorum. "You called for me?"

Immediately, she knew she had said something wrong because those closest to the king turned to gasp at him with a horrified and amused expression. She tossed a look back to Cefin, who nodded nervously, and then turned back to the king, who was studying her.

"Your impudence is amusing to me," he boomed, after an eternity. "My scholar says you are the empath. He has seen it with his own eyes."

"Yeah, he has," Lauren growled, narrowing her eyes at Probert, who still seemed high from their encounter that morning.

"I command you, empath, to heal me then," Idris commanded. A buzz of excitement rose from the group. "Demonstrate your powers for us all, and show us that you are who you say you are."

"I..." Lauren stammered. "There doesn't seem to be any tyllwyllwch around here—"

empath

"HEAL ME!" Idris barked, causing Lauren to jump backwards. "Or I will send you and your companion to the dungeons with the rest of the charlatans."

Lauren turned to look for Cefin, but the crowed had squeezed him out. They were closing in on her and she felt the beginnings of a panic attack in the bottom of her stomach. What if she saw some horrifying thing in the king's mind and he threw her in the dungeons anyway? What if he was as adept as Probert, and he pushed the painful feelings into her?

"I command you!" Idris said, as the murmur in the room grew at her inaction. "As your king!"

"Well I didn't vote for you," Lauren mumbled under her breath.

"*Bring her to me!*" Idris commanded.

Lauren saw the flash of metal before two completely different voices filled her brain, pulling her between thoughts about a drunken game of cards the night before, duty to the king, and the nervousness of the girl who was having a fit.

When she returned to her own mind, she was kneeling before the king, and she heard her own panting before she felt how winded she was.

"So..." Idris observed, his eyes roaming over her crouched form, "you would dare disobey the king?"

Lauren was pretty sure Idris wouldn't give a rat's ass about the way empathy felt, or how Probert had basically forced himself on her. But she remained unable to get to her feet, her hands clawed against the marble floor under her hands.

"Please don't make me do this," Lauren whispered.

"You will disobey me?" Idris asked, looking down at her.

"*Please*," Lauren repeated, hoping that it would resonate with the monarch.

"The empath is stalling," Probert growled to the king. "Take her, sire. She will not be able to resist."

"No," Idris said. "I do not know what kind of horrors this empath can work upon me. Put her in the dungeon until she is more amenable."

Lauren's mouth opened in shock, and she envisioned being trapped in a windowless room, forced to endure the whims and anxieties of the king and Probert. The panic lit in her heart and spread across her body like a wildfire.

Before she could open her mouth again, more hands grabbed her.

There were too many emotions, too many thoughts. She was going to explode from it all. She needed to get away, get away from their hands; their emotions were drowning her with too much, just too much.

"I will take it from you..."

The Anghenfil was there in her mind. It was a beacon, a talisman against the blowing winds of her mind. She could focus on it and ignore everything else.

"I am here for you, Lauren..."

She couldn't breathe. She felt trapped in everyone else's emotions and needed to get out of there. If she could just leave here, everything would be better, she'd feel better. There were too many people in there, too many voices, too crowded and she was afraid and scared and—

"Let me take your fear from you..."

She released her tight grip.

"Yes..."

She was on the floor; they had released her and she was gasping for air. Footsteps thundered around her, screams of fear and cries from soldiers echoed in the cavernous room. She lay on the steps of the king's throne, but the king was no where to be found, and neither was Probert. In fact, everyone seemed to have forgotten about her—but why?

Then she heard the beating wings and an earsplitting roar that carried through the giant hall.

It was the sound that she had been waiting to hear all this time.

She turned up to the stained glass window above them as a dark shadow crossed in front of it.

Then, with a mighty blast, it shattered, and the Anghenfil perched on the stone wall, opening its giant, dragon-like jaw and releasing a stream of fire into the room.

More screams, more cries, and more thundering footsteps as the crowd dispersed frantically, avoiding the creature's flames and the swords of the soldiers pouring into the room to defeat the monster.

Lauren could feel the Anghenfil's eyes on her and her heart sank into her stomach. *She* had called it here; *she* had finally given into the temptation. She couldn't tear her eyes away from the monster. It inhaled deeply and spewed red-hot fire into the room, lighting the tapestry-covered walls with bright flames.

This was it.

What she had been dreading for weeks.

She closed her eyes as the tears gathered in her eyes, and she bowed her head in acceptance—

"LAUREN!"

"Oh God, Cefin!" Lauren gasped, having completely forgotten about him. He stood in front of her with Bessie, holding the old mare's reins in his hands as she bucked angrily in the chaos. No one seemed to notice or care that he had ridden the horse into the great hall.

"Come on!" he cried. "We have to get out of here before the entire castle goes up in flames!"

Lauren knew that the right thing to do would be to stay there, to accept her punishment. She would submit to the fate she had been destined for since the moment she set foot in that world, and give herself to the beast.

But she was still a coward.

Slowly, painfully, she nodded and pulled herself to her feet, following Cefin as he led her and Bessie out of the burning castle.

***

"You should ride Bessie for a while," Cefin said, breaking the silent night air between them.

"No," Lauren said, wrapping her arms tighter around herself. She didn't want to touch anything, to open her mind to the Anghenfil in any way. In their rush out of the city, it soared overhead, a trail of ashen smoke billowing behind it. Lauren cowered behind Bessie, and Cefin comforted her the best he could, still not knowing the source of her fear and her misery.

Now, hours later, she wondered how many people died in Traegaron because of her, because she was too afraid to do what was needed.

Choking back tears, she prayed that Cefin wouldn't notice her anguish, but he seemed to be more attuned to her than ever.

"I won't let them hurt you," Cefin said, patting Bessie on the neck. "I promise. If they follow you to Rhianu—"

"It's not them I'm worried about."

"I will kill the Anghenfil for you," Cefin snarled. "When we get back, I shall—"

"Oh God," Lauren couldn't take it anymore and fell to her knees, sobbing. She didn't deserve any of the happiness that Cefin promised. She couldn't stand that others continued to march head-first into terrifying situations while she remained hidden on the sidelines.

Cefin dropped Bessie's reins and rushed over to her, kneeling beside her.

"I'm sorry," Lauren sniffed, as another sob shook through

her. But when she looked at Cefin's face, he was staring down at her necklace.

The stone was now a deep, ebony black.

"Lauren?"

Lauren couldn't take the questions in his eyes. With an angry cry, she yanked the chain hard, breaking it, and tossed the necklace as far away as she possibly could, before sinking down to sit in the cold grass.

She felt his hand slide across her back. Her whole body stiffened, but her mind remained clear.

"Wait a second," she said, sitting up, still feeling his hand on her back—and nothing else. Forgetting about the stone, she slid her hands under his cheeks to cup them gently.

"Oh my God," she said, her hands off and looking at them. "I don't...I don't...I don't have my powers anymore." She scrambled to her feet and ran to where she had thrown her necklace, searching the low grass for the stone. Her fingers came into contact with the cool rock and she rushed over to Cefin and touched his arm—

Her powers are gone?

Lauren came back into her own mind as the stone fell from her fingertips. She began laughing maniacally as she spun around the empty plain.

"Lauren?" Cefin said, rushing over to her. "What is it?"

"The *necklace!*" Lauren exclaimed, feeling happier than she'd felt in years. "Oh God, Cefin, it was the *necklace* the whole time!"

"Lauren, calm down," Cefin smiled. "I'm confused, what—"

In response, Lauren jumped into his arms, pressing her lips to him in the most long-awaited kiss of her life. He was shocked, his arms laying limply by his side and remaining there, even when she broke away from him and hung at his neck.

"You aren't reading me?" he said, finally catching on.

She shook her head happily, and his hands finally slid around her in the most amazing embrace she had ever felt.

"Your necklace was the source of your power?" he asked.

"All this time. All I had to do was just take off that stupid—"

Cefin pressed his lips to hers, cutting her off. Her head was spinning now, realizing that everything she had ever wanted was now here in her grasp.

Lauren wanted to say so much to him. To thank him for saving her, to tell him that she'd wanted him to hold her, to tell him she ached for him. But words seemed ineffective at this point. With a sly grin, she pulled him down to the uneven ground to show him exactly how she felt.

***

They lay under the bright moon curled in each others arms, covered with naught but Lauren's discarded dress and the night sky. She was pressed as close to him as she could be; she didn't realize how starved she'd been for human touch. It had been weeks since she'd touched anything other than a farm animal, and Cefin made her skin sing with happiness.

She was nearly bursting with emotion, but these were all hers —and it was better and more satisfying than anything she'd ever felt in her life. His arms were strong and held her against him, and she reveled in the fact that he *wanted* her. She didn't even mind that he seemed to be quite a novice kisser—something she missed the first time, but she was more than happy to show him what to do. And the sex...well, it wasn't really that good, if she were being honest. She was pretty sure Cefin was a virgin, and never learned the finer points of sex. Rug burn was an understatement.

As if on cue, he kissed her again, leaving a trail of slobber on her face. She tried to sound enthusiastic as she leaned into him, especially when he beamed down at her. This close to him, she could hear his thoughts, but they were a distant music, not front row at a rock concert.

But he noticed her reticence. "Is it back? Did I hurt you?"

"No, it just feels nice," she lied. "I forgot what it was like for someone to hold me like this."

"I've wanted to hold you for weeks now," he whispered, brushing her hair out of her eyes. "It's been painful not to."

"You're telling me," she said wryly. She hadn't had anyone hold her since—*Nope*, she hissed at her mind.

"I didn't hurt you, did I?" he asked, gently stroking her arm. "I've heard that the first time can be...painful."

Lauren blushed slightly, wondering if she should tell him she'd been sexually active for almost five years or if now was the time to show him what foreplay was. Instead, she shook her head with a plastered-on smile.

He could sense the hesitation. "Did I?"

"I mean," Lauren said, looking up at him. "It wasn't my... well...I've done this before..."

"Oh," Cefin said, and she could feel a flash of jealousy from him.

"I mean, he's gone now," Lauren said, quieter. Josh's face came to the forefront of her mind again and she wondered angrily why she still missed him. She had her *One*, so why was she still thinking of her old life? "He's gone now."

"Dead?" Cefin asked, sounding almost hopeful.

"No." Lauren shook her head. "We just..." She struggled to figure a way to say it. "We fell out of love, I guess."

"Impossible for anyone to fall out of love with you," Cefin stroked the hair out of her face. His unspoken affection was warming, but didn't quite encompass the sadness that had taken root suddenly.

"We were very close," Lauren continued. "But then it just..."

"How does one fall out of love?"

"I wanted to get married, and he wanted to explore the world." It was the simple explanation, and prevented going into too much detail about her complicated and miserable feelings about the whole matter.

"Wait," Cefin said, sitting up and looking at her. "You were to be married?"

"No." Lauren shook her head. "I wanted to be though. He didn't."

"What man in his right mind wouldn't want to marry you?"

Lauren shrugged; she'd asked herself that same question more times than she could count. Though when the question came from herself, it sounded much more accusatory than when Cefin said it. Almost like there was something wrong with her that made him leave. But those thoughts were banished to the back of her mind, and now that Cefin was here, she'd never have to think of them again.

"I would marry you," Cefin professed, a mischievous grin on his face. "And then we would explore the world together."

"I'd like that." She smiled, but it didn't quite reach her eyes. Here was what she wanted: a man who wanted to marry her and be with her, and yet she was still holding back. Something was still scaring her about all of this, about him. It was too perfect, and she hadn't done enough in her life to warrant this kind of perfection and love. And there was still the problem of the Anghenfil—their connection appeared severed (or it was not at home in the happy space that was her brain), there was still underlying fear that bringing the monster to Traegaron would come back to haunt her.

And there was also the problem of—

"Ssh," Cefin said, cupping her cheek. "You're thinking

again."

"I do that."

"Your heart is racing," he said, looking at her. "What are you worried about?"

There was the question again, the open door to let him in and share with him all of her problems and anxious thoughts. He loved her now, this vision of herself that she had put forth for him, but would he still love her if he knew the depth of her guilt? Would he still love her if he knew *she* was responsible for the Anghenfil's appearance at Traegaron?

"Lauren," Cefin interrupted again, placing his hand on her bare chest where her heart was. "You are so worried, my darling."

"Darling?" Lauren smiled, liking the sound of that. She placed her head on his chest, listening to his heartbeat, slow and steady.

"What concerns you? My proposal of marriage was too sudden?"

"No. No, it wasn't. I would love to marry you."

Worrying now was stupid and pointless. She had everything that she wanted right here, and she wasn't going to sabotage it. After all, Cefin had just proposed marriage to her—wasn't that all she'd been missing from Josh?

"Does that mean you'll stay?" Cefin asked sleepily.

"Stay," Lauren murmured against his chest. She tried to remember why she wanted to go home, and all she seemed to remember at that moment was Cefin. He would continue to protect her from all of the problems of this world and from the monsters in her own mind.

"Yes, I will stay with you," she whispered as they drifted off to sleep.

***

As the sun broke, Lauren awoke groggy and freezing and miserable, until she remembered where she was and with whom she'd been sleeping. She looked for Cefin, spying him a little ways away, fully dressed and standing next to Bessie, who was eating some grass. Lauren was still naked and lying on the itchy grass and stone, and so she quickly pulled on her dress to warm herself up.

"Morning," she said with a yawn as she strolled over to Cefin. His face lit up when he saw her and he pulled her into his arms, kissing her forehead lovingly. She sighed like an idiot; she missed having this kind of affection.

"Good morning, my love," he said.

"My love, hm?" Lauren whispered to herself before looking up at him. "Did you really mean it?"

"Mean what?"

Lauren's heart began to pound. Had she not heard him right? Was he just speaking in generalities?

"The whole...marriage...thing..." she muttered.

A smile blossomed on his face and he squeezed her again. "Of course I meant it. I love you."

Lauren grinned, all of her nerves disappearing just as quickly as they had arisen. She and Cefin were going to be *married*. Sure, she didn't have a ring or a Facebook to post to and shove it in everyone's face, but she had a man who was handsome as sin, who was crazy about her. So what if he wasn't good in bed? That was no big deal; she could teach him. And hey, she could even show him exactly what *she* wanted, instead of him trying to do what he wanted. That was something to be excited about.

Again, he was sloppy as he kissed her, his tongue ramming into her mouth. She tried her best to sound excited and added it to the list of things she needed to teach him.

"Well, my darling," he said, looking down at her. "We'd best get a move on before these plains become crowded with travelers."

Or the king's soldiers, she added silently. She was nervous about their escape; what if they came for her in the village? But she shoved that thought in the back of her mind as Cefin smiled down at her.

"I cannot believe I get to hold you every day," he whispered. Lauren giggled, not quite believing herself that her perfect Angelman was actually in love with *her*, wanted to marry *her*. He lifted her up on top of Bessie as if she weighed nothing.

"Are you going to join me, my good sir?" Lauren asked.

"Yes, just one moment." He bent down in the low grasses and picked something up off the ground.

Her necklace.

"Get rid of that," Lauren snapped, panic spreading across her at the very sight of it.

"We should bring this with us," Cefin said, examining it closely. "Perhaps Siors—"

"Get rid of it," Lauren repeated, and Bessie stomped her foot underneath her, probably sensing Lauren's agitation.

"My darling, I—"

"I don't want that thing." Lauren couldn't even *look* at it. "It's been nothing but misery."

"Darling—"

"I don't *want it*!" Lauren screamed, and Cefin nearly dropped the stone in surprise at her anger.

"All right, all right," he acquiesced, reaching back and hurling the stone into the plains. "It's gone now, my love."

Lauren nodded, looking down at Bessie's mane at her fingertips. The sight of that stone was a trigger to her, reminding her of all of the terrible things that she was keeping just beneath the surface. The protective structures she'd built over the past night crumbled and she struggled to remember why she'd been so happy before.

Cefin pulled himself up behind her and wrapped his strong arms around her, pulling her back closer to him.

"Ssh," he whispered against her head. "I didn't mean to upset you."

"I hate that thing," Lauren murmured, leaning back into him and letting his presence chase away her fears. "I never want to see it again. I never want to be an empath again."

"Then neither shall happen," he said, sliding his hands around her to hold onto the reins and nudging Bessie to walk forward.

chapter fifteen

Although the sight of the necklace had rattled Lauren, the slow plod across the plain was actually quite pleasant, snuggled as she was in Cefin's strong arms. The farther away they traveled from her stone, the happier she became, and the more she began to accept that it was really over. Every so often, Cefin would press his lips to her temple, and she would sigh happily.

It was too soon when they arrived in Heulog at the base of the mountains and had to deal with the merchant whose carriage they had left in Traegaron. He was none-too-pleased that Cefin hadn't made good on his promise to sell his goods, and even more upset that Cefin had left his unsold merchandise in the castle.

While Cefin argued with the man, Lauren placed her hand on her chest, reaching for her necklace out of habit. The movement reminded her of all the times she would call on it for support and for comfort, a reminder of the home she had left behind. She had worn it proudly every day, hoping that one day it would give her a way to get home.

But now, with the stone somewhere in the plains where she and Cefin made love, it was quite certain she would never get home. She tried to rationalize her own disappointment, hoping that she could find the right thing to say to herself to make it go away. Although she'd never get back to California, she'd also never have to sit at a computer and work a boring data entry job. She'd never see her mom and dad again, but she had Aerona, Siors, and even the little twins. They were her new family now.

And even better, with Cefin there, professing his undying love and devotion to her—and *marriage*—she would never have to think about how Josh hadn't loved her enough to marry her. She could secure that thought in the back of her mind with the other painful thoughts, like her underlying worry about the Anghenfil.

At once, fear swooped through her and she took a deep breath. She knew the connection between her and the Anghenfil was severed as long as the necklace remained in the plains. She knew she could get away with never having to tell Cefin about the connection, or that she'd called the dragon to Traegaron. It would be her own secret. She could outlast it and get over it.

The problem was that she couldn't seem to contain her worry about it. It was a violent storm in her brain, ripping and tearing all of the other thoughts until there was nothing but the fear. She grasped for her necklace again, remembering it was gone.

She placed her hand on Bessie's neck but felt nothing but horse hair. She bit her lip and took a deep, cleansing breath, but only filled half of her lungs before having to exhale. She clutched at her dress and—

"Lauren?"

Cefin was back and she nearly flew into his arms, his touch calming her down immediately.

"What is it?"

"Nothing," she whispered. "Just...missed you, is all."

"We should get moving," he said, stepping away from her. "If we stay here much longer, I might get thrown in jail for theft."

She slipped her hand into his, needing to be connected with

him to protect herself. He didn't seem to mind. He grabbed Bessie's reins and started up the mountain path to Rhianu.

But even with Cefin right there with her, holding her hand, she was unable to fully contain her worries about Traegaron. She knew she had not paid her consequence yet, and she deserved something for calling the monster to her. The thought settled in the bottom of her mind, moving around much like the Anghenfil used to. More than one time, she reached out to touch Bessie, hoping to get a calming connection from the horse, but remembering she had given up her powers.

She wrapped her hand around Cefin's arm, gripping it as the worries spiraled out of control in her mind again.

"I'm not going anywhere," he laughed, pulling his arm a little bit. "I fear you're going to tear my arm off."

"Sorry," she said, releasing it. "It's just...I was so lonely. I want to make up for lost time."

He kissed her forehead and they continued to walk, but she felt no release from her worries. Three or four times, she wondered if she should tell him everything. After all, the stone was gone, and there was nothing to fear anymore. But each time, the fear overpowered her desire to speak, and she remained quiet at his side.

They were almost into the village when a loud noise startled both of them.

"OY!"

A small head of red hair burst from the nearby bushes and flew at Lauren, wrapping his arms around her. She smiled down at Eddy, who seemed confused that she wasn't going into an empathetic fit.

"What's this?" he asked, stepping back from her. "Why aren't you...you know..." He shook and twitched like she probably did when reading another person.

"I guess I'm no longer an empath." Lauren grinned, winking at Cefin. "How's your sister?"

"She's better, I 'pose. Mum keeps me outta the house during the day." He cocked his head up at her. "How come you aren't an empath anymore?"

"Lost my powers. Don't quite miss it, to be honest."

"But wait..." Eddy's eyes grew large. "We need the empath!"

"You guys got along fine without one for a while," Lauren retorted, trying to keep her consternation at bay. It was just like when she faced the king; he had wanted to use her for his own twisted purpose. Why was she to suffer just because she was an empath?

What if they found another stone and forced her to—

"It's fine, Eddy," Cefin said, ruffling the boy's head. His voice cut through her panic, and she tried to relax.

"It's *not* fine!" Eddy cried, his eyes filling with tears. "What if Mairwan falls again?"

"She won't," Lauren waved him off.

"But what if she does! What if she falls and she—"

"Eddy," Lauren said, reaching down to cup his cheek. His skin felt strange in her hand, and she realized it was the first time she'd ever been herself while touching him. "Your sister is going to be fine. Don't worry, okay?"

But Eddy wasn't the only one who was worried about Lauren losing her powers. Siors nearly dropped the tome he was reading when Lauren and Cefin walked into Aerona's house hand-in-hand, and Aerona spilled the pail of water she had been holding.

"What is..." Siors gasped, coming quickly to his feet.

"I lost my powers!" Lauren grinned, sitting down at the table. Lauren tried to ignore the way Aerona's eyes lingered on their joined hands. Suddenly, she didn't want to tell Aerona that she and Cefin were getting married.

Siors, as well, seemed to be absorbing the situation slowly. "You...you're an empath. How can you lose your powers?"

"The necklace!" Lauren said, trying to ignore the concern on their faces. "*That* was the source of all my empath powers," she grinned at Cefin. "Should have taken it off weeks ago!"

"Slow down, Lauren, "Aerona asked, joining them at the table. "What happened in Traegaron?"

"Your buddy Probert's a real jackass," Lauren said darkly. "He forced himself on me."

"No!" Siors gasped, his hands coming over his mouth.

"It's true," Cefin nodded, squeezing her hand under the table. "I found them in the library."

"He said it was some kind of advanced empathy thing," Lauren said. "Instead of having me read all of his emotions, he focused on all of his negative thoughts. Did you know about this?"

"Of course not." Siors shook his head. "Lauren, when Brother Probert sent word for you, I was hoping to accompany you myself. But you left without me."

Lauren felt a twinge of guilt for leaving so suddenly, but she buried it. "I don't know if you would have been any help."

"I tried to convince her to leave Traegaron," Cefin said, "but we were summoned by the king."

"The king!" Aerona gasped again.

"And then..." Lauren trailed off, unable to tell the truth about how she had finally given in to the temptation of the Anghenfil. She could see the looks on their faces; she knew that telling the truth would help no one, and perhaps just make things worse.

"Then the Anghenfil appeared," Cefin finished for her. "We escaped in the ensuing chaos. The castle was burning."

Lauren remembered the library, and prayed that the Anghenfil's fire didn't reach it. Guilt swelled in her chest, too much for her to bury with the rest of the feelings about Traegaron. She was responsible for it all; she shouldn't have gotten out in time. Something bad was going to come out of it all, she just knew it.

"What called the beast to Traegaron?" Siors asked, tapping his finger to his chin. "It hasn't been seen in the king's castle since..."

"I don't know," Lauren shrugged, reaching for her nonexistent necklace again and hoping that could be the end of the discussion. She was beginning to panic with all of these questions again, and she couldn't take a breath. She needed something else—maybe to crawl into Cefin's arms to chase away all of her nerves.

"And your necklace, what of that?" Aerona asked, noticing Lauren's movement.

"It—" Cefin began.

"I just took it off," Lauren interrupted him before he spoke about how it had turned black. He looked surprised but didn't correct her. "Realized that it was the source of my power and chucked it."

"Where is it now?" Siors asked.

Lauren shifted nervously. "It doesn't matter. I'm not putting it back on again."

"I think it's for the best," Cefin agreed, and she smiled at him in gratitude.

"But your powers!" Siors continued, looking between Aerona and Cefin. "We must return them to you! The village needs you!"

"The village got along just fine without me," Lauren snapped. "For fifty years, you guys didn't have an empath. Why the hell do you need one now?"

"Because you have a gift," Siors said.

"A *gift*?" Lauren shook her head, unable to believe that Siors would value her powers over her mental well-being. Her guilt from calling the Anghenfil, the fear that she'd be made to put the necklace on again, the unending panic in her mind—it all combined to form a hurricane in her mind and she exploded in anger. "You have *no* idea what it's like to wear that thing! I'm better completely rid of it!"

"Lauren, dear," Aerona said, reaching across the table to take her other free hand. "We don't mean to upset you, but you've been a great asset to the village, and—"

"Is that all I am to you people?" Lauren asked, standing up so fast the chair fell behind her. "Just a freak that you can—"

"No, Lauren, that's not it at all!" Siors began.

Aerona leaned forward, concerned. "Lauren, sit back down."

"Why do *I* have to suffer? I'm already stuck here, and now you want to make me even more miserable by preventing me from being *normal*. I *hate* being an empath, I *hate* the pressure everyone's put on me to solve *their* problems." Lauren was on the verge of tears. "What about my problems, huh? What about my own tyllwyllwch?"

Lauren looked between Aerona and Siors. Even Cefin seemed unable to argue on her behalf.

"*Forget it*," she huffed, unable to stand being in the room another minute longer.

***

She was irrationally angry and she knew it, but it was easier to be angry at them. She brushed the tears away from her cheeks as two more dripped to the ground. Her angry tirade left her by the river, the only place she felt she could go without someone bothering her. She'd *sleep* out here if it meant never having to see their faces again, to have to deal with the consequences of—

"There you are."

Lauren's heart beat out of her chest when Aerona came to sit next to her. Aerona looked at the river and then began to laugh quietly.

"What?" Lauren asked.

"I'm just remembering the day I sent you to wash our laundry."

Lauren remembered all too well as well, and the ghost of a smile appeared at her lips.

"You have been an enigma since the moment you arrived here. And it has nothing to do with the world you came from." Aerona smiled when Lauren turned her head. "You have so much locked tightly in your head, it seems, and you don't share it with anyone else."

Lauren nodded and tried to play with the stone, remembering again it was gone. Why did she suddenly miss that stupid thing?

"I'm sorry if we upset you," Aerona said.

"And I'm sorry for acting like a child." Lauren nodded. "But after what Probert did to me...I just...I don't want anyone to ever take advantage of me like that again."

"We would never dream of taking advantage of you," Aerona said, looking at her strangely. "But you never mentioned any ill effects from being an empath, and so we assumed..."

"I couldn't touch *anyone*, Aerona. Do you know how lonely that is for me?"

"You aren't lonely anymore," Aerona whispered, and Lauren tried her best to ignore the feeling that Aerona may be jealous of her and Cefin. After all, Aerona and Cefin had grown up together, it fit for them to be together. And Lauren belonged somewhere else, at home.

Lauren shook her head, clearing it of these odd thoughts welling from somewhere deep inside her. *She* was with Cefin, although she still couldn't bring herself to tell Aerona that they were to be married. For someone who had been dreaming about it for so long, she was suddenly dreading the occurrence.

"You know how terrible it's been for me," Lauren said. "I'm in a strange land, and all of a sudden I have these powers that I don't understand."

"But you were helping people!"

"And I was drowning in it!" And the Anghenfil was always there, offering her a life jacket. Again, she pictured what would happen if she told Aerona about the monster, and glued her jaw shut.

"You should have told me," Aerona said, wrapping her arm around Lauren lovingly. "You seemed to be well. I had no idea you were struggling so much."

"Well I'm not anymore, as long as I don't have to be an empath."

"Very well then. We won't ask it of you anymore."

Lauren nodded, wishing that Aerona's words had made her feel better. But they only served to make her feel guiltier than before.

***

After a fitful night's sleep, Lauren helped Aerona with breakfast and with tending to Mairwan, who was still slowly recovering from her fall. Seeing Mairwan renewed the fear that she was going to tell everyone about the Anghenfil, but the little girl seemed to have no memory of it.

"So since you aren't going to be healing anyone today, what do you plan to do with yourself?" Aerona asked, tearing Lauren away from her bubbling fear.

"I don't know," Lauren said. "I'm not really much use to

Baltes anymore, am I?"

"Perhaps he could use an extra set of hands on the farm," Aerona suggested, with that same tone in her voice that reignited Lauren's guilt.

Lauren made an excuse to leave, taking a deep breath once she was out of the house. She surveyed the village of Rhianu, which was busy in the early morning. The people, now used to her, nodded and smiled at her. She was one of them now, a normal villager without some stupid superpower.

A young boy bumped into her and she sighed, not missing the way she would have known every little thing about what he was feeling. With a smile, she spun him around and sent him on his way.

She supposed she could go spend the day with Baltes, but she wouldn't be much use without her powers. She was pretty strong now, and could probably help out with laundry or some other manual labor. Aerona hadn't asked her to do anything this morning. Perhaps she hoped Lauren would change her mind about retrieving her necklace.

Lauren knew in her soul that she was taking the easy way out, but she didn't care. She'd spent so long living with her fears that it was pleasant to take a break from it, to give herself the freedom to just live without being constantly on edge. It was exhausting to constantly be afraid of everything.

A ruckus at the edge of town drew her attention, and she and other villagers walked over to see what was going on. Two children were slumped over an old mule, and a woman, perhaps their mother, was crying.

Even without her necklace, Lauren knew they had tyllwyllwch.

"Please, where is the empath!" she cried. "My children are sick with the tyllwyllwch."

empath

Lauren felt a few eyes move to her and she shook her head, hoping the woman didn't see. But she apparently recognized Lauren, as she came rushing over, grabbing her hands.

"The empath, you're here," the woman cried, tears falling down her face. "You have to help, my daughter she—"

"I'm not an empath." Lauren smiled nervously, taking her hands out of the woman's. "Sorry, I can't help you."

"I saw you," she begged, grabbing at Lauren again. "Down in Heulog, I saw you heal an entire village!"

"Sorry." Lauren stepped back, feeling very uncomfortable. "I don't have my powers anymore."

"But if you can't help me, no one else can!"

"I...don't..." Lauren looked around the village, feeling the eyes of everyone in the village on her. They were accusatory, curious, angry, all of them focused on her, wondering why she wasn't helping the woman.

Lauren's breath came in short spurts, and she became lightheaded from the lack of air. Without another word, she turned around and ran out of the village, up the trail to the watcher's post.

**

"Cefin!" Lauren cried, running into the clearing. The man in question was sitting against the rock, his spear by his side, but he was up in a minute, cradling Lauren in his arms as she flew into them. It felt so nice to be comforted, she breathed him in.

"What is it?" he said, rubbing her back.

"There was a lady in the village," Lauren said, burying her head into his chest. Could she tell him about the tyllwyllwch? She felt like a bad person, but she also felt selfishly and stubbornly like a good person, just trying to do things for herself.

"What did she want?" Cefin asked.

"Oh who cares?" Lauren said. "Kiss me?"

He complied happily and passionately, but she could not shake the nerves. She was avoiding reality again, her mind reminded her loudly, and she turned to kiss Cefin even harder.

"You're distracting me," Cefin said, burying his head in her neck. "I should be watching the village."

"You were working so hard," Lauren murmured, running her hands through his hair. "And I needed you."

"What's got you so upset?"

"It's silly. I probably overreacted." Lauren shook her head as she clung to him. "I mean, it's not like the Anghenfil returned or anything. That's what should worry me, right?"

Cefin stroked her hair gently. "There are other things that could bother you. If you feel something, you should honor that."

"I'd rather just not feel anything but you," Lauren smiled.

The sex with Cefin wasn't better the second time around, and didn't serve to sooth her nerves whatsoever. As the sun set on the ridge, she sat with him and oscillated between telling him everything that was on her mind and not saying a thing.

She stayed with him until his shift was over, when the old man Graves hobbled up the path to take his spot. She worried about returning to the village, about what people would say when they knew she decided *not* to help those two children with tyllwyllwch. The urge to bury her head in the sand came back, so she turned to Cefin with a smile.

"So...you and me getting married, right?"

"Yes?"

"I should probably stay at your place now, right?" Lauren asked, hoping he would say yes. She wasn't sure she could take another night of Aerona's guilt-inducing stares. If she stayed with Cefin, she could pretend none of it existed.

Cefin, however, seemed to be completely flabbergasted. "But we aren't married yet. Why would you ask such a thing?"

"Yeah, but we're gonna be. How about tomorrow? Just real quick, have Siors do the ceremony, then we can—"

"What is the matter with you?" Cefin asked again. "And don't say it's nothing, because you've barely let me breathe since you showed up at the watcher's post."

The tone of his words stung and she shrugged, loosening her grip on his hand.

"I just don't want to talk about it, okay?"

"You never want to talk about it," Cefin said, dropping her hand entirely. "You didn't want me to tell Aerona about the stone. You didn't even tell them that we're getting married, and now you want to marry me tomorrow?"

"I just..." Lauren shook her head. "It's just difficult and—"

"It's not difficult," Cefin snapped, for the first time sounding angry at her. "I let you see the darkest parts of my life, and you can't even be honest with me."

"I..." Lauren's eyes welled with tears at the way he was looking at her. If he was angry now, what would happen if she told him the truth? She couldn't risk it.

"Lauren,"—he took her hands gently and kissed them—"what are you so afraid of?"

"THERE SHE IS!"

Lauren's heart stopped.

Twim Probert and a hoard of the king's soldiers were waiting on the edge of Rhianu.

chapter sixteen

They had surrounded the village, a group of fifty knights in their full garb huddled in the small village. The gaggle of knights had drawn a crowd and Lauren did not think they looked too friendly towards her.

"Lauren, get back," Cefin growled, throwing a protective arm in front of her. She felt only a little relieved; maybe they could just run away now. Maybe she could close her eyes and this would all disappear.

But that knowing voice in her mind knew her chickens had come home to roost. Just as the Anghenfil appeared in Traegaron, she had known that this was coming. And she knew how it was going to end.

"Stand aside, son," Probert ordered. "We will be taking the empath back with us!"

"She no longer has her stone," Cefin hissed. "She is of no use to you."

"Matters not if she has her witch powers or not! She must pay for her crimes."

"Crimes?" Siors called, breaking through the crowd. Lauren felt no relief at the sight of him. His concern for her was about to disappear as soon as he discovered the truth. "She has committed no crime, Brother Probert—"

"Yes, she has," Probert continued, his beady little eyes

trained on Lauren. "She is responsible for the destruction of Traegaron."

"The Anghenfil did that," Cefin exclaimed as Lauren's began to feel lightheaded. "I was there."

"And who brought the Anghenfil to Traegaron?" Probert hissed, sending Lauren's panic to an all-time high as every eye in the village turned to her.

"And what proof do you have?" Siors asked.

"We have not seen the beast in Traegaron for fifty years, not since the last empath was in our castle," Probert announced to the murmuring crowd. "And then when we have another empath, it suddenly reappears!"

Lauren wished she could deny it all, as she had done for weeks and weeks, but she suddenly couldn't make a noise. Her throat felt like it had closed up, the same way she felt when she was buried under the rubble when she first arrived. She swayed and clung tighter to Cefin.

"That is preposterous!" Siors faced his scholar-brother. "She has been in this village for weeks, and the beast has not come for her. Why would it take her from Traegaron?"

"Because she *controls* it," Probert said. "The same way she controls the tyllwyllwch that infects this land."

Lauren closed her eyes. This was nothing but a dream. A big, terrible nightmare that she would wake up from. But when she opened her eyes again, all she could see was accusation and disbelief, and it stung her to her core.

"Lauren?" Cefin now sounded apprehensive, and her heart thudded in her ribcage.

"I don't! I swear!" Lauren stammered looking wildly between Cefin and Siors. "That thing is *evil* and I don't *want* to hear it in my head!"

She immediately knew she had said the absolutely wrong

thing.

"In your *head*?" Cefin exclaimed, stepping away from her.

"*YOU SEE?*" Probert barked wildly. "The empath admits that she hears the beast in her head. It came for the one before her, and it came for her in the castle of Traegaron!"

"No, I didn't mean to call it—" Lauren replied, gasping as the villagers began to talk amongst themselves.

"And I suppose you would like us all to think that the beast doesn't come to you on command?" Probert continued, his eyes wide. "Then tell us: how did you arrive in our land if not by the Anghenfil's magic?"

Lauren's mouth fell open as she struggled to find an answer that would placate the crowd.

"Am I lying?" he asked.

"I...I ..." she whimpered, searching for a friendly face. Siors was horrified. Aerona had two hands firmly on Eddy's shoulders. And Cefin...even Cefin looked disgusted with her.

"You said you didn't know how you got here, and you wanted to go back up to the cave," Cefin gasped. "I nearly *died*, and you can control that beast?"

"Cefin, I just wanted to go *home!* I can't control it, it just appears in my mind—" Lauren gasped.

"SO YOU ADMIT IT!" Probert screamed. "You admit that you and it have a connection!"

"Yes!" Lauren cried, tears spilling down her face. "I don't want it. It's terrifying and I'm afraid of it and..." She fell to her knees and began sobbing.

"Take the empath and put her in the cage," Probert ordered. "She will no longer be able to hurt anyone else."

"N-No!" she screamed as the soldiers closed in around her. "Aerona! Siors! Cefin, somebody...please!"

"We take her back to Traegaron," Probert sneered. "She dies

in two days."

***

Lauren wrapped her arms tighter around herself, sobbing softly. Probert and the king's soldiers had made themselves comfortable in Rhianu for the night, leaving her locked in this iron-barred carriage. The soldier assigned to keep watch over her had long since disappeared, though it didn't really matter. None of the villagers wanted anything to do with her now.

Lauren kept asking herself what would have happened if she'd just told everyone outright about the monster, if that would have stemmed their anger. She saw the hurt in their eyes, the fear, and the betrayal. Especially Cefin.

She felt lower than the day she and Josh broke up. She couldn't believe she'd convinced herself that she could just bury all of the things swimming beneath the surface, all of her worries about the Anghenfil, about what she really was. Yet again she had ignored her own intuition. She was going to die here without ever being able to see home again. She sobbed harder, letting the tears fall onto her dress without wiping them away.

Where was the Anghenfil now? She would be a perfect meal for it.

She heard a noise outside of the cage and looked up, wondering if her life was going to be made shorter by a wild animal. Instead, she saw the wild, frizzy hair of Owena emerging from a nearby bush.

Owena looked as crazy as ever, muttering to herself as she walked over to the carriage. She grasped something in her hand as she glanced around, first at the village in the distance and then back to Lauren.

"Hey," Lauren whispered, coming to the bars of her cage. "What are you doing here?"

Owena grumbled something, looking around and up at the

sky.

"Can you get me out of here?" Lauren said, hoping that she could get past Owena's insanity.

The old woman shook her head and pointed at Lauren.

"You," she mumbled.

"Me?" Lauren tossed another furtive look around her. "Can you get me out of here?"

"You," Owena repeated, thrusting her hands into the cage. She opened her palm, and Lauren's breath caught in her throat.

It was a ruby necklace.

Except instead of bright red, the stone was dark—as dark as Lauren's when she threw it away. But it wasn't Lauren's ruby. Something about it was different, and yet similar.

"Where did you get this?" Lauren gasped.

"No time. Touch." Owena shook the amulet in her hand.

Lauren hesitated. She was already on edge; reading this crazy woman's thoughts might be enough to send her over. Not only that, but if anyone saw her with the ruby, she'd be forced to wear it, forced to endure taking their emotions. It may stay the execution, but at what cost?

Owena jiggled the necklace again, her wrinkled face serious.

Whimpering, Lauren closed her eyes and covered the woman's hand with her own, wincing as foreign memories washed over her.

***

She was in a small, dark room, the walls plastered with posters of heavy metal bands. A little light streamed in from the windows, illuminating her hands as they stared at the little orange bottle in her hands. The name on the bottle was familiar, but it wasn't hers. The prescription was for oxycodone, prescribed for her father's bad back, but never taken. He said his side of the family had a problem with addiction and he never wanted to test the waters.

But things...they were bad. Ever since the divorce, everything had gone to shit. She couldn't concentrate, so her grades were slipping. Her mom didn't seem to understand. She was more interested in her new boyfriend, the one she'd been screwing when she walked out on her husband. He was coming over that night for dinner, or maybe he just lived there; she wasn't sure which was reality.

With trembling hands, she cracked open the top and looked at the pills inside.

She'd only meant to get high once, to dull the pain of failing a science test and having to suffer through her father's disappointment. But the draw was seductive, and she had refilled her father's prescription twice already.

She swallowed the first pill, closing her eyes and hoping it would hit her bloodstream before she was called downstairs. She just couldn't take the show her mother put on for everyone. Like they were one big happy family, when she was drowning inside.

She looked at the bottle and considered taking two, just to make sure she wouldn't remember anything.

She looked at the bottle again and counted the rest of the pills in the bottle. Fifteen, maybe more. She could take this entire bottle and end it completely.

She pushed the bottle away, that thought sending chills down her spine. She'd been keeping that thought at bay for months now, just dulling the pain instead of getting rid of it.

"I can take your pain..."

She heard a voice, but didn't react. She'd heard it almost every time she took one of these pills. At first, she'd thought she was imagining things, but it was now a familiar sound. Once the pills got her high, it would promise sweet release, if she'd just take another one.

The bottle was now a few inches from her hand. The temptation was so alluring, the idea that she could just stop all of the ridiculousness in her life. Let them deal with their problems, she could be free.

"Let me help you, let me take you away from all of this."

Her heart pounded and her fingers encircled the bottle. Tears splashed down her face. She wanted to throw the bottle across the room, but her body wouldn't listen. She was so afraid of what was going to happen.

"It will be all right. Let me take you away..."

She opened her mouth and swallowed the rest of the bottle.

***

"An empath?" She was standing in the castle at Traegaron. A man wearing purple robes stood in front of her, a smile on his face. He was young, perhaps in his early twenties, and he looked pleased to have her there.

She had been in this strange land for a month, with odd powers that she didn't understand. She couldn't touch another person without getting a mindful of their problems and feeling like she had to fix every one of them. It was infuriating, and she wanted no part of it.

But then she was summoned by the king, and for a little while, things were better. She was special here; these empath powers turned her into a celebrity. She was given a huge room in the castle and paraded around by the king as his new toy.

But then the king's scholar began taking advantage of her. He would bring her down to his office and force himself on her, pushing a storm of hateful emotions into her already fragile mind. She was overcome with pain, worse than she'd felt sitting in her bedroom. It became a voice, a hateful echo in the space of her heart, whispering the truth that she'd been trying hard to bury.

The scholar did his little experiments once a day, not caring that he left her curled into a ball or that she'd lost enough weight to see her own ribcage in the month that she'd been there. No one—not even the king—was willing to help her. She was just an empath; this was what she was expected to do.

Because nobody cared.

She grasped at her ruby necklace at her throat, a birthday present from her grandmother. It was the only thing that connected her back to her world, the only thing that reminded her that she was *real* and that this world, and all of the pain inside of it was not. The necklace was the one thing that kept her here, kept her from snapping.

She lay on the cold stone ground of the scholar's office, watching the tears drip off the edge of her nose, and prayed that someone—anyone—would come take her away from this.

But she had no one on her side, just as she had no one back in her world to run to.

She screamed in anger, her voice echoing off of the stone walls.

"I can take your pain away..."

She'd heard the voice for weeks now, when she was alone crying in her room. It was the same one that she'd heard in her bedroom. But she'd resisted for so long, hoping that things would get better before she had to give in to the temptation.

But she slipped into the darkness.

"Take it," she whispered.

***

The Anghenfil had come for her, and she thought it terribly amusing to see the destruction of that horrifying castle as they flew away. It cradled her gently in its giant tail, passing over the lands and the fields with ease. She felt better now, like all of her problems were going to disappear.

"Will it hurt?" she asked.

"No more than you hurt today..."

It watched her with ruby red eyes, the same color her ruby necklace had been when she received it. But weeks of slipping farther and farther into despair had darkened it.

The monster was waiting for her permission, and she was scared of what it would do to her. But she was drowning, and the monster promised her a hand.

"Do it."

The stone at her chest grew darker and darker until it blackened completely, a dark stone that shone no more. The chain made no sound as it broke, and the pendant fell to the ground. Her chest grew cold, like it was filling with tyllwyllwch. Her heart beat out of her chest in fear—

No, it was *actually beating out of her chest.*

The Anghenfil's tail wrapped around her, the tip sliding inside of her chest. It hurt but only for a second. She watched in horror as it pulled her heart from her chest. But it was the heart itself that shocked her; it pulsed with darkness, as if covered in tyllwyllwch. The tail unwound itself and returned to the Anghenfil with her heart in tow, and the monster tossed it into its mouth, swallowing her heart in one gulp.

Its belly, already burning a bright orange, warmed with the addition of her pain, her fear, and her misery, and her mind went blank.

***

Lauren gasped as she broke away from Owena, still holding onto the necklace.

"C-Cassidy," she whispered, staring into the old eyes of the woman before her. The vacant response was now even more terrifying, knowing the depths of pain and emotion her eyes had once held. And knowing how close Lauren herself had come to that same fate.

The Anghenfil was a truly evil creature, preying on those already on the edge of the abyss. And in the sweet promise of release, all it brought was more pain and more anger until there was nothing left.

That's when it devoured its prize and sought out another.

Lauren became furious at herself, but it was a different kind of fury than she'd ever felt before. She was angry with herself for allowing the monster to take advantage of her. She thought she was smarter than this, more aware than this. She thought she had a better handle on her problems. But now, in the cold light of day, she began to see reality.

Every time she "buried" something in the back of her mind, she was trying to avoid dealing with it. She was afraid to think so many things that she couldn't keep them all at bay, constantly living in fear. And she thought, stupidly, that if she ignored her problems, they would magically disappear.

Except *she* was the one who magically disappeared.

And yet, her problems remained. She continued to pretend that she was fine when she was obviously not, continued to dive into mind-numbing activities rather than live in the present moment, even here in Rhianu. The more she ran and the deeper she sank into her own misery, the more appetizing she was to the Anghenfil. It was content to let her spiral out of control, like fattening up a turkey for slaughter.

Lauren looked at Cassidy and was struck by similarities.

Cassidy was drowning in her loneliness, feeling like there was no one to turn to. But Cassidy was *actually* drowning, whereas Lauren was captive only by her fear. Lauren didn't have...

She stopped that thought, but not because she was afraid to think it, but because she realized how damaging that train of thought had been. She'd been downplaying her own misery, and yet, Lauren had felt as much sadness and as hopeless as Cassidy. Lauren may have only been afraid of things inside her head, but the fear was real. The anxiety, the panic, all of it was just as pronounced as Cassidy's. But Lauren was afraid to admit how far she had fallen into her own darkness.

Because admitting it would make it real.

She stared at the black stone in her hand and realized that fear had been the backbone of every decision she'd ever made. It had clouded her judgement, even making her fear her own thoughts because she never stood up and *faced* the very thing haunting her.

But not anymore.

chapter seventeen

A noise startled them both, and Lauren hissed at Owena (or should she call her Cassidy now) to disappear. The old woman seemed to have lost all of her lucidity again, humming to herself as she strolled away from the carriage.

Lauren slid the necklace around her neck and hid it in her dress, hoping no one would see it. The presence felt good against her skin, like coming home. But she now had other problems to think about—namely, how she could get out of this carriage?

She heard another noise, the same one, in fact. It sounded like something crashed in the village. Two soldiers ran up to the carriage, looking around for something, before another sound from the village sent them running.

"Damned children!"

"Children?" Lauren blinked, and she heard an explosion in the distance, followed by yelling. Could it be Eddy causing problems? But why?

"Lauren!"

Lauren's head nearly swiveled off of her neck. Aerona rushed up to the carriage and grasped at the iron bars. She looked relieved and anxious to see Lauren.

"Are you all right?" she asked.

"I...yes..." Lauren stammered. "Confused, but all right."

"Eddy is helping Siors distract the guards while I get you out of here," Aerona said, fussing over the lock.

"I don't understand. I thought you hated me?" She swallowed and felt the old fear creeping back into the back of her mind. "I almost got Mairwan killed—"

"You *saved* Mairwan," Aerona corrected.

Again, fear gripped at her, but she finally pushed out the words. "*I called the Anghenfil to me.*"

Aerona stopped her fussing with the lock. "Why?"

"Because...it told me that it could solve all of my problems and..." Lauren pressed her forehead against the bars. "And to be honest, it sounded nice."

"And you believe this would make me hate you?" Aerona tutted. "My darling, I'm offended you think so little of me."

Lauren's eyes popped open, and she stared at Aerona as if she'd never seen her before. Aerona was the kindest, most gentle person Lauren had ever met. She had taken Lauren in when she had no where else to go, and had become a calming presence in her life. What possessed Lauren to think that Aerona would reject her for something out of her control? The worry that she had been holding onto for weeks evaporated from her body like tyllwyllwch.

"I...I'm..." Lauren stammered, at a complete loss for words. "I'm a coward." She pressed her head against the bars again. "And an idiot."

"Fear is rarely rational," Aerona said, with a look behind her to the village where more yelling echoed.

"So what's your plan?"

"Just waiting on, ah, there he is," Aerona said, as Cefin appeared out of the bushes with his sword drawn. Some of his long hair had come out of the tie, and he had a cut on his cheek.

"We have to hurry," he said, without acknowledging Lauren's shocked face. With a mighty heave, he brought his sword down on the lock on the cage breaking it. Lauren scampered out of the cage and stood in the clearing, wavering between shock and appreciation.

"We need to get you out of the village," Aerona said. "Cefin will take you to the edge of the village, and then—"

"No," Lauren said, feeling the weight of the necklace around her neck.

"No?" Cefin looked stunned. "Lauren, they're coming for you—"

"I'm going after the Anghenfil."

Their stunned faces grew even more so and Aerona and Cefin launched into tirades about why that was a terrible idea. But Lauren held up her hand, a knowing calm settling over her. With all of her worries freed from the back of her mind, she could hear her intuition, that inner compass that always steered her in the right direction. It was the quiet, knowing voice that had spoken for her when she'd ended things with Josh.

Then, as now, she felt like a different person, as if someone were pulling the strings and she was merely doing what they instructed. She had fought reality for so long that now it was time to accept the truth. And although she was scared, shaking, terrified—this was the right thing to do.

"I know how to defeat it. I just..." She swallowed. "I needed to find the courage to do it." She tugged on the chain around her neck and pulled Cassidy's empath stone out.

"Your necklace," Cefin gasped.

"No, not mine. The other empath...it's a long story." She stared at the ebony stone and remembered the pain that Cassidy felt, the loneliness and desolation knowing that no one was ever coming for her. Lauren closed her eyes and imagined herself banishing the tyllwyllwch from Cassidy's soul, helping her to see that she was not as alone as she had thought.

The stone began to glow in her hand, and she concentrated on this feeling of control and determination. The glow grew white hot until the stone seared her skin, but she held on to it.

"Lauren..." Aerona gasped.

Lauren opened her eyes and shut them again, nearly blinded by the light from the stone. It dimmed as she lost her concentration; not to black, but to a beautiful bright red. The same clear color as Lauren's had been when she'd purchased it.

"How did you do that?" Cefin asked.

"I think it became dark because *I* allowed it to." She rubbed the stone again, the familiar ridges providing the same comfort that hers used to. "Because *I* let myself fall into the darkness. And that's what the Anghenfil wanted."

"D-darkness?" Cefin said, exchanging a confused glance with Aerona.

"Sadness," Lauren whispered. "Loneliness. Whatever you want to call it."

Cefin made a noise. Lauren was startled to see a tear fall down his face.

"My love, I'm sorry that—"

"It wasn't you, Cefin," Lauren said. "It was...well, it was my fault."

Aerona cleared her throat and took the signal that she needed to walk away for a moment.

"But *I'm* the one that left you when Probert..." Cefin stammered.

"Cefin, if Probert had never shown up, I would have been keeping this secret inside of me until it ate me alive. And it was close, let me tell you," she added with a wry smile. "I don't blame you for thinking that I was nuts."

Cefin looked at the ground.

"I'm sorry I wasn't honest with you. *Trust me*, I wish I had been honest with everyone up front."

"Why weren't you?"

"Because..." Lauren trailed off and looked out into the village. "Because I wasn't honest with myself. I was afraid to be. And that is why all of this just blew up in my face... as usual." She sighed heavily, closing her eyes and forcing herself to speak. "If I had just been brave enough to face reality in the first place, I might have gone home weeks ago."

The word home caused Cefin's head to snap upright. He suddenly realized what defeating the Anghenfil was going to mean for her.

"No," he said, grasping her hand desperately. "No, I don't want you to go. Lauren, I love you..."

"Cefin," Lauren said, feeing the familiar tug of uncertainty. It would be great to stay here with him. He was a guy that loved her.

And that was it.

She looked at him and realized she knew absolutely *nothing* about him. She may have read his hopes and fears, she definitely knew him physically, but she had been too wrapped up in her own insecurities to see the man in front of her. And somehow, she knew that he had done the same to her.

"How can you possibly love me when you don't even know me?" she heard herself ask him.

His mouth opened in shocked hurt. "You said you loved me."

"I lied," Lauren said. To Cefin's stunned face, she added, "If it makes you feel better, I was lying to myself too."

"This is...I don't understand why—"

"Cefin, you can't possibly love me. Maybe...maybe one day you could have, but not until I was brave enough to let you see me as I am—"

"Then let me see you!" Cefin exclaimed, stepping towards her. "Please, don't go."

"Cefin, I don't belong here," Lauren replied, brushing away the hair from his face. "I've never been happy here—not truly happy. If you look inside your soul, you'll know that's true."

He stared at her and she appreciated his handsome features one last time. She would never be completely impervious to them, but she could now see her own reactions for what they were, and what they weren't. And now that she had put aside her own fabricated love story, she could see the one that had been staring her in the face the whole time she'd been there.

"You need to make a move with Aerona," Lauren said.

"What?" Cefin seemed to get the gist of what she'd said, but the concept left him bewildered.

"Aerona and you—I think you two belong together."

A blush spread across his face. "I don't—"

That was all the proof Lauren needed. "She loves you, really loves you. Better than I ever could, actually."

"I don't deserve her," Cefin said, taking Lauren by surprise.

Lauren laughed, realizing that she and Cefin were more alike than even she realized. Everyone seemed to be living in fear, the way she had been. But just as she had come to realize her own foolishness, there wasn't anything she could say or do to get Cefin to understand. He would have to face his own demons and come to his own realizations the hard way.

Instead of speaking, she pulled him into a hug. It was more intimate and real than any physical contact they'd had before.

"I'm going to miss you, Lauren Dailey," he whispered into her hair.

"I would despair if you didn't." She winked at him as she stepped back, craning her head back to take in the mountain. "Go face your Anghenfil, Cefin," Lauren said, "now I'm going to go face mine."

❖

Lauren stepped into the dark cave and alarm bells went off in her head as fear bubbled inside of her. But she now knew the difference between fear of the unknown and the quiet knowledge that she was about to do something wrong. These bells, and the accompanying butterflies that exploded in her chest, this was simply *fear*. And she was no longer letting fear dictate her life.

As if emphasizing a point, her ruby began to glow, lighting her path in the darkness.

"Come on, you scaly son of a bitch," Lauren called, her voice echoing in the cave. "Show yourself."

She could hear it breathing, the same way she heard it moving in her mind. She saw the fire in the distance and kept walking as it grew brighter. Ash and smoke filled her nostrils, and she continued to fight the urge to turn tail and flee.

She could do this; she could defeat it. She had all of the tools in her arsenal, she just had to remember her purpose.

The cave opened into a cavern, tinted red by the fire glowing in the Anghenfil's stomach and crackling at its mouth. It was curled up in a ball, reminding her of a cat the size of a dinosaur. The long, serpentine tail was still, save the tip, which brushed against the floor lazily. Cefin had cut it off, and she never considered when or how it regrew. Perhaps her fear was its sustenance, the thing that allowed it to live for millennia, and why it feasted on a new empath every half century.

She could see one of the four giant, clawed feet, like a monstrous hawk's claws, relaxed on the floor. The neck was long and scaly, and perched on top of it was a long head with red eyes glinting in the low light. Smoke swirled from its jaw, where huge, bone-crushing white fangs jutted out. It surveyed her like a snake about to devour a mouse.

It did not move, but Lauren heard the familiar hissing in the back of her mind.

"There's no need to pretend."

Her body screamed to run away, but this time, she did not let it win. Running, she had learned, never solved anything, and the problems usually caught up to her sooner or later. She *would* see this to the end. She had all the power in the world over this beast.

"You have no power...it is easier if you give in to me."

"Right, because that worked so well with Cassidy," Lauren barked, her voice echoing in the cave. She wasn't sure why she spoke aloud, since the monster could very well hear inside of her head, but she had always had more control of her tongue than her mind. She kept her focus on the stone, and it grew brighter in the face of the Anghenfil.

"Cassidy was in pain...I took it from her...she suffers no more..."

"She *feels* no more, you mean," Lauren cried as the stone glowed even hotter. "She's an empty shell! You took her *heart!*"

"I take the hearts of those who give it freely, those who no longer wish to suffer. As you did."

Lauren's heart began to race, and she narrowed her eyes. "Why did you bring me here? To Rhianu, to this world?"

"You know the answer to that, but you are afraid to speak it aloud..."

"I'm not..." Lauren shook her head, but she couldn't finish the sentence. Not when the monster very clearly knew the truth. The chink in her armor was enough to dim the stone slightly, but she wasn't giving up.

"You are here because you asked me to bring you here. You asked me to take away your pain...because you aren't strong enough to overcome it..."

"I am s-strong," Lauren replied feebly as the panic exploded between her ears and the stone dimmed even more. The

Anghenfil laughed at her attempts to lie in the face of her open mind.

"You cannot even be truthful with yourself about what it is you fear. But the Anghenfil knows the darkest places of your mind...You know why he did not return."

Her eyes widened and she swore she saw the stupid monster smile. Why did the Anghenfil have to bring *him* up? Her fear swirled within her like Probert's cleansing; the sensation was unexpected and unnerving. Almost instantly, the box of forbidden thoughts exploded like fireworks, and her stone, now completely dull, grew blacker by the second.

"Yes...you know in your heart...and you fear it..."

"This isn't about that," Lauren said, struggling to keep the tears from spilling down her face.

"You wonder why he did not come for you, but you know why. You don't wish to believe it...and so you pine for him..."

She bit down on her tongue.

"You know you were never good enough for him. So good at lying to yourself..."

The stone was dark now and so was her soul.

"You are afraid no one will ever love you...even he didn't love you...the one person whom you trusted above all others to be there... left like everyone else.."

"S...stop..." Lauren cried, but the dam had broken, and she was on the edge of slipping again. All of these terrible, horrible, forbidden thoughts that she had been so afraid to think were in the open, taunting her and hissing at her the way the Anghenfil did.

"Yesss...now let the Anghenfil take that pain...you will never have to run again...you will never have to be rejected again..."

She hated the merciless glee in its eyes. It had broken her by speaking what she was most afraid of—the fear that she would never find someone to ever truly love her. The fear that Josh was her only chance at happiness and he left because she wasn't good enough.

And yet...vocalizing it, putting words to the fear, suddenly made it seem... ridiculous.

Thinking about it didn't hurt as much as she feared, not really. Just like in the dream with Mairwan, the flames were all in her mind. The ideas that she had been too afraid to even consider—these things that haunted her from a distance—they were just ideas.

Josh wasn't her only chance at happiness, he was *a* chance. And while they were happy, when she really thought about it, there was more to their dissolution than a lack of a diamond ring.

That one realization broke the dam of other thoughts—rational thoughts, and she felt the stone warm at her neck.

She *was* afraid of being alone, but being in a bad relationship wasn't much better. The end of her relationship with Josh was rocky and unfulfilling; not the romantic love story she'd painted it out to be in her mind. Even before they broke up, she had fooled herself into thinking that Josh was someone different, that he was ready to commit when he was obviously and vocally against it. But she'd been too afraid to see the truth, too afraid to face the reality that as much as she loved him and as much as he loved her, they were not right for each other.

She was too afraid of being alone, of having to risk the fear never finding another person to love her. So accepting their less-than-fulfilling relationship was less scary than the alternative.

She opened her eyes and the stone grew brighter. The Anghenfil hissed in anger and rage as it recoiled from the light.

"Yes...they will reject you...And there is nothing you can do to change it..."

She couldn't change it. She couldn't prevent getting hurt by someone else, that she would put her fragile love and faith in someone and they would break her heart. But to risk pain was also to enjoy love, and good, deep relationships with people. She had just spent a month in this land and she hadn't met one person she'd consider a friend—not because they'd rejected her, but because she'd *assumed* they would.

And when she finally allowed someone to see her for who she really was, they stood beside her.

The stone was hot now, and warmth spread out across her chest. Sparks flying from the monster's nostrils as it grew more agitated.

"YOU WILL NEVER BE ABLE TO CONTROL YOUR MIND!"

"You're right." Lauren smiled and the Anghenfil roared louder as the stone grew brighter.

Before she could ask others to accept her, she needed to accept her own imperfect self—that she had periods of depression —yes, depression—and could not control her anxiety. She had a mental illness and it wouldn't go away if she just buried it under the surface and hid from it. The very same way she was confronting this demon, she would have to take control and not suffer in silence.

It was all right to admit that she wasn't perfect all the time. It was all right to admit that she was anxious and sometimes low. It was all right to lean on someone else when she needed a friend. It was all right to ask for help; it would come when she needed it.

Even if came from within.

"You cannot defeat me—"

"I already have," Lauren said, and everything flashed a brilliant white.

chapter eighteen

Lauren's eyes blinked open and she saw white, nothing but white. Her eyes adjusted to the brightness of the room and focused on ceiling tiles and fluorescent lights. She became aware of something in her nose, and on her arm, and the *beep-beep-beep* of a machine nearby.

"L-Lauren?!"

"Momma?" she croaked, turning her head to the side. As if out of a dream, her mother was by her side, face pale with worry and lack of sleep. Lauren couldn't help the tears that appeared in her eyes and spilled down her cheeks.

"Oh baby," Lauren's mother whispered, "you're awake...we were so worried about you."

"What happened?"

"There was an earthquake," her mother explained, brushing the hair out of her face. "You were hit by a concrete beam. There was ... they had to put you into a coma." Her mother's voice cracked. "I was afraid you weren't going to make it—"

Lauren closed her eyes and leaned back, mentally paying herself twenty dollars for the original bet. It was nothing but a coma dream after all.

And yet...it *was* real wasn't it? In her groggy mental state, she still felt different. She had experienced fear, love, and elation. She had walked across a fantasy world and she had spent half of it in the throes of anxiety and terror. She had faced a fire-breathing monster and...survived.

She'd survived.

"H-how long was I out?" Lauren asked.

"Just a day. I was so worried about you. It was like you were..."

"A day?" Lauren blinked, looking around her. Everything was so *normal* and yet it was strange.

"I'll have the doctors come check on you."

"Yeah, get some of these tubes off me too." Lauren cracked with a weak smile. "I feel like I'm in *The Matrix* over here."

"There's my girl." Her mother kissed her on the forehead and disappeared through the door.

Lauren smiled; she was home.

***

She was held in the hospital for a few more days for observation and didn't complain in the least, especially after taking an hour-long hot and steamy shower. Real or no, she felt like she'd spent a month taking river baths, and it was nice to stand under the hot water for a while.

A few of her work friends dropped by with flowers and well-wishes, telling her that the building was decimated, but she was the only one who was seriously injured. The insurance company was considering moving the operating headquarters somewhere cheaper to maintain, which meant that most of them would be receiving buy-outs. Even if they'd decided to rebuild locally, Lauren had already decided she was leaving the company.

"Whatever you want, honey," her mom said. Something about her reminded Lauren of Aerona, and she wondered if the latter woman ever dug up the nerve to make a move on Cefin.

"I kind of think I want to go back to school," Lauren continued. "Or do something else. Something that actually *helps* people."

"Yes, honey."

"And Mom," Lauren said, biting her lip. "I think...I think I need to see someone."

"What?" Her mom turned to look at her sharply. "What kind of someone?"

"I mean...I'm having a real hard time getting over...well... Josh."

"I know, darling. I could tell."

Lauren was strongly reminded of Aerona and the feeling of relief when she finally came clean about the things that had been weighing on her. All of her fears and panic felt like wasted energy.

"I just...never wanted anyone to worry about me," Lauren said. "But you know, it really hurts. And I'm ready to admit that I can't get past it on my own." She remembered what the Anghenfil said, all of the fears it had dredged up. "There's a lot of stuff I can't seem to get past on my own."

"Sometimes the strongest thing we can do is to ask for help, darling."

Lauren nodded, and looked at her necklace lying on the table beside her. She hadn't put it on since she'd awoken, and wasn't sure she ever would again. For as long as she'd held onto it as an anchor when she was in Rhianu, now she felt moored within her own soul.

There was a knock at the door and Lauren heard her heart monitor spike.

Josh stood in the doorway. Familiar and foreign at the same time, he held a bouquet of flowers and wore an apprehensive look on his face. For the first time since she woke, her anxiety made a roaring return.

"I'll...leave you to it," Lauren's mother said, disappearing through the door.

"Hey," Lauren said, after the initial shock wore off. She was shaking and nervous but resisted the ever-present urge to run away. After all, she'd faced the Anghenfil; Josh was small potatoes compared to that. "Come on in."

"Hi," he said, walking into the room. He shoved the bouquet at her, which she took gently and placed on the table next to her. "Are you okay?"

She almost answered in the affirmative, as she had always done, but that was something the old Lauren would have done, and that's how she ended up in a fantasy land with the Anghenfil in her head. She spotted her necklace again and remembered the warmth and strength she found in it.

Terrified, shaking, nervous and against all of the screaming voices in her head, she answered, "You know, I'm not okay."

"Do you need me to get a nurse or—"

"No, physically, I'm fine," Lauren said. "But...ever since we broke up, I've been telling everyone that I'm fine when I'm really not. I've been lying to everyone, including myself."

Josh sat back a bit, unsure of what to do or say.

"You know, I knew we needed to break up two years ago," she said. This was one of the most forbidden of the forbidden thoughts, kept locked away by fear and stubbornness. "I knew it the first time we talked about getting married. Do you remember? We were in the old apartment, and we stood in the living room and I asked you if we were going to get married. I knew right then that we needed to end it, but...I was too afraid."

She could no longer look at him, instead focused on her feet.

"I tried to tell myself I was afraid of losing you, but I was actually afraid that no one else would love me. Of all the things I was afraid to admit, that's the one that I was the most afraid of." She took a deep breath. "So I pretended that things were better than they were, and I turned you into someone that you aren't. I convinced myself that if I just waited long enough, you'd come to your senses or whatever and we'd ride off into the sunset or something." She laughed softly. She'd done the same thing to poor Cefin, and he was *actually* a knight in shining armor. "Even after we broke up, I spent every day *waiting* for you to 'snap out of it' and come home to me. And it's been completely terrible, let me tell you." Again, she laughed at herself and all the misery she had put herself through. "But I've finally come to realize that holding onto the past because I'm afraid of the future isn't a way to live, you know?

"I'm still scared. I'm scared to date again, I hate the idea of you dating someone else. I'm scared that you'll love her more than you loved me..." She trailed off, the pain palpable. "But maybe that's okay. Maybe that's why we aren't together anymore, because you and I both deserve someone who is better for us than we ever were. And I just need to let go of what we had so I can find happiness." She felt two tears slip down her cheeks. "And I have to believe that I'll find that happiness."

She finally felt brave enough to look at him and was unsurprised to see him surveying her like she was certifiably insane.

She laughed, feeling more at peace than she had in years. "Look, that's a lot of words to say that I'm *not* okay, but that's okay. I've obviously got a lot of stuff to work through...and I don't want you to worry about me, all right?" She cleared her throat and cracked a smile. "So how about them Jets, huh?"

***

Lauren was discharged from the hospital that same afternoon, the doctors saying that she was going to make a full physical recovery within a few weeks. Lauren, however, made sure to get several recommendations for local therapists and made an appointment. She knew that it was going to be a very long road until she was at a point where she was completely out of the darkness, but these first few steps felt good, kind of like clearing the tyllwyllwch from a dark cave.

The nurse was in the room giving her final directions for care and check-in, when another girl was wheeled into the room, no older than sixteen.

Lauren locked eyes with her and was struck with the familiarity of the eyes, the curls, the face, and the sadness. The other girl, as well, was taken aback at the sight of Lauren.

"My apologies, Miss Dailey," the nurse wheeling the bed said. "I thought you had already been discharged."

"Just about to leave," Lauren said, unable to tear her eyes away from Cassidy. The girl she'd seen in her visions in Rhianu. The girl who the last time she saw had aged fifty years and was known as Owena.

And Cassidy was staring right back at Lauren as if the same thing ran through her mind.

"Do you two know each other?" the nurse asked.

"N-no," Lauren said, sliding into the wheelchair and breaking eye contact. "Just leaving."

Lauren's nurse wheeled her out of the room, and she threw one last look back to Cassidy, spying her mother and father waiting outside. She remembered them from Cassidy's vision, although they seemed haggard-looking. They spoke to each other in strained, hushed tones, as if neither wanted the other to be here right now.

"Well she's *your* problem, Martha."

"*You're* the one who gave her the pills, Dave."

"Hang on," Lauren said. With a mighty heave, she pulled herself to standing and walked back into the room.

Cassidy looked up at her, shocked.

"Listen," Lauren said, cutting Cassidy off before she could speak. She walked over to the hospital pad and jotted down her number. "Before you even *think* about doing something like that ever again, I want you to call me. You call me, and you talk to me, understand?"

Cassidy took the paper wordlessly. Lauren leaned down and enveloped her into a hug.

"I know what it's like to suffer in silence," Lauren whispered. "And I know what it's like to feel like you can't talk to anyone about your problems. So the next time you feel like no one is there for you, and you're drowning, you call me."

Cassidy swallowed.

"I'm here for you," Lauren said. She pulled out her necklace from her pocket and looked at it. Cassidy eyed it as well with the familiarity that came with wearing it for a long time. "I don't know where we were or if I made it all up in my head, but..." She wrapped her hand around the necklace and reached out to touch Cassidy's hand.

Even made up things can be real. But they can also be defeated.

Lauren lifted her hand and smiled at Cassidy, who was smiling right back.

And as Lauren left the hospital, she took in the beautiful late summer day and knew she was going to be just fine.

note from the author

New Year's Eve in 2013, I hit my rock bottom. I spent the night curled in a tiny ball, crying my eyes out and drowning in silent misery. Even though I was so far in my own darkness, I continued to pretend to everyone—including myself—that I was fine. I only had my heart broken; what was that in the scope of the rest of the world's problems?

After a conversation with a family friend who likened my broken heart to major surgery, I finally gave myself permission to ask for help. That one decision started a chain reaction leading to the rediscovery of my love of writing and finding the bravery to "come out" as an author. One year later, you have my *third* published book in your hands.

Funny how that works, huh?

During my so-called quarter-life crisis, I realized how much I had let fear guide my decisions. Once I noticed that fear, and realized that it was unfounded, I made drastic decisions about my career, my life, and my priorities as a human being. And yes, I was scared to make these changes—hell, I'm still scared—but I did it anyway.

This book was the hardest thing I have ever written, because I had to share the parts of myself that I am not very proud of. But my hope is that if you *are* silently suffering, if you think your problems aren't important, if you think nobody cares—you're wrong. And perhaps, through Lauren, you might have found the courage to face your own dragons.

You are braver than you think, stronger than you could ever imagine, and aren't in this alone.

/S.

acknowledgements

As always, thank you to the reader for reading all the way to the end. You are my sunshine, and you make me happy when skies are gray—or burning from a fire-breathing Anghenfil. Thank you for going on this personal journey with me. If you are so inclined, please consider leaving a review on your favorite bookstore website.

Because this book was so hard to write, a special thanks go to some amazing beta readers who helped me to center and focus. Michelle, Robyn, Wendy, and Nikki—I bow my head in gratitude. Thank you for giving me the warm fuzzy that I wasn't completely insane (or more so than usual) and for helping me buff out the rough edges.

Thanks also go to Gina, my line-editor extraordinaire, for taking a fine-toothed comb through this book. When writing through incredible pain and anxiety, we tend to forget our grammar rules. It was such a relief to hand this jumbled mess over to you for your expert opinion and guidance. I've said it before, and I'll say it a third time: You are my hero.

Cassondra, my darling-drawer-of-my-dragon: I am honored to showcase your magnificent work on such a personal book. You have such a bright future and I can't wait to see what is next for you. I love you, baby girl, and I am so proud of you.

Finally, a word for Adam: If you made it this far, as Peter would say, "You are a troopah." Thanks for the memories and six-and-a-half years of true bliss. But now, I think I can finally say goodbye.

also by s. usher evans

DEMON SPRING TRILOGY

Three years ago, Jack Grenard's wife was brutally murdered by demons. Now, along with his partner Cam Macarro, he's trying to rebuild his life in Atlanta. But on a routine investigation, they find a demon who saves instead of kills. They must discover who she is before Demon Spring, the quadrennial breach between the human world and demon realm, when all hell—literally—breaks loose.

The Demon Spring Trilogy is the first urban fantasy from S. Usher Evans and will be released in 2018 in eBook, Paperback, and Hardcover.

The Razia Series

Lyssa Peate is living a double life as a planet discovering scientist and a space pirate bounty hunter. Unfortunately, neither life is going very well. She's the least wanted pirate in the universe and her brand new scientist intern is spying on her. Things get worse when her intern is mistaken for her hostage by the Universal Police.

The Razia Series is a four-book space opera series and is available now for eBook, Audiobook. Paperback, and Hardcover.

also by s. usher evans

THE MADION WAR TRILOGY

He's a prince, she's a pilot, they're at war. But when they are marooned on a deserted island hundreds of miles from either nation, they must set aside their differences and work together if they want to survive.

The Madion War Trilogy is a fantasy romance available now in eBook, Paperback, and Hardcover.

The Lexie Carrigan Chronicles

Lexie Carrigan thought she was weird enough until her family drops a bomb on her—she's magical. Now the girl who's never made waves is blowing up her nightstand and no one seems to want to help her. That is, until a kindle gentleman shows up with all the answers. But Lexie finds out being magical is the least weird thing about her.

Spells and Sorcery is the first book in the Lexie Carrigan Chronicles, and is available now in eBook, audiobook, paperback, and hardcover.

about the author

S. Usher Evans was born and raised in Pensacola, Florida. After a decade of fighting bureaucratic battles as an IT consultant in Washington, DC, she suffered a massive quarter-life-crisis. She decided fighting dragons was more fun than writing policy, so she moved back to Pensacola to write books full-time. She currently resides with her two dogs, Zoe and Mr. Biscuit, and frequently can be found plotting on the beach.

Visit S. Usher Evans online at:
http://www.susherevans.com/

Twitter: www.twitter.com/susherevans
Facebook: www.facebook.com/susherevans
Instagram: www.instagram.com/susherevans

Made in the USA
Columbia, SC
28 January 2018